HER
FATHER'S
DAUGHTER

HER FATHER'S DAUGHTER

A THRILLER

T. M. DUNN

CROOKED
LANE

NEW YORK

Published in the United States by Crooked Lane Books, an imprint of The Quick Brown Fox & Company LLC.

Crooked Lane Books and its logo are trademarks of The Quick Brown Fox & Company LLC.

Library of Congress Catalog-in-Publication data available upon request.

ISBN (hardcover): 978-1-63910-327-0
ISBN (ebook): 978-1-63910-328-7

Cover design by Louisa Maggio

Printed in the United States.

www.crookedlanebooks.com

Crooked Lane Books
34 West 27th St., 10th Floor
New York, NY 10001

First Edition: July 2023

10 9 8 7 6 5 4 3 2 1

To Allan, my partner in life,
who makes it all possible

I cannot think of any need in childhood as strong as the need for a father's protection.

—Sigmund Freud

PROLOGUE

"DON'T YOU LIKE it?" Mother asked. "Your father spent all night putting it together, one hundred and two pieces."

I found the model train circling our Christmas tree—the kind not for playing but for collecting—tedious and redundant. Around and around and around. I didn't want to disappoint them. *It's a beauty*, I remembered the father on the commercial saying to the son. *This is the best present ever!* the son replied.

"This is the best present ever!" I jumped up and down with pretend glee, flashing a smile so wide it hurt. My father patted the top of my head, picked up the engine, slammed me in the face, and broke my nose.

"You have potential for greatness," Father told me on the drive home from the emergency room. "Acting is an art. The difference between a great actor and a good liar is commitment and sacrifice."

The pain medication had me in a semiconscious state, but I would never forget the two greatest gifts I'd ever receive: the inspiration to act, and though not as monumental but nevertheless life changing, a broken nose, which the doctor reset to be perfectly straight, an essential feature for an actor.

I would never develop an interest in model trains, but the one that circled our tree on Christmas morning the year I turned six was the reason I wanted to become an actor, a great one.

Which was also why, the first time Sal punched my ticket on the Metro-North New Haven Line, from Hartford to Grand Central, I knew he was the one.

Sal's side-to-side shuffle, his regional accent, which incrementally changed as we approached New York, the way he tipped his cap back each and every time he said, "Tickets, please," and the way he tipped it forward every time someone asked him a question about the time or the location of the nearest restroom—all made it abundantly clear that Sal, the Metro-North train conductor, would be the next character I studied, rehearsed, and became.

LINDA

CHAPTER

1

THE SMELL OF burnt eggs and sweet peppers woke me at 7:25 AM.

I didn't run. I walked to the kitchen. Flames shot up from the cast-iron skillet. I sighed and poured out the box of salt, kept close to the back burner for exactly this purpose. For the third time this month, the apartment building was saved from ruin and breakfast was charred to an inedible crisp. With one of our checkered, singed potholders, I grabbed the handle and dropped the frying pan into the sink.

Where the hell is he?

Dad might forget to shut off the stove before he left the apartment, but he never went anywhere before he had his coffee. I picked up the *Greatest Dad* mug, the only one my father ever used. The inside was clean. I turned it around and around, searching for answers, but there were no fortunes to be read in his empty cup.

He had to be home.

Could he still be sleeping? Dad never slept past seven AM. I thought maybe he wasn't feeling well again. Over the last few weeks, he'd been complaining of headaches and stomach issues. He blamed my cooking, but I knew something else wasn't right. He refused to see a doctor, because there was nothing bottles of Pepto-Bismol and handfuls of Advil couldn't fix.

I had managed to get one of our customers, a primary care doctor, to look him over when we exterminated her apartment for silverfish. She said that without tests she couldn't say for sure, but she asked if he was feeling stressed. He shook his head no, and I almost lost it. Dad was always worried about something. The something usually related to me.

His latest concern was that I, his reason for living, would be off to college in a few weeks. He pretended to be happy for me, but I knew he wasn't. I was all he had in the world.

What was I supposed to do? Instead of going to college after high school, I'd helped Dad run his business for the past seven years. If a full scholarship hadn't fallen in my lap, I probably would have put my life on hold for another seven years. The only out-of-state school I'd applied to was in California, a long shot, but they'd offered me a full ride. Dad agreed it was an opportunity of a lifetime and I couldn't turn it down.

But now I was worried. How would he survive without me? I had been his entire life since my mother died.

Ah, that was it. Today was August 2. I couldn't believe I had forgotten, but I was grateful I had.

I walked to his room, tugging on my right earlobe, which was shorter than the left. Dad called this idiosyncrasy my "tell," a nervous tic that showed I was worried.

I banged hard on Dad's bedroom door, waiting for him to open, but when he didn't, fear scratched the back of my throat. I was sure he was fine, but what if . . . ?

I touched my earlobe, turned the knob, and went inside. "Thank God," I said.

Dad sat on the edge of his bed in his usual discombobulated state. His mismatched pajamas and worn socks (retrieved three times from the trash) made me sad. As did his half-in/half-out ponytail that I swore I would cut off some night while he slept.

He was good-looking, sweet, but too shy ever to show his teeth when he smiled. Dad had no interest in dating. "You're the only person I need," was how he deflected it. At five, ten, even fifteen years old, I found this comforting. At twenty-five, I was suffocating. Two weeks from tomorrow, I'd be off to California for my freshman orientation at USC, and I refused to feel guilty for leaving Dad, but it pinched the back of my eyeballs to see him sitting with the photo album he retrieved from the back of his closet every year on the anniversary of Mom's death. Thirty-six pages filled with happy pictures of my parents from the time before I was born.

Dad obsessed over only one photo, a Polaroid of Mom with clay-speckled hair and a belly protruding from under a white T-shirt too small for her preggo bod. Dad had snapped the photo the day she finished what he thought was her best work: a three-foot sculpture of our family—Mom, Dad, and their imagined baby. The piece was still stationed between his bed and dresser, the epicenter of the room, under a spotlight angled at thirty degrees, the best position to see the details.

All I ever saw was an orange blob of clay. A dust collector.

Dad said my mother was a great artist. Maybe she was. I didn't know a lot about art, and I had never known my mother. She killed herself three days after I was born.

"Fire," I said, and he looked up from the album. "Breakfast is burnt."

He didn't react as expected. No apologies. No running to the kitchen to try to save what was already too late to be saved. Instead, he patted his bed for me to take a seat next to him.

We had no time to go down memory lane—his lane, his memories. We had a job to do. One of the luxury buildings we serviced on Park Avenue had mice. People, especially those of means, lose their shit at the mere mention of a mouse sighting. But the fact is, if you live in NYC, you'll have mice. Unless you have a good exterminator.

Donovan and Daughter Exterminating was the best. We were a small, family-run business and took care of any and all situations with a personal touch. Our customers weren't digits in a spreadsheet; they were people who depended on us to make their problems go away.

"Credo," I said. "We have to get to work."

"Forget Credo." Dad patted the bed again.

Michael Credo was the building manager of all the Park Avenue buildings we serviced. He was a pompous ass, but he had the power to hire and fire contractors like us. His buildings brought in half our income.

"Please," I said.

"Not today." Dad patted the bed again.

I knew arguing would get me nowhere. I sat.

Dad opened his nightstand drawer, stuffed with the laminated wallet-sized cards he collected at funerals.

Whenever someone died in the neighborhood, whether we knew them or not, we were there. While some fathers took their children to parks or to Dairy Queen for ice cream or ignored them altogether, my father took me to funeral parlors. I'd seen more dead bodies before the age of five than episodes of *Sesame Street* and *Barney* combined.

Dad palmed a card in each hand. "Right or left?"

Oh lord. Each card had a picture of a saint on one side. On the flip side was the name of the dearly departed along with a special prayer, and often the name and address of the funeral home.

I pinched my lips. I wanted to eat. "Breakfast," I said.

"Right or left," he repeated.

Dad never raised his voice. When he was upset, he whispered, and when he was furious, he didn't say a word. Dad had given me the silent treatment only twice. The first time I was so young that I can't currently remember why, and the second time was when I'd sent him a text, intended for a friend, in which I noted that it'd been five weeks since my last cigarette. Dad had asked me a week before if I smoked, and I'd told him, "Not once."

Dad shoved the cards under my nose. "Pick one." He acted as if I had a choice, but there was only one answer that would satisfy him.

I sighed and pointed. "Right."

Dad revealed St. Raphael, the patron saint of soul mates and happy times, on the front; on the flip side, the name of the dearly departed, Rebecca Charlotte Donovan—died August 2, twenty-five years ago today.

My mother.

The details of that day had been branded into my memory as if I had been the one to live it and not her.

It was overcast, but so humid you sweated in the shower, when my mother went to the NICU unit to say good-bye to her daughter, born nine weeks too soon, weighing one ounce under two pounds, fighting for her life inside the plastic walls of an incubator.

I knew how my mother had died—an overdose; she swallowed the whole bottle, save for three pills. Whenever I asked why she'd committed suicide, Dad would only say, "The weight of her love was more than she could bear."

In middle school, the snarky teen in me added to the story: "Three pills, one for the father, the daughter, and the mother." A joke that was not well received, as Dad didn't simply love my mother—he worshipped her. I wanted nothing more than to forget this story and the woman who'd abandoned us, but as long as my father lived, that would be impossible.

I glimpsed a tear in the corner of Dad's right eye, and I decided I wouldn't play the part of the grieving daughter. Crying was a luxury we couldn't afford, especially not today, with our biggest customer scheduled for service.

"I love you," I whispered. "She's gone, Dad. Let her go, please."

"Never."

That was it. I'd had enough. I tore my mother's death card straight down its worn laminated center, one half for Dad and the other half for the wastebasket at his bedside. I didn't want to hurt my father, but he'd wasted years of his life pining over a woman who'd abandoned both of us. It was time for him to move on. I left him and went to the kitchen.

I gulped down a strong cup of coffee, spitting the coffee grounds that had slipped through the filter into Dad's empty mug.

Before I could make Dad a coffee to go, he was standing in front of me, dressed, with his ponytail pulled back and neat. At least it wasn't a man-bun.

"Thank you," I said.

Dad glanced over at the burnt pan in the sink. "What was it?" I asked.

"Your favorite," he said.

Dad kissed my forehead, and I smiled, relieved he wouldn't spend the day reenacting his annual wallow-fest but instead would go to work with me. I walked to the apartment door, grabbing the set of keys attached to the dyed-blue rabbit's foot Dad had owned since he was a kid, and grasped the doorknob. Then I stopped. I heard *her* on the other side of the door and froze, keys in one hand, doorknob in the other, sucking down my breath.

Dad didn't ask me what the holdup was or why I was no longer in a rush to get to Credo, the account we couldn't afford to lose. Now we both heard our neighbor Mrs. Camberi's health aide fumbling with her keys in the hall. I had managed to avoid Anne since the night we'd slept together, and there was no way I was going to face her now in front of my father.

I waited until I heard Mrs. Camberi's heavy metal door slam shut before I opened our door to leave.

We were in the elevator, the doors a half inch from closing shut, when we heard, "Hold it, please."

Dad pressed the OPEN button, and Anne stepped inside. I kept my eyes on the full trash bag in her hands. She and Dad exchanged pleasantries. I was certain it would make the situation worse if I said anything. The doors opened at the basement; neither Dad nor I had remembered to press *L* for the lobby. Anne stepped out and walked toward the room where the trash and recycling bins were stored.

Dad nudged me.

"Have a great one," I called out.

The elevator doors shut. Dad tapped me on the shoulder. He wasn't going to let this go. I turned to face him.

"Not involved," I said, meaning *Anne and I are not screwing.*

Dad shook his head, registering doubt regarding my claim.

A one-night stand with a woman who worked next door turned out to be riddled with complications. For one thing, it would be on my head if Anne quit and Mrs. Camberi's daughter put her mother in a facility, the worst possible outcome. As Dad had told me, "If I ever get to that stage where you can't take care of me, shoot me."

"After the last one had quit, you promised you wouldn't have relations with any other of Mrs. Camberi's caretakers," Dad said, barely above a whisper.

But Anne wasn't like the other aides. Those affairs were on me. This one was on Anne. She'd invited me in for a drink. I could have said no, but it had been a long day of termite inspections for a pain-in-the-ass Realtor in Scarsdale. The job had been routine, but on the drive back, I heard on the radio there had been a train accident that day. A bad one. Five people in the first car died and twenty others were badly injured. If Dad hadn't had the stomach flu and I hadn't been forced to skip the college-info session, I would have been on that train, and I always rode in the first car.

The one person I was desperate to call, I couldn't. We were over. I'd ended it. Badly too. Sharing the last slice of cold pizza in her queen bed, with her dozen coordinated throw pillows and her bulldog Sam snoring between us, I'd told her I loved her, and she'd said she loved me too. The next day I texted her I wasn't ready for a relationship. Texted. Not called. An email would have been less cold.

Jess was the only person I'd ever seen more than one or two times. It wasn't about sex with Jess, though it had started that way, and it was good, the best. But what we shared soon became so much more. We were together for almost six months. She was the first big secret I ever kept from Dad.

My life revolved around my father. One didn't need to take an intro to psych class to know I had daddy issues, which for me meant every choice I made took my father's needs into account. He always came first. I'm sure having a mother who had killed herself and a father who'd devoted his life to raising me had a lot to do with it. For the most part, I was okay with that.

On the day of the train wreck, I was hurting, missing Jess more than ever, and by the time I got to my apartment, my resistance was down and my head and heart hurt—pathetic, I know—so when Anne opened Mrs. Camberi's door and invited me inside, I accepted.

Three bourbon and sodas later, we moved from Mrs. Camberi's couch to the guest room where Anne slept Monday through Friday evenings. Anne had a child monitor with her in case Mrs. Camberi woke up and needed something. We played it responsibly. At least I thought we had.

The next morning, Anne told me she had never cheated on her wife before. I hadn't realized she was married. She told me we could never do it again.

That was more than okay with me. I didn't mess around with married people knowingly. We agreed to never speak of it again, and we'd both kept our bargain.

I was saved from any further commentary by the arrival of a text. It was from Jack, the head doorman at Credo's building: *Miss Linda. Can't reach Mr. Anthony. There's been a cockroach sighting. We need you here now.*

This could be bad.

I lifted the screen to Dad's eyes. He shrugged.

"We can't lose this account." I heard the desperation in my voice, but I couldn't control it. Dad didn't respond.

I texted back: *On our way.*

"Dad, I know this is a hard day for you . . ."

"Enough," he said.

CHAPTER

2

O UR VAN HAD been vandalized again, right in front of our building.

"This is the third time this summer." I banged my palm against the spray-painted tag on the windshield, which made it impossible to see the road. The truck with the giant rubber rat stationed on the roof and the rainbow-colored roaches (Dad's tribute to the Grateful Dead) painted on the side panels was an obvious target for bored teenagers roaming our neighborhood. Calling the police wasn't an option. Not with my father. To him, there were two types of cops—the lazy good-for-nothings counting the days to their retirement and fat pensions, and the sociopaths with weapons and license to kill.

I had never been a fan of the police either, unless you counted Jess. I didn't know she was a cop when we first met, and by the time I found out, I was so taken by her, she could have been a serial killer and I still would have wanted her. But if we didn't report the incident to the police, the insurance company wouldn't pay.

I sighed and turned to Dad. "We've already spent a couple grand out of our own pockets . . ."

I didn't need Dad to say a word or give me one of his *You should know better* looks. I knew what he was thinking: *No good ever comes from calling a cop.*

"Fine," I said, "but there's no seeing through the windshield." We'd have to take the train, with our equipment strapped to our backs, into the city yet again.

Dad slid open the side door of the van. I grabbed my green coveralls with our company name, *Donovan and Daughter Exterminating*, embroidered on the back, and slipped into them. Dad pulled out one of the Trail Wilderness backpacks filled with all the poisons, traps, and other accoutrements needed to take care of any situation and helped me hoist it onto my back.

He slid the side door shut.

"You're not taking the other pack? I don't know if we'll have enough traps."

"I'm not working today," he said.

"Anne was a mistake," I said. "I'm sorry."

"Not my concern," he said, "but I am saddened by your actions this morning."

"This is about Mom?"

"This is about the woman who gave you life." Tears were threatening to arrive in full force.

"Dad, we can do everything we always do. We can go to the cemetery in NJ and stay in our usual motel."

Dad wiped his eyes with the handkerchief he carried in his pocket. "Thank you."

"Today we have to do this job. We have a slow schedule tomorrow. We can take the trip then."

Dad took a step closer to me, and when he raised his hand to return the handkerchief to his pocket, I flinched. Dad had never once put a hand on me, not even given me a slap on the butt, but I'd never seen this look in his eyes before. It scared me.

"Dad, even if the traps in the basement could wait another day, the text. The roach sighting."

"Ignore it."

"We can't. Credo doesn't care about our personal lives," I continued. "If we don't show up today, it will give him the excuse he wants to go with one of the bigger companies that can afford to undercut us."

Dad nodded like he understood, but he wouldn't make eye contact with me. His disappointment felt like a knife in my gut.

"We can go and take care of the roach situation, the one apartment, and leave. We need to make an appearance. It will be quick. I promise."

Without another word, he walked away.

I wanted to call after him but didn't. He had to do what he had to do, and I had to take care of business so we wouldn't lose it.

As I walked away, I wondered for the hundredth time: *What will you do without me?*

ACT I

My dear daughter,

I know my disappearance has left you feeling abandoned.
On my word, I've been close by, watching you.

By the time you've read Act I, your world, as you've
known it, will have been turned upside down. You are
confused and hurt. I regret the pain I have caused you. If I
am anything, I am human. In my desperation to preserve the
past, to keep my relationship with you as it always has been,
I've acted selfishly. Today, circumstances have forced me to
do what I should have done long ago. In these notebooks, you
will soon discover the story that belongs to you.

In the beginning . . .

The first time I met your mother, I was mediocre at best, only
I didn't know it. I didn't even know anything stood between
me and the role of a lifetime until the day I saw her standing
in the middle of Grand Central Terminal, looking up.

I was on my way to work. Not exterminating back then,
though the rehearsal space I was using was infested with rats.
It was 1993, three years before the restoration of the magnificent vaulted ceiling would begin and a year before you would
be born.

On the day I met your mother, there wasn't anything to see, so it seemed. Years of cigarette smoke and other pollutants had destroyed the celestial ceiling's beauty. Ordinary people moved quickly through the terminal, avoiding the smells of sweat and despair and contact with the inhabitants: folks down on their luck, or with no luck at all—the homeless, the runaways, the undesirables.

Your mother was neither ordinary nor undesirable. In her stillness, there was heat; she was visibly angry, shaking her head and muttering under her breath as she looked skyward. Of course, angry, muttering people abound in Grand Central, and I had learned to keep my distance. Your mother was different. I felt this in my throat. I would soon discover she was a woman who could see beauty in a lump of clay and the potential in all things, alive or dead.

I moved close enough to hear what the woman was saying. It was one word.

"Fake, fake, *fake*," she repeated over and over, each time with more conviction. It was as though this one word was enough to tell the whole story. I thought she was talking to me.

"Fake?" I repeated back to her.

Her eyes dropped from the ceiling to me. She was close to my height, almost five foot ten. Our eyes met: mine the perfect distance apart, gray blue, average in size; hers big, black holes that I feared would pull me in with no chance for escape. There was no spark, no magic, at first. In fact, I found her facial features nice but plain, though her nose was a flawless shape and size. I had seen enough nose jobs, or what we in the business called facial enhancements, to know it was a real nose. There was one flaw, a small thing—her right earlobe was shorter than her left, but not by much. Still, if I had simply walked away then, I could never have picked her out of a lineup later.

Something was happening in the space between us. I couldn't name what that was at the time. I don't know if I could now. The energy I was feeling told me my work could wait; it would have to. I didn't know it then, but I was in a state of inertia, the same routine, the same roles, trying to change, to move me from a craftsman to an artist to a master. To paraphrase

Newton's first law of motion, only an external force could propel me to act, to change. Your mother was that force.

"It's a fake." Her accent was subtle, and I couldn't tell from where, though I was certain it was not from New York, and her voice was deeper than I had expected from a woman whose neck looked as if it would fit within the circumference of my fist.

Her dyed-black hair fell at the center of her back, the bottom edge a diagonal line, not straight across. I found this perplexing. It was as if the stylist hadn't cared.

"I'm sorry?" I said, not having any idea why or for what I was apologizing.

"The original mural wasn't restored. They covered it with panels, completely redid it, and got rid of so many details. It's the details that matter."

"I agree. But perhaps this rendition, though not the original, is a masterpiece of its own."

She remained silent for several long breaths. "I do love the triangle." She pointed to a spot, but I couldn't see the shape to which she was referring. She took hold of my hand, and it was all I could do to keep myself grounded; her touch . . . well, it was electric. Using my pinkie as a pointer, she said, "Right there. There's a small constellation." I nodded to please her, but all I could see was soot. "Triangulum," she said. "It wasn't in the original mural."

"Isn't it an artist's prerogative to take the facts and assumptions of the world and make their own truths?"

"Do you like playing with trains?"

I followed her eyes down to my black loafers and up to my blue cap and thought, *Of course.* The conductor's uniform. I wasn't quite used to its fit—loose at the waist, too tight around the thighs. My work with Sal was in the early stages. We still had a month of rehearsal left before showtime. I knew that walking in the world as "Sal" this soon was taking a risk. But we were low on supplies. Sal was a bigger eater than I'd anticipated.

Today was my first solo dress rehearsal, so to speak. Father always said, "On the stage there is no producer, director, or writer; there is only the actor responsible for the audience's experience."

This meant that in order for me to give a stellar performance, I had to employ any and all resources at my disposal to help me live inside the character's skin, hence the itchy wool uniform.

"Call me Sal," I said, my lines flooding back to me.

"Salvatore," she said.

"That was my father. I'm just Sal. Simply Sal."

"Simple Sal."

From anyone else I would have found this insulting, but every word she spoke rang endearing.

"Italian?" she asked.

At first, it sounded like an invitation to dine with her. I felt panic drop into my gut but quickly came to my senses and realized she was asking if my name was Italian. I didn't know if the original Sal was of Italian descent. I would have to ask him when I returned.

"Legend has it my great-great-grandmother had a sordid affair with a man from Naples, and though they never married, she took his name and gave it to their son," I improvised.

"How did she die?"

This question was startling, but the right one to ask. How a relative had died might tell her something about the man standing in front of her. A character's backstory is crucial to playing a role authentically. Death holds more truths than lives lived.

"She stepped off a train platform," I said.

"Anna Karenina–style." She paused for a long moment. "I meant no disrespect. Things just fly out of my mouth sometimes."

"I'm familiar with all of Chekhov's plays, but I've never read Tolstoy."

She raised her brow and squinted at me. "You don't know how it ends?"

"I don't."

She let out a deep breath and laughed. I didn't understand why, but I knew she expected me to do the same, so

I did, though I hadn't yet perfected a working-class man's laugh—the kind of deep laugh that comes from the gut of someone who likes all-you-can eat buffets and a few beers while watching the game.

"What's it like to be a train man?" she asked, with such bravado I knew my answer should be one that showed I didn't take myself too seriously.

"Sometimes it feels like I'm a glorified ticket taker." This was firmer ground for me, in line with my preparation. "But I like the different people I meet," I said with a smile.

"My name is Rebecca." She extended her hand to me. "Never, not ever, Becky."

"Nice to meet you, Rebecca Never, Not Ever, Becky." We shook. Her hand felt rough, coarse. She clearly used her hands to make a living, but her Chanel shoes told me the roughness wasn't from scrubbing toilets. She used her hands to feel alive.

"You're an artist?" I asked.

"I paint," she said. "I hope to someday sculpt." This time when she smiled, I could see her perfectly straight teeth were an illusion. In fact, she had the slightest overbite. I liked that.

Looking up, I said, "Maybe they can restore the original painting?"

"Not possible."

The light in your mother's eyes, the same I see in your eyes now, burned a hole in my soul. I never for a moment believed that light would go out forever.

"Anything's possible." This was not a line. It was the truth, and it made my skin tingle to share a moment of honesty in a public place.

She shook her head. "Too much damage to the ceiling. Sometimes you can't go back." She smiled again. "You're right, though, the new mural is its own work of art."

Her words seemed an apt description of me. I was not the original Sal, or Frank, or any of the characters I'd studied and embodied over the last two decades. I wasn't a mere carbon copy either. I was different, fresh, a work of art in progress.

"I've taken enough of your time," she said. "A pleasure."

I watched her walking away, and the farther she got, the harder it was to breathe. The thought of my never seeing her again was unbearable. So, I did what I had never done before, what Father had warned me never to do: I deviated from the script and chased after her.

I caught up to her at the exit to West Forty-Second Street, the armpits of my bargain-basement shirt soaked in perspiration under my wool uniform jacket, and asked, "May I buy you a cup of coffee?"

At the nearest diner, Rebecca ordered two coffees and pointed to a cake stand with a chocolate cupcake.

We sat and talked. Your mother was a talker, a trait I typically despised in a woman, in everyone. But she spoke with such authority, without a hint of arrogance, that I found myself leaning in so as not to miss a word of what she had to say. She talked and I listened until our waitress delivered a small white plate with a chocolate cupcake time had forgotten. In her other hand, she held a coffeepot. I followed Rebecca's lead and turned my chipped white mug over for a fill.

"Room for milk?" the waitress asked me.

I wasn't sure. I didn't do caffeine or any drugs, but I knew the coffee would keep us talking.

"Black for me," Rebecca said.

"Me too."

The waitress filled our mugs to the brim and went back to her place behind the counter.

She took a sip of coffee and said, "You must have loved trains as a kid."

I was thrown by this non sequitur, and it took me a moment to get myself back into character.

"Riding the train with my grandfather was some of my happiest times. He would let me punch the tickets for him. He always bought me ice cream at the end of his shift, even though it was close to dinnertime. It's our secret, he would say."

"Your grandfather, a conductor too?"

"Forty-seven years," I said. "He never missed a day of work except the day my grandmother died. Married fifty years." I was impressed with how easily the lines flowed, and with how much I had committed Sal's story to memory.

"Where did you grow up?" she asked. I was certain she was auditioning me, though I didn't know for what part yet.

"Outside of Syracuse," I said.

"Are you an only child?"

"I had a brother, but he died in Iraq. A new recruit mistook him for the enemy and machine-gunned him and a young boy."

"That war was wrong," she said.

"All are," I said.

She nodded. "What do you like to do on your days off?"

This stumped me. I couldn't imagine what Sal did on his days off. I couldn't picture him outside his uniform. She sipped her coffee and waited.

As harmless as this question appeared, I knew my answer mattered. The future of our relationship depended on it. Sal struck me as someone who went to an occasional baseball game, but only if someone else had bought the tickets and he tagged along for the company.

I did something else I had never done before: I drew from my own backstory and childhood. One of the few happy memories connected to my mother.

"I rescue dogs, pit bulls mostly. It was a cause my mother was passionate about."

"Really?" She leaned in, and I knew I had given the right answer.

"There are so many dogs used as untrained guard dogs, kept behind garages or junkyards or any other business some idiot owner wants protected from theft but is too cheap to install alarm systems for. Those poor animals are left outside in harsh weather, fed very little to keep them hungry and mean."

"Must be hard to find homes for them," she said. "Pit bulls get a bad rap."

"They can be very sweet," I said. "We do our best, but it's not so easy getting people to adopt a pit bull."

"Can I trust you?" Rebecca asked.

I was taken aback but pleased with her forwardness. "Of course," I said.

She smiled, showing her overbite with confidence. "Okay, then: not a nibble." She lifted the plate with the cupcake and put it under my nose, as if to tempt me.

"Too delicious to resist." I held back my disgust.

"Not one lick of frosting until I return."

"You're leaving?" I tried to disguise the panic in my voice.

"I have a surprise for you," she said.

I deplore surprises, but before I could protest, she was up and out the door.

Our waitress didn't seem to care and continued whatever it was she was doing with those ketchup bottles. It took all the willpower I could muster to not go after your mother. But if Rebecca and I were destined to do great work together, then she had to return to me of her own volition. So, I waited, watching our coffees grow cold.

Waiting for your mother to return stirred something in me I couldn't name until she came back, her eyes as wide as her smile. Grief. I was grieving your mother's absence. Already. The possibility she wouldn't return cut me deeper than my father, alive or dead, ever had.

If she could get me to access emotions so raw, so real, there was no question in my mind and heart: she had to become my mentor. With her directing me, I could achieve the most authentic performance of my career.

"Close your eyes," she said upon returning. I did as she directed.

"Now open."

Her hands cradled the chocolate cupcake, now with a lit candle in it. "Make a wish."

"It's not my birthday," I said, though it could have been. I had embodied so many characters over the past two decades that I had long forgotten my own birthday. Sal's birthday was April 22.

"Wishes aren't just for birthdays. They're for new beginnings too."

That night I returned to the hidden room in the wall adjacent to the subway tracks where the No. 4 express and No. 6 local trains ran. With a firm but gentle hand, I ended my work with the original Sal.

* * *

And that was the start of us. Your mother and me.

When it ended, it wasn't my decision. It was hers. Her fault. She ran away. She ended us.

* * *

Your mother and I had agreed to meet by the clock tower in the center of Grand Central Terminal at three fifteen PM. She was teaching an art class that week for middle school children in Yonkers. I connected to the artist in her, but her love for children was a red flag. I didn't hate children; I feared them. No matter how much foundation you applied, a child could see all your cracks, slither through to your insides, and with the gusto of a starved rat, gnaw you hollow.

I overslept, something you know I never do. Ending my work with Sal had taken its toll. Sal didn't want to say goodbye, but they never do. I'm a professional, and I've always managed to sever ties with ease. I was also in peak condition in those days, stronger and more agile than I'd ever been. I could overpower a man twice my size, and Sal was small in stature. My mind wasn't as focused as it should have been, though. I was distracted by thoughts of your mother, and what I know now to be love. In the end, I was fortunate to walk away that night with only a bruised rib.

The hard part was done, or so I thought, but there was still the matter of disposing of the shell. It's because of these logistical nightmares that I almost always did my work at the brownstone. My great-grandfather had purchased the building for precisely this purpose. A former funeral parlor with a crematorium in the basement made the grueling effort it took to perfect one's craft less of a burden.

I loved the city, and so did Father. He had no interest in moving to Connecticut, the place Mother yammered on and on about. "The city is no place to raise a child," she repeated over and over.

Father understood it was the only place to raise a child actor. I wish you could have met your grandfather. You have his wit and keen eye for seeing the details that most don't notice. It's in those details where lives are saved and destroyed. When I jumped onto the tracks where the No. 6 local and the No. 4 express trains ran, it was already past one AM, but it might have been later—the cheap watch I'd bought from a street vendor had stopped working. All I knew was I didn't have a lot of time to finish the job.

The lighting in the tunnel was always weak, but my vision was strong: twenty-twenty in the right eye and twenty-thirty in the left. This rehearsal space Sal and I used, I had discovered six months prior, when I followed a homeless man who had refused my dinner invitation. I'd studied many homeless people before and wasn't interested in this man as my next character study. I only wanted to help him, and I was asking for nothing in return.

I followed him to the platform for the No. 6 line, and when he jumped onto the tracks without a second thought, I did too. It was exhilarating to act without foresight or plan.

About halfway to the next subway stop, the homeless man slid through a space in the wall and slipped into a hidden room equipped with the basic necessities to live . . . or rehearse. It even had a sink with running water. The man wanted not a thing from me but to be left alone. I complied. I didn't return until after I met Sal.

I chose to use that hidden room because of Sal. A creature of habit, he was impossible to coax to my brownstone for dinner or a drink, or to watch a ball game.

After he declined my invitation to watch a pay-per-view prizefight—he needed to be in bed by eight PM for his five AM shift—I realized that if there was to be any hope of my working with Sal, I'd have to find something that his by-the-book, scheduled-to-the-minute character could not resist.

My daughter, I can imagine your face scrunched up the way it does when you're curious or confused. You're wondering what was so special about a man who punched tiny holes into card paper for a living. But there was much more to this everyman than one could see at first or even third glance. Do you know a Metro-North train conductor is responsible for the lives of dozens of passengers at any given time? I had the honor of watching Sal evacuate to safety three full cars of passengers from the back of the train after a fire started in one of the restrooms. Sal was an everyman hero.

Call it serendipity, fate, divine intervention, or luck. Weeks after I'd followed the homeless man who didn't need my help to the secret room behind the subway walls, a paperback fell from Sal's satchel while I followed him. The book was a mystery set in an abandoned underground station in London. I took it as a sign.

The next day, when I returned the book to Sal, who agreed that the character development was somewhat lacking, I mentioned the secret room in the wall adjacent to the subway track, and his curiosity as a conductor and avid mystery reader was piqued. He was eager for me to take him there. He practically begged me.

There was the matter of the current occupant. I'd have to inform him of my intentions before bringing Sal there. After all, it was the polite thing to do.

When I returned to the humble dwelling in the subway tunnel, the door to the room was open, the dresser empty, the hot plate gone, the mattress on the floor bare, and the two buckets, one for urination, the other for defecation, had been cleaned out. The space was clearly available.

At the end of Sal's next shift, I brought him to the space in which we would spend the next six weeks, rehearsing lines, intonations, inflections, gestures, postures, until the day I met your mother.

After the arduous task of saying good-bye to Sal, I knew that clearing the space would be a breeze. I left what should have been done the night before to the next morning, and even after waking late, I still had three hours to strike set.

This would have been more than enough time. As I have taught you, the keys to doing any job well are the right tools and mindset. The salesclerk at the restaurant supply store sold me a cleaver he said was sharp enough to cut through bone like it was soft-serve ice cream. I had the body bag obtained from a coroner I had done character work with years prior. The last tool I needed to move the vessel from the subway room to the brownstone, where I would finish the job, was the steamer trunk I'd inherited from my father. It was a thing of beauty. (Everything your grandfather designed was flawless.) In fact, it was so airtight I could have skipped the body bag altogether, but I wanted to protect the lining. It was washable—soap, water, a little bleach—but why create unnecessary work?

Unfortunately, I get my lack of aptitude for math and science from your grandmother. Your grandfather was a mathematical genius, a magician of physics. He would have been a mechanical engineer if his parents hadn't thought the work beneath his station in life. With no formal training, only a brilliant mind and the ability to design to exact specifications tools to complete any task with the least amount of energy exerted, your grandfather crafted a trunk with wheels positioned in such a way that one could transport three hundred pounds of dead weight as if the trunk contained nothing but air.

I had my tools and a plan.

Five chops. Four limbs, head, and torso placed into the body bag, zipped, and dropped into the trunk. I would roll the trunk to the street, hail a cab downtown to the brownstone, and after I returned from my meeting with your mother, take care of the rest in the same way I had all the other characters I'd worked with.

You might wonder how I managed to roll a steamer-size trunk through the station, drop it from the subway platform onto the tracks, and roll it to the room, the set, without anyone noticing. I am quite sure people noticed. My father taught me that if you play a role with confidence, act with determination, and never hesitate, no one will question your motives. I recall passing two police officers on my way through the station; I tipped my cap and nodded and went on my way. I was wearing my own conductor's uniform, and unlike the day before, the fit was perfect.

Seeing Sal's body lying on the mattress, I had the urge to wake him. I rarely missed my characters once I had become them, but Sal was different. In some ways, before your mother, Sal was the closest I had ever come to having a friend. But there was no time for sentimentality. The clock was ticking, and I didn't want to be late for my meeting with your mother.

I opened the trunk and pulled out my vinyl suit, another one of your grandfather's designs. The material didn't breathe, but it did protect one's clothes and skin from excrement and bloodstains. It was also light and flexible and made it easy to move around in the cramped space.

Suited up, I went to work.

Well, my daughter, as we both know, we make plans, and God decides to go another way. It didn't take long—only one cut, in fact—for me to realize the man at the kitchen supply store had taken advantage of me. He'd sold me a cleaver that wasn't sharp enough to cut through butter, never mind bone. I had to take it back and get a refund, then go to a more trustworthy kitchen supply store closer to the Meatpacking District, then return and do the work as it needed to be done.

I looked down at the watch on Sal's wrist, the only part of his uniform I hadn't taken yet. "Nothing fancy, but it helps me keep the trains running on time," he'd said the first time he punched my ticket. To make conversation, I complimented him.

I'd discovered later it was engraved *Love, Mom, January 3, 1972*. It had been a gift from his mother on his first day as a Metro-North conductor. At first, he spoke of her as if she'd died, but after days of working together, he told me she was in a nursing facility in Queens. He was all she had. I envied his relationship with his mother, almost to the point where when he spoke of her, it angered me.

I hadn't wanted his watch before, but now I felt sure that Sal would have wanted me to have it. I removed the watch from his wrist and put it on mine. It was a perfect fit.

His timepiece reminded me that I'd run out of time. If I was going to meet your mother, I'd have to finish striking the set later.

Without his watch, Sal was fully naked; out of respect, I put his body into the black bag and zipped it closed. It was quite the chore and strain on my lower back, which had never been an issue at the brownstone, where I had pulley systems and other devices Father had designed to make the work and cleanup less backbreaking.

Nothing about my work with Sal had been like my earlier studies. Sal was the only character I had worked with outside the brownstone. But now I realized that it was because I'd broken my routine, moved outside my comfort zone, that I'd met your mother. You could say Sal was our unofficial matchmaker. For this, I am forever grateful to him.

I removed my vinyl outfit and kitchen gloves and left them alongside Father's trunk with Sal.

The plan was to return that night and finish the work.

*   *   *

It was 3:18 PM when I arrived.

I was five minutes late.

As you know, my dear daughter, I am never late.

A woman I had known for less than a day was already transforming me from a meticulous, controlled master of precision into a distracted, discombobulated, tardy mess of a man. I hadn't felt such discomfort since my father died.

I saw her before she saw me. She scanned the plaza, and when her eyes settled in my direction, her smile widened. She rushed over, and before I had a chance to say one of the witty conductor-isms I had memorized—*Trains always run on time; it's people who run slow*—she invited me to her place for coffee. She said she needed to be there to let in the exterminator. The last time he'd skipped a visit, her apartment had become a refuge for every roach in the building.

I'd never said yes to a woman's invitation before Rebecca, and I've never done so since. I find women who ask men out to be pushy and overly pragmatic. Rebecca was different. She had no hidden agendas. I could see that. She just wanted to have coffee with me. With *me*.

"It's uptown. We can take the subway," she said.

I hesitated.

"Something the matter?"

Father insisted subways were for peons. When times were financially trying, he said, it was better to walk ten miles than ride a subway ten minutes with the ordinary people. "Why don't we take a cab? On me, of course."

"A cab will take longer with traffic." She took hold of my hand, and the sweat from her palm stung and felt good too.

I was trying to process the crisscross of emotions charging through me when, *bang*, a small child, a boy, ran right into me.

From nowhere, another boy child only a few inches taller shouted, "Got ya!" and pushed the other kid into my gut again.

"Stop it!" The first boy slapped at the taller one but missed, and the two ran circles around me. All I could do was close my eyes and wish them away.

"Boys, stop it, now!"

I opened my eyes to see a woman with bags the color of eggplants under her eyes clutching at both boys' hands.

"How many times do I have to tell you not to run off?" Before either could answer, she said, "I don't want to hear who started it!" The boys both glanced down at the floor. It was like she could read their minds. "I'm sorry," the tired woman told me.

"Why are you sorry?" I asked.

Her face winced with gratitude. She treated my question as if it were rhetorical. I was sincerely curious as to why she was apologizing for the actions of her children. Back then I had no understanding of ordinary parent-child relationships. Mother . . . well, she was a ghost who hovered about but had little direct interaction with me. Father did all of the directing, but he never took responsibility for my actions, good or bad. My performances were on me.

Rebecca stood outside the circle in which the woman, her boys, and I were now engaged. She observed us, and I felt as if I were auditioning for a part without having any idea of the role.

The woman tightened her grip on both children and said, "Tell the nice man you're sorry."

Why did she assume I was a nice man? I was bewildered that she'd trust me, a stranger, over her own flesh and blood.

"Sorry," the boys mumbled in unison.

"Would you direct me to the train that stops nearest the Natural History Museum?"

Why was she asking *me*?

Oh. Of course, the uniform.

I knew everything about the Metro line, the routes Sal worked, all the local stops and the schedule weekdays, weekends, and holidays, but I didn't know one subway line from another.

"You can take a cab," I said.

"That would be expensive." She sighed.

I almost went into Sal's wallet and took out a twenty to give to her; she did look tired. But Rebecca came to my rescue.

"You can catch the shuttle to the West Side." She pointed at a sign. "When it stops, the subway you need will be on your left before the street exit." Rebecca knelt and asked the smaller boy, "Where are you visiting from?"

He poked his head out from the back of his mother's dress, but before he could answer, the taller one said, "Durham."

"We're on vacation while my dad goes to work," the little one said.

"Not work," the taller one corrected. "Dad's here for a conference."

"Fun," Rebecca said. "Well, you both help your mom find the B or the C trains. Can you remember B or C?"

They nodded earnestly.

"Then you get off at West Eighty-First, and the dinosaurs' house is a short walk from there. Come closer," Rebecca whispered. They both moved right up to her face, close enough to kiss her. "Dinosaurs are tricky creatures." The boys nodded together again, like this was a statement of fact everyone should know. "You can't leave your mother's side for a second. Okay?"

"Okay," they said in unison.

Rebecca stood. "If you get turned around, just ask someone. Most New Yorkers don't bite."

The tired woman mouthed a *thank you* as the boys dragged her away.

"You were pretty taken with those kids," Rebecca said to me.

"They were adorable." I gave her the response I thought she'd expect.

"I thought they were bratty." She smiled, showing the right amount of teeth to display confidence, not arrogance.

"Me too." I returned her smile, but with closed lips. A humble, shy workingman didn't show his teeth, not so much as an incisor.

Now she took hold of my hand and dragged me in the direction of the No. 4 and No. 6 lines. She rushed us through the hordes of commuters and tourists. I could barely keep up, and for a time I was convinced she was taking me back to the secret space where Sal's shell still lay. The No. 4 train arrived, the doors opened, and she pulled me inside. I followed her to two empty seats at the far end of the car.

We sat, not exchanging a word, not a glance, but her hand wrapped tightly around my fist bubbled a feeling inside me so foreign that it took several stops before I could name it.

Safety.

I felt safe.

She tilted her head at an angle so only her right eye met my left. Emerging from our silence came a question that you might call a game changer. "What's your story?"

"I told you most of it. It's rather boring."

"Your real story," she said.

Before I had the chance to ask her to explain, she did. "You're no train conductor."

I didn't know what had given me away—not knowing the directions to the Natural History Museum or the way I'd cut the cupcake with a knife at the diner yesterday. I'd known right away it was the wrong move; Sal always broke his bread with his hands. But I didn't ask her how she knew. It didn't matter. What mattered, what intrigued me, was that she knew.

"If I'm not a train conductor," I said, "then what am I?"

"Something tells me there are many answers to that question." The train stopped. She removed her hand from mine. "This is us." She exited the train quickly, and I hurried behind, barely making it through before the doors shut.

*   *   *

By the time we surfaced from the subway, the summer night air had taken a turn from bearable to beautiful—seventy-two degrees with an intermittent cool breeze, a rarity in a city that could easily suffocate you if you let it.

Rebecca was leading me to her place. I knew going there would be a risk, but I couldn't bring myself to leave her.

When we stepped onto the red carpet leading to the entrance of her Park Avenue, Upper East Side building, the doorman was there to greet us with an open door and pleasantries.

"What a beautiful evening, Miss Rebecca."

"Thank you, Jack," she said.

Jack touched the tip of his hat, nodded, and returned to his post behind the desk in the lobby.

At that moment I knew I had to walk away and never see my Rebecca again.

I had a stronger stomach than most, but still, the rarefied world behind doors held open by poor schmucks for the self-absorbed and entitled nauseated me.

"Good night, Rebecca," I said. "It was a pleasure."

I'd started to make my exit when she asked, "You're not coming up?"

"It's best I be on my way."

She stood silent, as if willing me to change my mind.

I should have walked away then, but her stillness drew me closer.

"Have you lived here long?" I already knew the answer (and I'll explain how I knew shortly, Linda), but I needed to break the silence.

"Me? Live here?" She laughed that sexy, throaty, utterly enchanting laugh. "I'm apartment-sitting. I have a place . . . well, I did, in the Bronx."

"My father was from the Bronx," I said.

"Where?"

I didn't answer. Didn't know how to explain that my father was from the Bronx but only in a metaphysical sense. It was where he'd begged my mother that we move. Father wanted us to leave the brownstone and live in a small two-bedroom apartment in the Bronx. He believed a world where cheaper cuts of meat, more gristle than flesh, and generic brands were one's only choices gave a person character. A great artist couldn't pretend to have character; they needed to live an authentic life.

"It's a big borough," she said, filling the silence. "The only one with an article in front of its name."

"Excuse me?"

"You know, it's not The Brooklyn, or The Manhattan, or The Queens . . . it's only The Bronx."

"Did you like it there?"

"The Bronx? I didn't not like it. But when this woman who bought a few of my pieces—"

"You had a showing?"

"If you can call on the street outside the Met a showing. A bunch of us artists would set up and try to hawk our work until the cops showed up and chased us off. One day this attractive woman, maybe in her fifties, bought three of my pieces, and the next day she was back and said she wanted to sponsor me. I had no idea what that meant."

I knew what it meant. "A patron of the arts."

"So, the pretend train conductor knows about the art world . . ."

"Mother was a collector." I didn't mean to let that slip, but Rebecca had that effect on me. I couldn't control my thoughts and words around her.

"It's a sweet deal. My 'patron'"—Rebecca used air quotes—"doesn't have pets, not even a plant to water. All I have to do is make my art. She gets to help the starving artist, though I'm far from starving." She pinched the flesh at the side of her waist.

"You have the perfect amount of meat on your bones." This came out wrong. I had meant it to be flattering; instead, I made her sound like a rib roast.

Still, she thanked me and returned the compliment. "You have the right amount of meat on your bones too."

She laughed, and this time I laughed as me.

"She travels a lot. When I don't go with her, I have the whole place to myself." She opened the door for me, and we went inside.

Jack the doorman raced to the elevator so it would be waiting for us. I reached into my uniform pocket, but Jack lowered his gaze and let me know a tip was not necessary, maybe inappropriate. He was an expert reader of body language.

Doorman, I thought. *A character worth studying*. I made a mental note.

Inside Ms. Patron of the Arts' apartment, Rebecca sniffed. There was a faint smell of pesticide. "I guess Jack must have let the exterminator in with his passkey. So I didn't need to rush back after all."

Hmm. The exterminator had been a ploy to get me to her apartment. I was a little disturbed by the deceit but also flattered by her effort.

The decor was as expected: exorbitantly priced minimalist. Very few pieces of furniture but each one custom-made by hand. Quaker style. On the wall facing the straight-back couch hung two Picassos—sketches from his early years, before he established his own style. The man had produced in such quantity that his work was valued at far less than most would expect from an artist with his universal name recognition.

"It's a Picasso," she said.

I pretended to be impressed, of course. She had already figured out I wasn't a train conductor, but I didn't yet want her to know that my background had gifted me with up-close exposure to famous artists, even hacks like Picasso.

"I think he's given more credit than he deserved," she said.

I had to bite my tongue so as not to tell her how much I agreed. I had so few opportunities to discuss art in a meaningful way. One of my characters had been a curator, but she'd lost her passion for art and artists. I'd had to crack her open to get to her deeper truth. That's when I discovered she had only one kidney. Right away, I regretted that I hadn't gotten her whole story. Based on the work we had done, I was sure she had given her kidney to save the life of someone she loved. Not a child or sibling; she was too bitter to have had a deep family connection like that. Maybe it had been one of her colleagues, or an artist. Whoever it was had accepted her sacrifice, then left her.

"These two are fascinating." I pointed to two mirror-image oil paintings that hung over the fireplace. They were abstract, but it was clear to me they were self-portraits.

"Some of my early stuff." Rebecca blushed. She walked over to the liquor cabinet and opened the door. "Would you like a drink? There's just about everything."

Clearly, she wanted us to move on from her work. "Water, room temperature."

"Is Bill your friend?" she asked.

Bill? Did I know a Bill? My mind raced through all the characters I had ever been, and I remembered Bill, a carpenter, from my college days. That had been in Rhode Island and more than five years ago. How did she know him?

Before I could respond, she said, "I'm sorry. I heard that's what you say to people who are in AA. Something about protecting their anonymity."

I swallowed the sigh of relief before it escaped. "No. I never liked the taste."

"Cool. You okay if I have a glass of wine?"

I told her it was no problem, but I wasn't sure if I was okay with it. If she was going to direct me and get me to reach inside to pull out real emotion, like all the greats do, she needed to be clearheaded.

I followed her into the kitchen and watched as she poured a glass of Chardonnay. I came up behind her, and she jumped.

"Sorry." She put her hand to her chest. "You startled me."

"Would you mind not drinking?"

Her expression told me she wanted an explanation, so I reached into my bag of tricks and pulled out a detail from my own backstory. "I wish my mother had been a friend of Bill's," I told her. "Mother was a blackout drunk, but it was my father who died of cirrhosis."

Rebecca put the cork back in the bottle.

I realized that it was time I told her the truth.

"The uniform . . . I owe you an explanation." I was ready to tell her everything. It was time to confess that I was an actor.

Why? Because Rebecca's patron was none other than my mother. They were one and the same.

Yes, Linda, I know: *What the fuck?* Let me explain:

I hadn't spoken to my mother since Father's death when I was sixteen. Mother and I still lived in the brownstone together at that point, and would for the next two years until I went away to college, but we scarcely exchanged a word, not of any substance. I blamed her for my father's death, and she never attempted to convince me otherwise. She was a smart woman; I had to give her that. She knew her efforts would have been futile. I hated my mother, but I respected her for this. Her silence was evidence. She owned the sins she'd committed against my father and accepted the consequences: losing her son.

Mother did come to my college graduation. I don't know if she was there for the ceremony, but at the champagne-and-strawberries reception, she handed me a manila envelope. Inside were the keys to the brownstone, which had been in my father's family for over a century, and a copy of Father's will, which stipulated that after completing college or turning twenty-two, I was to be given the brownstone and access to a moderate trust fund. Father had left nothing to Mother, which made sense: she'd always been the one with greater means and was much better at managing her financial affairs. Father, like son, was horrible with money. But you already know this about me, my sweet Linda.

Inside the envelope was also an original Picasso sketch, postcard sized. On the back was a note, written in Mother's sloppy handwriting—*Someday, I hope we can manage to have some sort of relationship. After all, I am your mother.*

That was where she was mistaken. She was no longer my mother, and after that day she was nothing to me, not even an afterthought. That is, until one summer day seven years later, when I received a call from a Mr. Franklin Reynolds, who claimed he was a close friend of my father's. I hadn't known my father to have any friends. Not what Father would have called "real" friends. People who gave without expectation of gain.

After I pushed, and not very hard, Mr. Reynolds explained he was my family's attorney. Apparently, Mr. Reynolds had an unmanageable gambling problem. In return for my father bailing him out of several financial fiascos, Mr. Reynolds had promised to keep an eye out for me should anything happen to Father.

"I thought you should know that your mother recently changed her will, leaving a considerable amount of her estate to some street artist." He didn't say, and I didn't ask, what the previous will had stated. I had no interest in my mother's estate, but my curiosity was piqued. The woman I'd once called my mother never gave anything without the guarantee of a substantial return on her investment. She suffered from what Father called the *conundrums of the wealthy*, or from being a member of the "one percent," as they're called today. She never gave to charities that needed her money, only to those with proven track records of financial success. Doing so elevated one's status in a society that Father had loathed, as did I.

"What can you tell me about the artist?" I asked Reynolds.

"She has no criminal record. From outside of Rochester. Graduated from community college. She recently gave up her basement apartment in the North Bronx."

"My father was from the Bronx," I said.

"I thought your father was from . . ." There was a long pause, after which the attorney continued with more useless data on my mother's beneficiary. "Only child. Parents deceased—drunk driver. Nothing noteworthy or extraordinary about her. In a word, unremarkable."

Oh, how Mr. Reynolds underestimated your mother.

*   *   *

Well . . . I had to know more about this "unremarkable person" and what she had to offer that had been so enticing to Mother, a woman who could buy anything and—almost—anyone she wanted.

Mr. Reynolds gave me Mother's address, and I told him his debt to my father was paid and to please not contact me again.

From across the avenue, using my bird-watching binoculars, I witnessed, on several occasions, Mother come and go from her Park Avenue dwelling. Her facial expression had grown more serious, more strained, and more stick-up-the-ass than ever. She appeared as I had expected. In life, unlike in great plays, characters don't have arcs through which revelations and grand transformations occur. They stay the same. Mother looked as miserable as she always had.

On the day the latest heat wave broke, she exited the building with her arm hooked into the arm of a young woman with shoe-polish-black hair. Mother appeared radiant, walking with what I can only describe as a skip in her step. I almost dropped my binoculars. Who was this young woman? Saint or sorcerer?

I trailed her.

For four days in a row between 8:45 and 8:48 in the morning, the young artist exited the Park Avenue building and power-walked thirty-two blocks to Grand Central Terminal. If I hadn't been in peak condition, I would have lost her, or maybe had a heart attack. Each day she bought from one of two newsstands a cup of coffee, black no sugar, and sipped her way to the 10:15 AM commuter train, the Metro-North Hudson Line.

On the fifth day, I followed her onto the train. That was the day I met Sal, my next character study. When your mother got off at Dobbs Ferry station, I stayed to the end of the line.

LINDA

3

I ENTERED GRAND CENTRAL Terminal. A man wearing a Brioni, at least a $10,000 suit, blocked me from moving forward and said, "Who you gonna call?"

I wasn't in the mood. I tried to step around him, but every time I moved right, he moved right; when I moved left, he moved left.

"Come on," he said. "Who you gonna call? Say it."

"Fuck off," I said.

"Where's your sense of humor?"

After the remake of *Ghostbusters* with the all-female cast came out, people would often spot Dad and me wearing our oversized backpacks and coveralls and make references to the film. For a time, I laughed along. Now I wanted this entitled fuck to get out of my way.

"Move," I said.

Gray Suit took a step closer to my face, and now I had what I wanted: probable cause to kick his ass. I lifted my left fist (southpaw), and he laughed.

"Aren't you cute."

The asshole patted my head and I grabbed his wrist, and in one move I had him on his knees.

"Want to know who I'm gonna call now?"

"You're crazy, bitch."

I twisted his arm harder. I was a moment away from doing some real physical harm when, in my peripheral vision, I saw a uniform rushing toward us. I thought it was a cop, but as he approached, I could see he was a train conductor.

"What is going on?" He looked down at Gray Suit on his knees with his arm held tight behind his back.

I couldn't risk an arrest or any trouble. I let him go. The jerk got up on his feet, moving his mouth but not saying a word. What was he going to say? He'd never imagined a four-foot-eleven girl, 105 pounds, giving off a vulnerable vibe no predator could resist, would kick his ass.

He also had no clue he was messing with a woman who was only three black belts away from the highest rank in judo. The only woman who'd ever reached the top level was even smaller than I: Keido Fukuda, four nine and ninety-five pounds. Dad always said size didn't matter. Except to assholes like Gray Suit, of course.

I was feeling generous, and I had to get going. "It's cool," I told the conductor, who looked from me to Gray Suit.

Gray Suit nodded and took a big step back.

"Who you gonna call?" I smiled at him and walked away.

* * *

When I got to the Park Avenue building, Jack, the building's doorman of many decades, waved me over. I pointed to my pack. I tugged on the front of my coveralls. Credo had very clear rules: all service people, especially those who specialized in vermin and insect infestation, used the rear service entrance. Under no circumstance were we to enter through the main entrance. Most of the building's residents never even knew we were in their apartments invading their privacy every week. If they did know, it was too unpleasant for them to think about. The upside was our skin-crawling-grotesque work gave us the superpower of invisibility. If Dad and I had any interest in a life of crime, the residents would never be able to pick us out in a lineup.

Jack continued to wave his arms like he was guiding me in for a landing.

I walked over to him. Jack was always impeccably dressed, uniform pressed, pants creased in a precise line, and all this was true today. But his doorman cap was off-center, which made me think the situation was serious and maybe there was a bigger infestation problem than we'd thought.

"Where's Mr. Donovan?" Jack asked.

"He had some other business to deal with, but I can handle whatever the situation is."

Jack held the door open for me and then rushed me to the main resident elevator, framed in gold plate. Jack pressed the up button three times, and we waited for the car to arrive. I had never seen Jack like this. In all the years I had helped Dad service this building, Jack had been the epitome of calm and collected.

When the elevator door finally opened, a woman in her seventies, wearing an apricot-colored fur coat and carrying a matching ball of fur that looked like something we would trap and drown, eyeballed me up and down as she exited.

"Is the service elevator broken?" Her tone dropped the room temperature several degrees.

"It's working fine, Mrs. Rendeer," Jack said.

"I will be reporting this to the building manager."

We both ignored her and got in the elevator. Jack pressed the button for the twelfth floor.

"Mrs. Ludwig's apartment." Jack paused. I nodded, though I didn't know the name, but I didn't know the names of most of the residents of our high-end buildings. On the days we come to spray, the residents typically stay away. If they don't see the exterminators, they don't have to acknowledge that all their wealth and status can't protect them from the roaches and vermin that infest the city. Dad, on the other hand, knows the name and face of every resident in each of his buildings. He memorizes the photos he finds on their shelves or in their drawers. While I keep an Excel spreadsheet on our desktop of schedules and payments, Dad keeps personal notes and anecdotes about customers in black, marbled notebooks with lined pages.

He has a reasonable explanation for his nosiness. For him, it's a matter of respect. They have histories. They aren't faceless, nameless occupants.

"During her morning tea," Jack continued. "Saw a creepy-crawly."

"A roach by any other name will still stink." I repeated what Dad had said more times than I, and I'm sure Jack, could count.

Jack pressed *12* again, as if this would get us to the floor faster. "She is out for the day and expects the situation to be handled before she returns this evening."

Jack exited the elevator. I followed him to apartment 12B.

He unclipped from his belt the large ring of keys to every apartment in the building. It must have weighed close to two pounds. On the first try, without taking a breath, Jack found the right key and let us inside. I knew each one was marked and color coded by floor, but when Dad was in possession of the master key ring, he always took a minute or two to find the right match.

Was Jack escorting me because he didn't trust me to do the job alone?

He stayed in the living room perusing the large collection of rare books, paper, cardboard—a roach's wet dream. I went to the kitchen, pulled my metal tank from my pack, connected the hose, and sprayed pesticide into every nook and cranny in the apartment. A few roaches scattered from behind the bathroom sink. I was now sure I had made the right choice to come today.

When I returned to the living room, Jack clicked his tongue, the way he did when taken off guard. He raised over his head, like someone accepting an Oscar, a book probably older than both of our combined ages.

"What you reading?"

"This is a first edition of Mary Shelley's *Frankenstein*."

"You're a fan?"

"Do you know what this is worth?"

"A lot?"

"I wouldn't be surprised if this would auction well, for quite a lot of money."

"You have to be kidding me." I reached for the book.

Jack raised it even higher. "My apologies, Miss Linda, but if anything happens . . ."

"You don't trust me?"

"There are few people with as much integrity as you and your father."

"You don't shadow my father; you give him the keys, and we work on our own."

"I'm afraid I gave you the wrong impression," he said. "There are those rare days where, well"—he glanced down at the book he was now holding close to his chest—"I need what I believe your generation would call . . . a mental health break."

"I think your generation calls it the same, but I get it. You're on the front line." Mrs. Rendeer and her powder-puff rodent she called a dog were among the easygoing tenants in this building.

Jack nodded. "Please." He lifted the book in my direction. "It is quite beautiful."

I waved *Frankenstein* away. "I appreciate it. Honest. I don't want to be responsible for anything worth that much."

Jack carefully returned the book to the shelf. He turned to me. "All good."

I eyed the grandfather clock in the corner of the room. I had to go. I had promised Dad one apartment and I would leave and meet up with him. "Jack, if it's all the same with you, I am going to take off, and Dad and I will be back tomorrow to finish the job."

"Miss Donovan, I am afraid that may not end well."

Jack was right. If I didn't exterminate the rest of the building, especially the neighboring apartments, the "creepy crawlies" would make their home there.

I lifted my tank. "Of course."

"Onward," Jack said.

Jack stopped in front of apartment 12C.

I put my hand on Jack's wrist. "Dad always serviced this apartment alone. He said the woman who lived here . . ."

"Mrs. Lyons."

"Mrs. Lyons was a bit craz . . . eccentric. Wouldn't want someone she didn't know in her home. Even if I was his daughter."

"True. But we both know what will happen if you don't service her today."

"This place will be party city for every roach looking for a safe haven."

Jack rang the bell and knocked three times. No answer. He inserted the key into the lock, and the ominous song from the old horror movie with the girl who spewed green pea soup began to play.

"It's Mr. Credo."

Appropriate ringtone for him, I almost said out loud.

Jack took his cell from his pocket. "Mr. Credo, Sir, yes, of course," Jack said. "Right away." He clicked off. "It would seem Mrs. Rendeer wasted no time."

"Sorry."

"Front line." He flashed a weak smile. "I would appreciate it if you would be so kind as to finish on your own."

"Of course." I couldn't help smiling. Jack did trust me.

"You can bring me the keys when you're done." He walked toward the elevator.

I turned the key, opened the door, and was punched in the face with a scent vile enough to make cockroaches smell like roses.

Chanel No. 5 and Death.

INSIDE THE APARTMENT, the air was sweet, pungent, harsh but bearable, until I reached the door to the master bedroom. The stench of perfume and decaying flesh almost knocked me over. I unzipped my backpack, took out the gas mask I was grateful Dad insisted we always pack, placed it over my face, and went inside.

There, lying on a California king bed, was a woman in a black cocktail dress. From where I stood, I couldn't see her face, but even with the mask I could smell the gases her body was emitting. She was definitely dead. A scream scratched at my throat.

I was ready to get out of there and call the police when I caught site of its tail, wagging.

I walked closer to Mrs. Lyons and saw a fat rat dining on the right side of her bloated, blue-tinted face. The scream escaped. The rat jumped in my direction. I lifted my tank and whacked it across the room. It laid motionless on the hardwood floor, but most likely it wasn't dead, just stunned, and soon it would be ready to attack again. I pushed the heavy oak armoire, letting it crash down on top of it.

The walls were so thick no one could have heard anything. No one could have heard Mrs. Lyons if she called for help. Had she been eaten alive? My heart started to punch its way through my chest cavity. I needed air, to breathe. I ripped off the gas mask; it crashed to the floor, and I ran to the living room. I had to call the police. I rummaged through my backpack, finally remembering my cell was in the front pocket of my coveralls. I took it out and dialed 911. "Rat. Ate a woman. She's dead. Very dead." I gave them my name and address and clicked off.

If possible, the air was more nauseating than before. I supposed I could have waited for the police outside the apartment, but I didn't feel right leaving Mrs. Lyons alone. I paced the faded Persian rug, stopping each time at the bedroom door.

I wondered if she was Catholic and an open casket was important to her. Dad had made me promise he would be buried, not cremated, and that his casket would be open for people to say their good-byes to him. "If it's not open, you can never really be certain who's inside," he would say.

I have witnessed the magic of many morticians. Some perform miracles, making the deceased look better than when they were alive. I couldn't imagine anyone who would be able to make Mrs. Lyons presentable enough for an open casket.

I continued to pace and prayed she was dead before she was dinner.

Poor Mrs. Lyons. My heart hurt for her. She wasn't the first corpse we'd discovered on the job. On more than one occasion, Dad and I had shown up to exterminate a building and found a person, usually elderly, with no family, no friends, dead, a heart attack, an aneurysm, a cracked skull from slipping in the shower, and no one knew until we, the exterminators, showed up to service the building. Whenever the death smell was in the air, Dad would insist I wait outside. He'd wanted to protect me from seeing a decaying corpse. An image, he said, "hard to erase from memory."

Today, Dad wasn't here to protect me.

My phone vibrated in my hand. It was Dad. FaceTiming?

I pressed the green button. There was Dad. His chin. "Dad, move the phone up." There was his once-again-messy ponytail that I now found calming.

"Dad, now the phone is facing the back of your head."

"Had to pick this up." He held a penny in front of the screen. "All day long I'll have good luck."

"I have to tell you something."

I could now see his face.

"You're tugging your ear," he said. "It must be bad."

I dropped my hand.

"You're still at Park?" he said. "You promised. One apartment and you'd leave. Forget Credo."

Credo. If I was worried about him firing us over a few roaches, what would he do when he heard one of his long-term residents had been partially eaten by a rat? He'll probably sue us for negligence. If word got out, Donovan and Daughter Exterminating would never work in this town, or any town, again.

"I'm in her apartment . . ."

"Whose apartment?"

"Twelve C."

"Mrs. Lyons."

Hearing her name, a name I hadn't even been able to remember a little over an hour ago, brought me back to a state of panic. My breathing was racing, and I couldn't speak.

"Linda, do you hear me?"

I rapidly nodded.

"There's a guest bathroom off the right of the living room. Go there. Now."

I hesitated.

"Now."

I did as he instructed.

"Do exactly what I say. Put the phone down."

I placed the phone on top of the toilet tank.

"Turn on the cold water. Splash your face three times, and in between, take a slow, deep breath, in through the nose and out through the mouth."

I did this four, maybe five times, until I was able to talk.

I picked up the phone.

"Dry your face on the pink towel."

I took the towel, which looked like it had never been used, wiped it across my face, and dropped it into the sink.

"Make sure you put the towel back as it was. Mrs. Lyons is very particular about her guest towels."

"She's dead, Dad."

This was the first time I couldn't read my father's expression. It was blank. Completely. Shock? Despair?

"Dad? Did you hear me?"

"It's part of the business."

"She's not just dead. Her face. Eaten."

"A rat?"

"How is that possible?" I could feel the panic, a choke hold around my neck. "We have mice. Mice and rats don't coexist." I repeated what Dad had said to me more times than I could count.

"Where's your mask?"

"I dropped it."

"Use the towel to cover your nose and mouth."

"I'm fine." This wasn't true, but after what Dad had said about Mrs. Lyons's guest towels, it didn't feel right to use one as a barrier between me and her stench.

"Let me see her."

I didn't have to ask why. Dad was a sleuth when it came to vermin, and I was sure he might be able to determine something, anything, from seeing the body.

Cupping my hand over my nose and holding the phone at my side, I walked Dad to Mrs. Lyons's bedroom and aimed the phone in her direction.

"Get closer," Dad called out.

I took a step toward her.

"Closer, Linda, closer."

I couldn't bring myself to look again. With my face turned away, I aimed the phone inches from where Mrs. Lyons's cheek should have been.

"Are there bites anywhere else?"

"I don't know," I said.

"Linda, please look."

"I can't," I said. "I can't."

"You are my daughter. You can and will. You were born for this." Dad had never spoken of exterminating like it was a birthright. I knew this wasn't the time to question him.

I forced myself to see she was also bitten on her neck and arm. I aimed the phone inches away from the bites.

"They seem to be the same in circumference."

"That means there may be only one rat," I said.

"A beta. Probably abandoned by its pack."

"I only saw one."

"You saw it?"

"It was still feasting." I gagged at the image burned into my brain.

"Linda, where is it now?" I could hear him struggling to hide his panic.

I turned the phone toward the tipped-over armoire.

"Linda, bring the phone up to your face."

I obeyed.

"What else do we know about rats?"

I was in no mood for exterminating trivia, but Dad wouldn't tell me what his point was without doing it this way, his way.

"A lot."

"If they don't keep chewing . . ."

"Their teeth will grow through their skulls."

"If that rat isn't dead, and there's a good chance it isn't . . ."

"I know," I said. "They are very resilient and pliable creatures."

"It will eat right through the dresser." The phone was shaking in my hand.

"Get out of the apartment," Dad said.

"I can't," I said.

"You called the police?"

"Nine-one-one."

Every muscle in Dad's face stiffened.

"Had no choice."

"You always have a choice."

"Dad, I have to get the rat poison and the cage from the basement. I don't want someone to get hurt."

"I don't want you to get hurt."

"Dad, I'll be fine."

"Leave *now*," Dad shouted, and I dropped the phone.

"Linda, where are you?"

I picked up my cell, and my hand brushed against Mrs. Lyons's bare foot. It was cold, like she needed a blanket to warm up.

"Linda, are you there?"

I wished I were anywhere else.

"I didn't mean to raise my voice."

I could hear the remorse.

"Do you trust me?" he asked.

"You know I do," I said.

"Then listen to me. Leave the apartment now. Meet me at Penn Station. The only thing that matters today is that we see your mother. Promise you will leave right now."

"Okay," I said, though I already knew this was another promise I would break.

"When you leave, don't forget the mask, under the bed."

How had he seen that?

Dad clicked off, and my screen saver popped up, the pic of Dad and me standing in front of our used but new-to-us van, freshly painted with our logo: *Donovan and Daughter Exterminating*. That had been weeks before my fifteenth birthday, ten years ago. The day I went from Anthony Donovan's daughter to Anthony Donovan's business partner. Looking over at poor Mrs. Lyons, I'd never felt more ready to get out, to finally get my degree. To get out of New York. If we lost this account, there was no way Dad would be able to support himself. I would never get to college. I couldn't walk away and pretend I'd never seen Mrs. Lyons's dead body. Besides, I'd told the 911 operator my name.

The police would be here soon, and there would be no explaining any of this to Credo. He would terminate us before I had a chance to speak, though I wasn't sure what I would say anyway.

I needed to call someone I could trust to help me figure all this out. I opened my phone.

In my contacts, there she was, the second of only two people I had on speed dial, the only person I'd ever let touch my feet. I wouldn't even let Dad give me a foot massage. She was my ex now. Every time I went to hit the trash icon to erase her from my contacts, a shooting pain traveled from my head down to my toes.

Her name, number, one push away.

Jess.

Jessica Jones, named after my favorite Marvel Universe superhero, really antihero. The badass of superheroes. Jess's parents owned a comic book store in Seattle. She called them eccentric and hippie. They sounded cool to me. They couldn't have chosen a more appropriate name for their daughter. Real Jess wasn't sullen like the comic book character; if anything, she was too perky, especially given her profession. She was the sweetest, sexiest person I had ever known. It had taken our breaking up, and my missing her so hard it hurt to brush my teeth some days, to realize she also had superhuman strength. She couldn't lift cars over her head, but she could pick me up and make me laugh, no matter how low to the ground I felt.

Jess.

My pointer finger hovered over the number two. I couldn't do it. I hit my saved messages instead. "Why are you doing this . . . I love you. You love me. We can take it slow. Call me. Let's talk this out. Sam misses you. I miss you . . ."

Then, a few weeks ago, she'd finally stopped. To call her now would be nothing less than cruel. I was no superhero antihero, and certainly no angel. I had done a lot of shitty things to some very nice women, but I couldn't do this to Jess. I'd caused her enough pain, and to bring her back into my life after pushing her out the way I had would be screwed up, even for me. Besides, Jess was a homicide detective, and this was a case of a poor old lady who'd died, probably of natural causes, though I wasn't sure if a rat eating her corpse was all that natural. But then again, maybe one creature feeding off another for survival was the most natural act in the world.

I picked up the mask from the floor and shoved it into my backpack. Maybe if I talked to Credo before the police arrived . . . or maybe if I went to Jack, who'd always liked Dad and me, he could help convince Credo this wasn't our fault. These things happened. Didn't they? I would assure him that there would be no other sighting or incidents with rats. I didn't see that conversation ending well, but I had to try.

I opened the front door, and standing in front of me, arms folded, eyes squinting with distrust, was a woman with more-salt-than-pepper hair, a wrinkled brow, and a complexion untouched by antiaging measures such as moisturizer and sunscreen: Detective Rita Frascon from the Homicide Division and Jess's partner. I respected her for her willingness to display signs of aging and feared her because she was tough—and because she hated me. She'd had the same serious expression on her face the night she warned me, "Partners have each other's backs. Hurt Jess, and I hurt you."

Was she here to follow up on her promise?

5

DETECTIVE RITA FRASCON extended her hand like we had never met, never fallen down drunk on our asses outside the bar where we had spent three hours waiting on Jess the night she was stranded on the No. 6 train between Thirty-Fourth and Forty-Second Streets. A jumper, the third one that month, had caused the delay. February, filled with short, cold days, took its toll on the residents of the city that never sleeps, which translated to the sleep deprived and depressed roaming the streets and subway platforms.

Frascon still had the handshake of someone who had nothing to prove but wanted it known she meant business.

I pulled my hand from her grip. "Rita . . ." I quickly corrected myself. "Detective Frascon. Surprised to see you here." I was relieved, but disappointed, Jess wasn't with her.

She pushed past me. "Where's the body?"

I pointed to the bedroom.

She took a paisley handkerchief from her circa-1986 navy shoulder-padded blazer, which was old, not vintage. "I will never get used to that smell." She lifted her chin toward my pack. "You got a mask in there?"

Before I could respond, she told me to forget it. "Once that smell gets up your nose, mask or no mask, you're tasting it for weeks."

She walked into the bedroom. "Jesus fucking Christ!"

The rat could still be alive. I ran to her.

Frascon was bent over the body, clicking her phone. Photos?

"Did you touch anything?"

"Only that." I pointed to the armoire on the floor.

She glared at it and then at me.

"I tried to kill—"

She jumped back. "There's a rat under there?"

"It's probably dead."

"Probably?" Her voice rose an octave. She backed away from the armoire. "One of the highest-priced buildings in the city has rats." She half smiled.

"Rat," I said. "I only saw one rat."

Frascon shoved her paisley handkerchief back into her right blazer pocket and snapped on blue latex gloves. She went back to Mrs. Lyons and, in a swift circular motion, tapped around her scalp. "Doesn't seem to be any swelling, head trauma," she said to herself. She clicked more photos, this time of the unbitten side of the neck and face, all the while humming the tune to "Ben," a song about friendship with a rat. I had forgotten her sick sense of humor.

Frascon took a step back. "Forensics will have to confirm the official cause of death, but given the condition of the body, she's probably been dead at least three days."

"Then she was already dead when . . ."

"She became the main course." She glanced over at the armoire. "I'd assume so."

I let out the breath I didn't realize I was holding.

"They think this is a possible homicide?" I asked.

"They?"

"Nine-one-one. Isn't that why you're here?"

"I'm here as a favor," she said.

I couldn't imagine why she would be doing anything to help me, but I was grateful. "Thank you," I said.

"She's the one you should be thanking." Rita nodded toward the bedroom doorway. I looked up, and there was Jess.

"Good to see you, Linda."

She walked past me, and despite the perfumed rotting flesh permeating the air, I could smell her clean, citrus, not-lemon-but-grapefruit soap, which I desperately missed. "You want to use my mask?" I offered.

"That one has the nose of bloodhound but a stomach that could handle food poisoning on the *Titanic* and still not get nauseous," Rita said. "Surprised you don't know that. But I guess you weren't together very long." She punched me right in the chest.

Jess ignored her, or agreed. I couldn't tell.

Jess walked over to Mrs. Lyons, her back to me, I couldn't see the expression on her face, but she made no sound to indicate the horror I assumed she felt.

She bent over the body, and there was that butt that matched her personality, hard and sweet. She wasn't skinny, a deal breaker for me. She was beautiful in a way that had always been too traditional for my taste. Great hair, long and thick, which was why instead of cutting it short, she kept it neatly tied back. If it weren't for her right eye appearing a tad smaller than her left, her face would have been symmetrically perfect and her looks boringly model-like.

I was okay with my looks. I didn't want a different nose or better skin, and I liked my ordinary brown hair, which now grew past my shoulders. I was a solid "cute," but women told me it was my confidence that they were attracted to. Jess had said it was my vulnerability, and the way I worked so hard to hide it.

She was wearing what I hadn't known until right then was my favorite of her suits: black, pin-striped, well fitted, no shoulder pads. Not designer, but not cheap. Made to last. She'd worn it the night we met in that hipster-posing-as-a-dive bar. It wasn't love at first sight; lust, for damn sure. Now all I wanted to do was insert myself between that suit and her skin and tell her how my ending us was a mistake. How I was a huge idiot.

"You with us?" Frascon snapped her fingers in front of my nose.

I had no idea what she'd said.

"So, are you going to tell us?"

"Tell you?"

"Why were you here today?" Jess asked.

"I came in to spray for roaches."

"Big roach problem?" Frascon said.

"We keep it under control."

"Where is father Donovan?" She made Dad sound like a priest. He had been celibate since my mother's death, so she wasn't too far off.

"Visiting my mother," I said.

"Today is the anniversary of her mother's death." Jess stopped examining the body and tilted her head in my direction.

"You remembered." I couldn't have told her more than once. I now regretted never introducing Jess to Dad. I had told myself that was the kind of thing you did when you were serious about each other. We were just having a casual fling. No big deal.

Right from the start Jess had acted like I, we, were the biggest deal. She'd insisted I meet the two most important people in her life here in New York: her partner, Rita, and Sam, her dog.

Sam was my buddy from day one. Doggy treats helped. Rita was a different story. It took several nights of bar hopping and listening to her gripe about life before she and I connected. Buying more than my share of rounds of vodka martinis, her beverage of choice, also helped. When I'd ghosted Jess, I'd ghosted Rita too.

Then again, Jess was a cop, so I'd known there was no way she'd win Dad over.

"How are you?" Jess's brown eyes had speckles of green and a sincerity that her professional tone and posture worked hard to hide but couldn't. Unconsciously, I pulled at my earlobe. This woman still turned me on, and that made me almost as nervous as the thought of Credo, who I was certain by now knew the police were here and would be rushing through the door any minute to discover his top-notch exterminating team couldn't stop a rat from entering his building, reaching the twelfth floor, and attacking a resident's dead body. Hearing this play out in my head, I realized that if I were in his shoes, *I* would fire us. How could this have happened?

"You're probably better than this one." Frascon snapped off the blue glove from her right hand in the direction of poor Mrs. Lyons's cold, dead body.

Jess made eye contact with Rita only. I told myself she wasn't here as my friend or my ex. This was business. Her job.

Jess pulled her phone from her pocket and waved me over. I walked to her side and looked at the image on her phone of the rat bites on Mrs. Lyons's neck.

"What do you make of this?" Jess asked.

"They say no two rats' bites are alike," I said.

"These look identical. The same shape and size."

"Exactly," I said. "The bites are from the same rat."

"The one under the armoire," Rita added.

The tops of Jess's shoulders scrunched up to the bottoms of her earlobes. I remembered how she would do this whenever I talked about my day. When I'd ask if I was making her uncomfortable, she'd say, "Of course," then insist I keep talking. She claimed my enthusiasm was a turn-on. She was being kind. She knew I needed to talk about work with someone other than Dad. Someone I could impress; someone I could show that I was tough and together and not the frightened mess I couldn't let myself see.

"They'll attack without cause." Frascon unbuttoned her jacket and pulled up the plain white T-shirt she was wearing underneath, exposing a nasty scar. "Back alley. I was chasing a suspect. Never saw this guy coming. The fuck jumped straight up, super rat, was going for my throat, but luckily I tripped and he got me above the abdomen instead."

I pulled my right pant leg up. "This, I asked for. Cornered the little guy and gave him no choice."

"Never corner a rat," Frascon said.

"I hadn't realized you knew your vermin," I said.

"Maybe if you had stuck around, it would have come up." She sounded more hurt than angry. I had been so wrapped up in how Jess was doing after the breakup that I'd never considered Frascon's feelings.

Before I could tell her, tell Jess, tell them both, I was sorry, Jess interjected. "Did you know the victim well?" Reminding me they were here on police business.

"I never met her." I glanced over at Mrs. Lyons, and for some reason I wished I had.

"How long have you been servicing this building?" Frascon asked.

"My father started the business soon after I was born. He wanted to set his own hours. He was a single parent and needed to be flexible."

"You're twenty-three," Frascon said.

Before I could correct her, Jess jumped in. "She just turned twenty-five."

I was touched she remembered my birthday.

Frascon rolled her eyes, and I knew why: never contradict your partner in front of a civilian, especially not one you loved who then ghosted your ass. I'd learned from all the cop shows Dad insisted I watch with him that this was a rookie move.

"My father serviced Mrs. Lyons's apartment alone. She was particular about who was allowed in."

"You're here today?"

"Jack—"

"The doorman?"

"I sprayed the apartment next door, and he insisted."

"He didn't want this place turning into a roach motel." Frascon knew her shit, at least when it came to pests.

"What did you eat for lunch?" Jess was sniffing around Mrs. Lyons's head.

"What?" Frascon and I said in unison.

"Peanut butter."

Frascon moved to Jess's side. "I can't smell anything over . . ." She circled her finger in the direction of the body. "And what is that perfume?"

"Chanel No. 5," I said.

Frascon and Jess eyeballed me. I knew they were thinking, *What do you know about perfume?* I was your deodorant-only kind of girl. I had dated a lot of different-smelling women, but no one smelled like Jess.

"Let's hope we're dealing with a beta," Jess said.

"Sounds like software for my computer." Rita laughed, and Jess smiled. Her right incisor stuck out. I remembered how I loved to rub my tongue along the tooth's edges.

Needing to stop the feelings of want from boiling over inside me, I turned to vermin-speak. "Betas are the subservient ones. They take orders. They will be sent out to get food for the pack, and sometimes they'll get lost, or when they return the rest have been scared off. That's how you run into solo rats."

I couldn't help myself and moved closer to Jess. "I think I smell peanut butter," I lied. I wanted to support her in some way. Besides, if she said she smelled peanut butter, I was sure she did. "Rats love peanut butter."

Frascon slipped back on a blue glove and ran her pointer finger down Mrs. Lyons's neck and arm. She smelled the dead woman's hand. "Nothing." She sniffed around the head again. "Maybe, but it's faint."

"Maybe that's why our little friend only bit her arm and neck but went to town on her face," Jess said.

"You think someone smeared peanut butter on her face intentionally?" The possibility was too insane to believe.

Jess got down on her hands and knees. I had no idea why, but I followed suit.

"I know you two have history, but Detective Jones, this is a police investigation," Frascon scolded her.

"Checking for holes," Jess said.

"Oh," I said. "If you're looking for how it got in here, it could have been a number of ways that would seem innocuous to the untrained eye." I was putting it on a little heavy, but I still cared about impressing her.

"Well, Ms. Exterminator, or should I call you Columbo?"

I ignored Frascon's spitting sarcasm, got back on my feet and walked over to the radiator, and pulled off the metal decorative cover. "The hole around the steam pipe."

Frascon nodded and *mm-hmm*ed. I opened the door to the connecting bathroom and lifted the toilet seat. "Rats are strong swimmers."

"Enough," Frascon said. "You made your point."

"It could be an alpha," Jess called out from underneath the bed. "The leader of the pack—a street gang, if you will." She was repeating something I had told her.

"Freaking fantastic." Frascon gently kicked the back of Jess's sensible but stylish shoe. "There could be a whole horde of rats."

"This building has mice," I blurted out.

"Mice, roaches, rats. Crackerjack job you're doing here."

"Mice and rats don't coexist," Jess shouted, coming to my defense, or so I wanted to believe.

"I guess you got rid of your mouse problem." Frascon's sarcasm bit harder this time.

"Look what I found." Jess crawled out from under the bed.

"Please, don't tell me another rat." Frascon said it, but I thought it.

Jess stood holding two pieces of glass. "A broken perfume bottle," she said.

"Maybe there was a struggle," Frascon said.

"Or she threw it at her attacker," Jess said. "We can't rule out someone brought the rat with them."

"Who would do that?" I asked. "Murder? Is that a real possibility?"

Before Jess could respond, Frascon raised her hand to signal *shut up*.

Jess nodded. "We need to bring in a forensics team." She spoke with an over-the-top professional tone.

"Shush." Frascon put her pointer finger to her lips. "Coming from the armoire," she whispered.

Jess and I moved closer to the six-foot wooden box. I could hear claws scratching.

"It's alive," I said.

Frascon drew her gun.

Jess shook her head, and Frascon put her gun away.

"I have rat poison and a cage in the basement."

"Go get it," Frascon shouted. The scratching now sounded more like chewing.

I looked over at Mrs. Lyons, and I couldn't imagine anyone doing anything to deserve this.

"Now," Frascon shouted. "Go."

The three of us rushed into the living room, and I slammed the bedroom door behind me—and my body right into the one thing that scared me more than a horde of rats. Credo, and what looked like half the NYC Police Department.

6

CREDO AND FRASCON talked in hushed tones. All I could hear was "not a robbery" when Credo pointed to the Picassos on the wall near the fireplace.

Jess was nowhere in sight. This time she'd been the one to leave. I supposed I had that coming to me.

Credo waved me over. Frascon walked away, dialing her cell phone. I assumed she was calling in Mrs. Lyons's death, or murder, to whomever one called this sort of thing in to.

"How are you doing?" I knew it was a stupid question.

Credo made it clear that he agreed. "How do you expect me to be doing?" he said. "This smell will haunt me. And I can only imagine the cost to get that stink out of this place. It permeates everything, the upholster . . ." He interrupted himself to pull me closer to him. "And on top of all of this, I have the police showing up in the lobby of my building because they got a call from *you* about a dead resident. You should have come to me first."

"She did the right thing" Frascon was back. Could she actually be defending me?

He turned to Frascon. "Overdose?"

"What makes you think that?" Frascon asked.

"She had a bit of a history of mixing her meds with gin. She called it her special Gin Fizz."

He didn't know about the rat?

Frascon shook her head, and I was certain this was where she would give me up. Instead, she handed me my backpack. "Don't you have to take care of something?"

"Are you still not done with spraying today?" Credo asked.

"Dead bodies can slow a person down," Frascon said.

"Of course, Detective," Credo said, but it was clear from the drop of blood he drew from biting his lip he wasn't happy.

On my way out of the apartment, Frascon handed me her card. "If I miss you before you're done, call me."

I nodded.

"Have your father call me too when he's back."

I nodded again.

"And don't leave town."

She reached up and took my hand from my earlobe.

"That was a joke," she said.

I forced a smile.

I had just reached the elevator and hit the DOWN button when Credo came up behind me. He moved faster than a water bug when the lights switched on.

"Where is your father?" he asked.

"With my mother."

"I thought she was dead."

"I mean at her grave site."

"Ah, yes, the anniversary."

Was there anyone Dad didn't share this with? I was surprised he hadn't tried to make it a public holiday, so schools and banks would close in her honor. Okay, I wasn't angry with Dad. I was pissed off at myself for not going with him this morning. Maybe a part of me was also really mad at my mother. I didn't believe in ghosts, but I certainly felt cursed. I couldn't help but feel this was her doing.

"This is a matter you will need to answer for." He pressed the DOWN button as well.

I took a deep breath and waited for the imminent death of Donovan and Daughter Exterminating. Clearly, I was no Credo fan, but how could I blame him for firing us? Even if he didn't yet know about the rat, there was the roach sighting, the mice, and I'd called 911 without giving any warning about the dead woman in 12C.

He hit the DOWN button again. "Why are these elevators running so slow today? They were just serviced."

As we continued to wait for the elevator to arrive, Credo didn't say another word. This was his game of torture. Dad had always said the pain was far worse in the anticipation of what was to come. He was right.

I couldn't bear it any longer.

"Get on with it," I said. "Say it."

"How do you explain what happened?"

"Did Detective Frascon say anything else?"

"The tight-ass in the tacky jacket?" Credo dressed impeccably, and he acted as if this were a personal affront. "Why would she have anything to say about Mrs. Rendeer?"

"The tenant with the fluff-dog." I was proud of myself for remembering her.

"She was just in my office complaining about the exterminator using the residents' elevator. What were you thinking?"

"It will never happen again," I said.

He hit the button again. "Listen, I know our residents can be, well . . ."

"High maintenance," I interjected.

"Pains in the derrière. We must not forget they are the reason we have jobs." This was the first time Credo had ever used *we* when talking about Dad and me, the help. Maybe he wasn't such an—

"If you ever take the resident elevator again—"

On cue, the doors opened. Credo stepped inside and pressed what I assumed was *L* for the lobby.

"Got it," I said. "Service elevator only."

"Don't let that detective and her partner take you away from your work. Cooperate as much and as little as necessary. A waste of taxpayer money, if you ask me. Homicide. Don't they have real cases—" The elevator door closed.

I wished I had cooperated with Frascon's partner when I had the chance.

I walked to the service elevator on the opposite end of the floor, where there were no apartments, only a storage closet for maintenance.

I hit the button. This elevator moved a lot faster, or maybe it only felt that way because I was dreading what I had to do next: go to the basement alone.

I'd stepped onto the elevator, tapping Frascon's card, when I noticed a handwritten note on the back: *You broke her heart. Do it again, and I will break you.*

Frascon had nothing to worry about. Jess's leaving without even a good-bye told me she was over me, and from the pain pulsating between my ribs, it was clear I would never be over her.

I took out my phone to call Dad. He would be worried about me. It went straight to voice mail. It was all too much to leave in a voice message. I'd try again later.

The elevator door opened. It was Jess. I was still on the twelfth floor, having forgotten to press the basement button.

"We meet so soon." She half smiled.

I nodded, resisting an urge to tug on my earlobe. To kiss her.

"I think it's okay for cops to take the regular people's elevator."

"You know I'm not your 'regular' people."

"I thought you left."

"I wouldn't leave you." I couldn't tell if this was a dig or not.

"Detective Frascon is pretty pissed off," I said.

"You can call her Rita."

"She cares about you."

"She wouldn't be this angry with you if you didn't matter to her. When we were together, you and her got pretty tight."

"She did me a solid right now with Credo, but I don't think there's any love lost on her end."

Other than Dad, Rita and Jess were the only real friends I'd ever had. I could have choked on the amount of regret I tried right then to shove down my throat.

"Jess," I said.

"Linda," she said.

"I know it's your job, but still, I appreciate you coming."

"You think the reason I'm here is because of my job?"

"Isn't it?"

She didn't answer me. It was hard not to push her to tell me what she was thinking. Unlike me, who shot my mouth off, Jess went inward when she was upset, stayed silent until she had time to think, and chose her words carefully. I respected her process and kept my mouth shut the whole way down.

The elevator door opened to the back end of the lobby, where we servicepeople would not be seen or heard. I made way for Jess to step out. She put her hand out to block the door from closing on her and, with her back to me, said, "For what it's worth, this isn't even my jurisdiction."

"How did you know to come?"

"Your father. He called and said you might need my help."

"I never told Dad about you. Us."

She stepped out of the elevator. "When you love someone, you figure things out."

Dad had known about Jess all this time? He'd never said a word. Then again, he did always know when I needed help.

The doors closed. I tugged on my earlobe, my hands slick with perspiration. I pulled out Frascon's card again and reread her note. *You broke her heart . . .*

Tell me something I don't know.

CHAPTER

7

THE BASEMENT'S LONE overhead fluorescent light blinked on and off, a signal in every horror movie I'd ever seen to beware. An indicator to anyone in the real world of a ballast failure, a potential fire hazard. I hated basements.

I'd complained to Credo about this several times. Each time he'd said it was maintenance's job to change broken bulbs and that flickering lights were still working. Credo was Santa Claus to his residents, Scrooge to those on his payroll, and a cheap prick to independent contractors like Dad and me.

I crept down the maddening, strobe-lit corridor. Something I was sure was a rodent—mouse or rat, I couldn't tell which—moved across my feet. I stumbled headfirst into the door to the utility room. Ignoring the lump rising between my eyebrows, I retrieved the keys with Dad's lucky rabbit's foot from the inside zippered pocket of my backpack and unlocked the four-by-six-foot room with two shelves and a sink where Dad and I stored and mixed our chemicals.

The light in the utility room was strong and steady, because I replaced its bulbs on a regular basis.

I used a step stool to reach the rat poison and cages we kept on the top shelf. I didn't remember ever needing either in this building before.

With the poison in my pack and holding the cage in my right hand, I was ready to get out of there and return to apartment 12C.

As I reached over to shut off the light, I saw that the blue pocket-size notebook with the list of codes to the combination locks on the residents' storage spaces—wire cages filled with everything from outdated furniture and discarded books to winter skis and snowboards—was right out in the open, resting on top of the extra metal tank.

Hmm. Dad and I kept that notebook in the locked desk drawer, always. Dad was absent-minded when it came to leaving food cooking on the stove and paying bills, but he never forgot birthdays, anniversaries, or anything related to work. He was a stickler for details. Then again, he had been more absent-minded than usual these days.

As much as I wanted to get the hell out of there, I decided I should check the glue traps Dad and I had set in the storage units. If there were mice, I could feel confident our little friend in 12C was acting on its own, a beta. If there were no mice, there was a high probability there were more, many more, rats roaming this building. They would for sure be in the storage area, with so many units packed with crap for them to chew on and nest in. I grabbed the notebook, an industrial-strength Hefty garbage bag, and a flashlight and rushed to the area Dad called an homage to *Storage Wars* meets *Hoarders*. He wouldn't have approved of me going in alone. "Always call for backup," he'd say, like he was a sergeant on one of his cop shows. (For a man who hated the police, he loved his cop shows.)

It took everything in me to not hyperventilate. I wasn't so afraid of the possibility of facing another rat, but the anticipation of it was nearly impossible to handle.

Dad wasn't here, though. What other choice did I have?

I flipped the switch; as expected, the bulb was out. I stuck the notebook and Hefty bag into the crevice of my half-cup-size-too-small bra. Gripping the flashlight the same way Jess had trained me to hold a gun at the shooting range—in both hands to handle the kick—I shined my light inside the various storage units, repeating the mantra *If we have mice, we don't have rats.*

There was not one glue trap in sight. Had Dad thrown the used ones away and forgotten to replace them? If I'd been worried about him before, now I was on the edge of panic.

He hadn't been himself since the news about my going away to school. I had even considered deferring until spring, but the conditions of the scholarship were clear—I use it now or lose it.

I was now glad he hadn't come with me today. Seeing Mom always grounded him. Maybe when he got home tomorrow, he'd be more accepting of my leaving in a few weeks and back to his regular self, who burned breakfast and forgot the to pay the Visa bill.

Usually, it was a relief when we found the traps empty, but today I needed one squealing-for-its-life mouse to believe 12C was a fluke, a lone rat sent out to bring food back to the pack that had returned to an empty nest. I almost felt sorry thinking of the poor abandoned creature, and then my light hit the cage tagged *12C*, Mrs. Lyons's storage unit. The image of her face, or what was left of it, was pounding against the interior walls of my skull when I heard it: the heart-crushing squeal of a mouse stuck to a glue trap.

I removed the black Hefty bag and blue notebook from my bra and, using the crook of my chin to hold the flashlight, aimed its light down at the middle of the second page. The combination—11 right, 33 left, all around twice, and 42 right. I unlocked the cage, stuck the notebook back into my bra, and stepped inside.

The squealing grew louder. The trapped mouse was somewhere between stacks of boxes marked *Donate*. I had to move them to get to the trap, but when I lifted the first box, its contents fell out through the bottom. Art supplies. Paints, oils and watercolors, never opened. All the other boxes that I moved had their sides chewed (mice love their cardboard) and were filled with brushes and blank canvases. I wondered if Mrs. Lyons owned some sort of art supply business, or if she was an artist who didn't have the time to live her passion because she was too busy living for others. I sighed, imagining her unfulfilled dreams rotting her insides.

Maybe along with her life, her suffering had ended too.

I let out another deep sigh, this for all the appreciation I felt for Jess. If she hadn't submitted the application for the full scholarship I hadn't known existed, I'd too have been living a life of abandoned dreams. She pretended to have nothing to do with it, but Jess was like Dad: they both believed a good deed counted only if it went without recognition. Also, like Dad, she was a terrible actor. Couldn't lie to save her life. They had more in common than I thought.

After moving six boxes out of the cage, I found the mouse, squealing to be freed and looking so tiny, helpless, and sweet. I understood why some customers wanted us to catch and release them to what they imagined was the country, with idyllic pastures where mice frolicked their days away. The well intentioned were clueless and didn't want to hear how these seemingly innocuous creatures, like rats, attacked when cornered, and bit, hard, with saliva that carried thirty diseases.

Still, the first time I saw one and heard its cries, I'd started to set it free when Dad stopped me. "It's impossible to detach without peeling off the skin from its underbelly." The humane act was to end its life as quickly as possible. Dad had taught me how to drown them under hot water in the utility room sink, but then I'd seen a more humane way on YouTube.

I quickly picked up the glue trap and shoved it into the Hefty bag, double knotted it closed, and smashed it hard against the concrete floor.

I heard a scream. It was Jess.

I dropped the trash bag and was running toward the exit when my flashlight went out.

I hoped the batteries were only loose, but after several hard shots to the palm and nothing, it was clear: the Energizer bunny was dead. My phone would give off enough light to lead me in the direction of the screaming. I reached into my pocket but couldn't find it. I wondered if I had left it in the utility room or dropped it in Mrs. Lyons's cage.

The screaming continued. I had no choice but to feel my way through the dark.

The screaming stopped. I was out of my mind with fear. "Jess," I shouted. "I'm coming." I was coming to save her, but from what I had no clue.

CHAPTER

8

I RUSHED OUT THE door to the corridor. The flickering fluorescent bulbs were out, another horror movie trope warning that something bad was about to happen. I was no longer
afraid for myself.

"Jess," I shouted. "Where are you!"

"You're tugging." She aimed her flashlight app at me.
"What's wrong?" She gently took my hand away from my
earlobe and placed it in hers.

Jess was the only other person I'd ever let get close enough
to see the chinks in my armor. Not even Dad could peer
inside me the way Jess could. It was impossible to lie to her.

"You were screaming."

"Screaming?"

"Jess, I heard you."

"What you heard was singing. It helps calm me," she
said. "I'm not a fan of dark basements."

"This was why Rita discouraged me when I tried to convince you to go to karaoke?"

"My voice isn't for everyone."

"Not even a mother could love."

"If she was tone deaf," she said. I laughed, for the first
time in . . . well, too long.

"I miss that." She aimed the light on my mouth and
leaned in, and I jerked my head back.

"I'm sorry," she said. "I just thought, maybe—"

"We could get back together?" I snapped my hand from hers.

"I thought you, we, were good."

"Great."

"Then what happened?" She shined her phone directly in my face. It was interrogation time.

"It's complicated," I said.

"It's complicated? I deserve more than that. We deserve more than that."

I used my forearm to shield my eyes from her flashlight app. "I'm sorry."

"I don't want your apologies, Linda." She pulled my arm away from my face. "I want answers."

"What do you want me to say? I have commitment issues? It's not you, it's me?" I could feel the tears coming. "Would you get that out of my face." I slapped her phone out of her hand. I heard it hit the floor and crack. The light went out. "I didn't mean to . . . I'll find it." I got on my knees and used both hands to sweep the surface of the floor within arm's reach in every direction, but all I felt was cold cement. Cold, dirty, stupid cement.

"Get up."

"It has to be here somewhere. It couldn't have just disappeared." I reached a few inches farther and felt Jess's pant leg. This time there was no mistaking her scream.

"It was just me." I got to my feet, and before I could reach for her, she was in my arms, resting her head on my shoulder. I'd held her so many times before, but never like this. Never to comfort her.

During the time Jess and I spent together, she was always taking care of me and my needs. I'd liked it at first, a lot, but when Jess had this particularly gut-wrenching day on the job—a mother shot in the head by her four-year-old, who'd found the gun in her mother's nightstand, a means of protecting her daughter, and thought it was a toy for playing with Mommy—I'd asked her what she needed, how I could help. She repeated that she was fine, that it had been one of those days. I went home early that night; Jess said she needed her rest. I didn't realize until maybe right now that she'd needed me to be there for her, no questions asked. Just be there.

I was glad I could be there for her now.

"Linda," she mumbled into the crook of my neck. "Please get me out of this place." I could taste her pain, sharp and bitter.

She grabbed on to my hand. We'd taken maybe three steps when I heard the crushing sound of an iPhone under my right boot. I bent to pick it up. Jess squeezed my hand tighter.

I might have fumbled my way around in the dark to try to see if the phone still worked, but Jess wasn't letting go and I didn't want her to.

With my left hand feeling the way and my right hand holding on to Jess, with all the impending doom waiting on the borders of my life, my body tingled not with dread but with joy. There in the dark basement, Jess's citrus scent seeped into my pores, and the two of us breathed the same musty air. My head was clear enough to know that when Jess and I had been together, preteens experiencing their first crushes had nothing on me; I was the epitome of a love-sick sap. But whatever this was that was happening between us now was something else, unprecedented, big. Not just big-girl love. Yes, I loved Jess, but it was more than that. I needed her, and I finally believed she needed me.

"Stay close," I said.

"That's the plan," she said.

"I will get us out of here."

Three or four steps later, Jess said, "There's a light."

"The utility closet," I said. She dropped my hand and took the lead, or rather she ran ahead. We were back where we started: Jess, the superhero, leading the way, and me, her adoring fan, following her every step.

We reached the closet, and Jess slammed the door behind us. "What happened back there . . ."

"You don't have to explain," I said.

"I do," she said. She took her phone from my hand.

"I will buy you a new one."

She took her phone out of its case. "The phone's fine." She used face recognition to turn the phone back on. "Rita thought I was crazy paying so much to protect a phone."

"I guess it was worth it," I said.

"The case cracked, but it did its job. Protected my phone."

I had no clue where she was going, but I knew if her approach was anything like Dad's, she would beat her phone-case metaphor to death and eventually get to her point.

"Why did I feel my phone might break?"

I assumed this was a rhetorical question, so I stayed silent.

"I had phones before, and they broke because I didn't protect them. As a cop, I see all the bad shit that happens, and I have my training, my gun." She put her hand on her holster. "We're not phones, and there's no case in the world that can protect us from—"

"Heartbreak," I said.

She smiled, but instead of showing her right incisor, she cried.

This time she turned her back to me, and when I tried to hold her from behind, she pushed me off. This utility closet had never felt claustrophobic the way it did now, and Dad had at least sixty pounds on her. I was sweating, but my skin, my scalp, the nails on my toes and fingers burned. I thought I was having a panic attack, and then Jess turned to me, wiped her eyes on the sleeve of my coveralls, and said, "Thank you."

"I didn't do anything," I said.

"Exactly," she said.

I was right. Sometimes what she needed from me was to do nothing. To just be there. I never could have imagined how hard it was to watch someone you loved express pain and not try to fix it, make it better.

"We better get back," Jess said.

I reached into my bra for the small blue notebook and returned it to the drawer. "The locker combinations for the cages are in there," I said. I could hear Dad's warning: *Never give up more than you have to.* I knew with Jess I didn't have to give up anything. I wanted to give her everything.

I picked up my pack and the rat cage.

"Shut your eyes," Jess said.

"Shut my eyes?"

"Trust me."

I trusted her, and we kissed.

I opened my eyes first. "That was nice," I said. "I missed you."

"Back there," she said. "Right before, The crying. It wasn't just about us. Just something about dark basements."

"Watch too many horror movies as a kid?"

"Yeah, that's it. Too many horror movies."

ACT II

YOUR MOTHER AND I were standing at the kitchen sink of her patron's apartment. I wanted nothing more than to share everything about me, and how she and I had truly come to meet on the day I'd been ready to say good-bye to Sal, but when I tried, she pressed her pointer finger against my lips and said, "If I don't ask, you don't tell."

A good actor is nothing if not a good listener. I didn't say another word about the matter.

Rebecca filled two glasses of water from the tap. She handed me one.

"Cheers," I said.

Before we clinked, she pulled back her glass. "I heard it's bad luck to toast with water."

"This isn't just water," I said. "It's NYC water, the best. You know, a man once made hundreds of thousands of dollars filling up bottles with water from his NYC apartment tap and selling it in New Jersey."

"That can't be true," she said.

"Swear." I made the cross-your-heart-and-hope-to-die gesture I had often seen. "His landlord tried to stop him, but he wasn't doing anything illegal."

"Is he still doing it?"

"Eventually, he just stopped. I guess he made enough money."

"Here's to NYC water and making our dreams come true." Rebecca clinked her glass against mine. "We can sit in the living room."

I followed her back to the handcrafted couch and noticed it again: Rebecca's hair. The bottom edge wasn't cut straight. I had been perplexed when we first met by her stylist's incompetence, but now the shoddy work angered me. There were few things I respected my mother for, but she had a sense of style and made sure a job was done right. Why would she allow this poor young artist to wear her hair like this?

"Make yourself comfortable." Rebecca set her glass of water on a wooden coaster on the coffee table.

I flashed to a table in the living room of the brownstone. Mother had taken only two pieces of furniture when she moved out: an ugly desk lamp and this coffee table.

"Are you going to sit?"

I was too agitated to join her. Something had to be done about her hair.

"Is everything okay?" She took my glass and placed it on a coaster next to her.

"Who cuts your hair?" I asked.

"My hair?" She smoothed the palm of her hand over her head.

"Is the hairdresser local?"

"I do it myself." She tightened her brow, clearly self-conscious. She knew her hair wasn't right. Not as it should be. This error in judgment, I could forgive.

"Where are your scissors?"

"You're going to cut my hair?" She twisted her lips into a half smile, half smirk.

"Just a trim."

"A hair stylist in a conductor's uniform who knows about the art world?"

"My mother was a hairdresser," I said, thinking of Louis, a character I'd worked with years ago. He'd taught me how to cut, dye, and style any type of hair. I was a master of color, which also was something we needed to fix. This

black-shoe-polish punk look was too harsh for her features.
But . . . one hair-fiasco fix at a time.

She wrapped her hair around her palm and examined the
ends. "They are a little split."

And crooked.

"They're in the bathroom," she said at last.

I followed her to an exceptionally large bathroom with
a lion-clawed tub. I could almost see Paul, the plumber, ass
crack showing, the whole cliché. He was the reason I'd had a
Jacuzzi tub installed in the brownstone. He had been a great
character study, a gentle soul who taught me so much until
he drowned unexpectedly.

Rebecca opened the medicine cabinet, which was filled
with half bottles of sticky red liquids, cold and cough medi-
cines, the stuff Mother had poured liberally down my throat
whenever she needed me to sleep.

"That stuff is bad for your health," I said.

"Just covers the symptoms," she agreed. Rebecca was
smart, but not in a preachy way. I was liking her more and
more. "Scissors." She handed me what looked like professional stylist scissors.

I ran one of its blades across my palm and sighed. The
scissors were in desperate need of sharpening.

I told her the scissors weren't cutting it. It took me a
moment to understand why she was laughing. I'd made a
pun. She thought it'd been intentional, but it was purely acci-
dental. Humor was hard for me.

Rebecca took the scissors from me and dragged a dull
blade along the scar I managed to hide by keeping the front
of my hair longer on the right side. Then she kissed my cheek.

For the first time, I had the desire to kiss someone back,
but I restrained myself.

I knew the right moment was yet to come.

* * *

The next morning, I folded Sal's uniform in a manner similar to the way military personnel handled the American flag
before draping it over the coffin of a lost solider. I went to the

far back end of the brownstone, stopping at the faux-wood paneled wall, and pressed the spot that opened the hidden keypad. I punched in the numbers *234581*, the code no one still alive, other than me, knew, and heard the loud click. With a gentle tap, the panel swung open, and I entered the only place in the world I felt safe.

It was here I'd discovered childish fears were characters hiding in the corners of our minds. If we were willing to seek them out, the bogeymen and monsters would teach us how to see through what others defined as evil.

I opened the chute that led to the crematorium in the basement, then rolled up the Metro-North conductor uniform and sent it on its way. I regretted having not been able to give Sal the proper send-off all my character studies deserved when our work had at come to an end.

It was somewhat of a conundrum as to what to wear for my date with Rebecca. I didn't want to appear rich and prestigious, but I also didn't want her to think I was a poor slob. I wanted neither envy nor pity. Simple and innocuous was best. I chose a blue cotton short-sleeved shirt and a pair of beige khakis, perfectly creased in the front, that I'd bought at a department store for those of working- to middle-income status.

Rebecca met me at the salon. She commented on how she liked me out of uniform but then insisted there were cheaper places to get her hair cut and she couldn't allow me to pay for such an expensive salon, but I explained that I had a gift certificate and it would expire if I didn't use it soon. She agreed.

I gave the stylist explicit instructions on how to cut so her hair would fall across the front of her face to make her look alluring without covering her eyes. I also insisted on changing the color to something lighter, more natural. The stylist did as I said, and Rebecca looked stunning. No woman, or man, had ever stirred such feelings in me. I'd never had any interest in sex. After Father died, watching Mother negotiate her relationships and many affairs had made sex seem overly complicated, painful even, and never worth the trouble.

As I watched the stylist blow out your mother's light-brown hair with red highlights, I felt my father's hands around my neck, choking me back to reality. Thinking Rebecca had come into my life to direct me so that I could engage more deeply with the work was a lie. The biggest lie, the only lie, I had ever told myself. I had fooled myself into thinking our burgeoning relationship was professional, but when I caught her smiling at me in the mirror, the explosion inside me was, without a doubt, personal.

I knew I didn't want to learn Rebecca's secrets in order to become her. I wanted to learn her secrets so I could love her, share my life with her.

But Father had warned that doing so would destroy me. A relationship would be the death of my acting career. "Marriage, children, family will hold you back from taking risks, from giving everything to your craft, and everything is what you need to give to be flawless, to be truly great."

I had to get out of there, now. I paid the woman at the front desk in cash for the cut and dye, adding a very generous tip, and walked out.

I didn't make it two blocks before Rebecca came running up behind me, still wearing the salon's smock. "Stop! Wait!"

I stopped.

She pulled my arm to get me to face her. Anger boiled up inside me. I hated to be touched and grabbed, and I almost raised my hand to crack her across the face, but seeing her in that ridiculous black smock, with her hair half blown out and half wet, erased the rage. I laughed. Not a fake laugh. It was real.

"Where are you going? Is something wrong? Do you hate the hair?"

I reached out and took a strand, still wet, in my right hand, and another strand, less wet, in my left, and made sure the sides were even. "It's perfect," I said.

"Why are you leaving?" She slapped the front of my jacket.

Her gesture was playful, I knew that, so I stifled a more hostile response and instead said, "I needed some air."

She scrunched her nose, and it was clear she didn't believe me, but she didn't say so. "Thank you for the haircut," she said, and walked back toward the salon.

I watched her for about a half a block, weaving through lunch-hour pedestrian traffic. Most people were oblivious to her, but a few, tourists, curious as to why she looked like she had just run out of a hair salon, stopped to watch her pass.

I tried, but I couldn't stop myself from following her. This time I took hold of her arm. She stopped walking. Hordes of people rushed around us in both directions. It was at once exhilarating and threatening. I usually hated people swarming like gnats around me, but there on Fifth Avenue, Rebecca and I had reached the climax of a romantic film where the two leads realize they're in love. That's when she kissed me—on the mouth this time. And almost instantly, I was kissing her back. The few minutes we stood in each other's embrace made up for all the love I'd never known I was missing. The music swelled, the soundtrack to the ultimate love story, and I was ready for anything.

She stepped back and said, "My place or yours?"

"You live closer," I told her, knowing it wouldn't be long before I'd take her to my home, but not yet.

She nodded and stepped in the direction of the salon. "Hey, wrong way," I said.

She tugged at her smock. "I should return this."

"It's covered," I said, not telling her I'd given a $200 tip on a $125 haircut.

A new, younger doorman was on duty at her building. This doorman didn't run over and open the door for us, though. He remained seated, slouched over his desk, never looking up from the newspaper hiding him from the world or vice versa. I could see the headlines but had no interest in reading them. I didn't want the outside world intruding upon us.

Rebecca opened the door and held it, which irritated me. It was the doorman's job, not hers.

"This is unacceptable." I walked over to the desk and stood there, waiting for the doorman to raise his head and acknowledge my presence. After a few long seconds, I pinched his paper down the middle, right between the winning and losing scores of one of those insipid ball teams that the city's so crazy about.

Now he looked up. He was even younger than I'd thought. He looked more like a doorboy. His round face gave me an arrogant, *fuck you* expression. This I had to admire. It told me so much about how little he thought of me.

He raised his left eyebrow, holding it only for a nanosecond. "Can I help you, sir?"

I looked at his name tag. "Gerald, you're the doorman on duty?"

"Yes, sir."

"Isn't your job to open the door?"

He didn't answer. He didn't appear to be catching my meaning. That was a shame. He looked smarter than he apparently was.

Rebecca stood close behind me. Her breathing moistened the nape of my neck.

"Get on your feet." My voice was calm but deadly serious. "Open the door."

"I'm sorry?"

This time I tore the paper from his grip, crumpled it into a ball, and pitched it against the glass door. "Get up. Let's start again."

He hesitated but obeyed. I turned to Rebecca, latched my arm into hers, and we walked back through the entrance onto the street. We waited for Doorboy to open the door for us. I counted to ten and, with Rebecca on my arm, stepped over the threshold. I nodded a thank-you to Gerald and put a ten in his palm. A free lesson for the young man: with hard work comes great reward.

When we reached apartment 12C, Rebecca put the key in the door's lock, but it wouldn't turn.

"Damn," she said, with her back to me. "I took the wrong key from the hook." She banged her fist against the door. "Ouch."

I took her hand into mine and blew.

"I'm always doing this kind of shit," she said.

"What shit is that?"

"Losing things, forgetting places, and"—she lifted my chin with the fingers I had just blown on—"making bad choices in men." She pulled my mouth to hers and put the tip of her tongue through my closed lips, touching the inside of my cheek. It was nice. She'd surprised me. I'd thought I would dislike kissing, especially when it involved sharing saliva. But Rebecca's kiss was pleasing. I would go as far as to say it was pleasurable.

She broke away first. "Wait here. I'll get the manager to let us in."

She took off down the stairs, and in that moment alone, without Rebecca's intoxicating presence, it hit me, a blow to the frontal lobe, triggering the trauma in my brain. Apartment 12C was not Rebecca's or her art-loving patron's. It was the home of the woman responsible for my father's early death. The woman I'd successfully managed to erase from my life for the past seven years. Father always said there were no coincidences, only opportunities to take advantage of, and calamities to escape.

I wanted nothing more than to once again have someone in my life to direct me, and my heart knew Rebecca could be the one. At the same time, I wanted nothing less than for my mother, the woman who had given me life, to destroy the one person who'd made my life worth living. The bond between Rebecca and Mother, her patron . . . was it breakable? Bendable? I feared their close connection would lead down a road that, if I took it, would surely end in disaster.

I had to leave.

*   *   *

Before Rebecca returned, I took the stairs to the lobby. I couldn't not say good-bye. I owed her that much.

Doorboy Gerald stood when he saw me.

"Stay seated. I need paper and pen for a note."

There was a stationery pad with the building's logo right in front of him on his desk, and still he took precious seconds to locate it. Then he searched his body and the top drawer of the desk, unable to locate a writing instrument.

"Try the bottom drawer," I said.

He checked and, with great pride and satisfaction, handed me a pen.

"Thank you," I said.

It didn't write. Not a mark on the paper, and it leaked ink onto my blue cotton shirt. I threw the pen on the ground and crushed it under my shoe. Doorboy jumped up, but I waved him off. I had no use for apologies.

I couldn't leave Rebecca without some explanation.

Father had raised me better than that.

I didn't wait for the elevator. I took the stairs, running up all twelve flights without taking a pause or a second to reconsider.

The apartment's front door was slightly ajar. I knocked.

No answer. I stuck my head in and called out, "Rebecca?"

"I'm in the bedroom," she called back. "Lock the front door behind you."

Her intentions were clear. Sexual relations might be part of her process as a director, but the pressure to perform would inhibit my own process as an actor. I simply wasn't ready for any of this. Leaving wasn't an option now, though. I would go into the bedroom, discreetly keep my eyes from her physical form, and tell her that my mother and her patron were one and the same. She would have to choose between us.

The bedroom door was half-open.

"Please, come in," she said. "I need you."

"Rebecca, I'm sorry, but—"

"Why are you talking through the door?"

I stepped inside, prepared to ask her to please put on her clothes, but she was dressed in more clothes than she'd been wearing before. Instead of the strapless sundress, she was wearing an old white T-shirt, the same brand Sal and I wore, and a pair of painter's pants, not the kind worn for style but for work. She held a paintbrush in one hand and a bucket of paint in the other.

"I thought I'd spruce the place up a bit. Do something nice for all Marilynn has done for me."

"Your patron," I said, cloaking my distaste at hearing Mother's name.

She smiled. Her right incisor jutted out, making her irresistible, and I tried my hardest to forget her connection to Mother.

"What do you think of this color?" she asked, holding up the paint can.

"Is it purple?"

"It's tangerine."

"I'm color-blind," I said. I wanted to take it back, but it was too late. Around Rebecca, I kept slipping back into me.

"That's fascinating." She tugged at her shirt and asked, "What color is this?"

"Orange?"

"Green," she said. "What about the carpet?" She pointed down.

"Blue," I said.

"It *is* blue," she said.

"I can see some color."

"It's fascinating," she said again.

"Frustrating," I told her.

She reached up and touched my cheek. I flinched. "Who hurt you?"

A ringing in my ears started, its pitch piercing my eardrums. I banged the heel of my fist against my right ear and then the left and kept banging, but it wouldn't stop. I'd never had anything like this happen before, not that I could remember.

"What's wrong? Tell me." Her voice came to me faintly. "Are you okay?"

I wasn't okay. My body was screaming. I had to go.

"I need to get to work." I rushed out of the apartment.

She didn't come after me. I wanted her to, but I also knew she was the director, and directors don't run after their actors, not the greats. I stepped into the elevator, the doors closed, and the ringing became a siren, an ambulance racing to save a life. Covering my ears only made it worse. I raised my unmanicured fingernails to both ears, ready to jab and pierce my eardrums.

The elevator doors opened. Doorboy Gerald was standing there. One look at his goofy boy-man face, and suddenly silence reigned.

I dropped my hands to my side.

"I'm on it." He dashed for the front door.

I needed to compose myself, so I paused, inhaled, and slowly let out my breath before following Gerald, who showed great patience standing at attention, holding the door open for me.

"This is for you." I slipped him another ten and stepped into the breeze. I looked over my shoulder at Gerald. "What time does your shift end?"

"Nine," he said.

"Have a good evening, then." I hurried home. I had a lot to prepare for and not a lot of time.

*　*　*

At ten to nine, the doorman arriving for his shift entered Rebecca's building, and at five to nine, Gerald exited. It was no surprise to me that he would leave before his shift was over. He was lazy and undisciplined. I followed him several blocks along an avenue and down the stairs into the subway. I waited close by as he struggled with the ticket machine. I was certain this wasn't his first time buying a Metro pass, and I was equally certain he had a problem getting it right every time.

Our elbows touched as we entered the car, but he didn't notice me until we were sitting across from each other and I said, "Heading home?"

It took a moment before recognition flashed across his face. He looked more pleased than surprised.

"Meeting a few friends for drinks."

"That sounds nice," I said.

"Join us," he said. "You can buy the first round."

"New-guy rules," I said, parroting something Sal had once said.

"Of course," he said.

"Need to stop at my apartment for more cash," I told him. "There's my insulin too." This I'd borrowed from my

Wall Street broke character's backstory. He was a cutthroat on the trading floor, risk-taker, daredevil, the kind of guy who jumped from planes and pulled the rip cord at the last possible moment.

"Type one," he said knowingly.

"You're diabetic?"

He nodded. "I'm as healthy as shit. I work out and eat well."

"You drink hard liquor, the stuff with less sugar." Another tidbit from my Wall Street character.

"Low carb, like vodka, tequila."

The train began to slow. "This is my stop," I said.

He nodded. "Well, I hope things work out with you and your friend."

"Pardon me?"

"You two had a fight."

"Why do you think that?"

"I read people pretty good, and your whole way, your face, your walk from the elevator to me, everything about you told me, *This dude just had some bad shit go down, relationship kind of shit.*"

"There's other kinds of shit?"

"Of course, man. Money shit. Bro shit. Lots of kinds of shit. The kind of shit that goes down between a couple— I'm talking any two people that are into each other—well, that's some deep-in-your-body shit. It gets into the muscle. You know?"

Now I was intrigued. Impressed. And interested in getting to know this character. Reading body language wasn't easy for anyone, but it would be essential to a doorman's station in life. There was a whole new level of maturity and wisdom our Mr. Gerald could teach me. Besides, from the way my body reacted in his presence, calm and yet charged, it already knew he had to be my next character.

The subway stopped. "Maybe next time," he said.

"If you don't mind coming with me to my place, I can change and we can take a cab to the bar. Drinks on me."

"An offer I can't refuse." He said this with his tongue pressed against the inside of his cheek.

Not a very good impression of Marlon Brando's God-father, but I delivered the expected movie line in response: "One day there will be a time when I come to you and ask you for a favor."

He laughed as we exited the train.

On the six-block walk to my brownstone, Doorboy talked about women and how hard they were to understand, and about his recent ex-girlfriend, whom he'd been planning to marry, except she had no interest in children.

"What woman doesn't want to have kids?" he asked me.

I had an answer for him, but he asked another question before I had a chance to speak. "You have kids?"

"I don't," I said.

"You want them, right?"

Me? A father? That could be the role of a lifetime. Then I remembered children were not possible for me. "No, I don't want them," I said. "This is it." I put the key in the door and opened it. I didn't have to see the expression on his face to know what he was thinking: *This guy must be loaded to afford a place like this.* "Family money," I said.

"I have a confession," he said.

Intriguing. We'd met only today, and he was already offering secrets.

"You can tell me anything," I said.

"Gerald isn't my name. I borrowed the name tag from the last guy who worked there, and, well, I didn't want to invest in buying one if I wasn't staying . . ."

He extended his hand to me. I shook it. "Rocco," he said.

"Pleasure to meet you." I was tickled by this news. He was comfortable with taking on another's identity.

"You're an actor," I said.

"I wouldn't say that."

I would, I thought.

I opened the door and hit the light switch, and the last working bulb in the chandelier popped.

"Got any spare bulbs?" Rocco laughed.

I hadn't any idea what he found humorous. "No," I said.

"Seriously, man?"

I shook my head.

"I'll wait for you outside," he said.

"Afraid of the dark?" I asked, though his shallow breathing made it evident. There was too much cool guy in his ego for him to admit to fear.

"Fuck that." He pushed me out of his way and, using a tiny flashlight on his key chain, guided us to the top of the stairs.

"I can take it from here." I stepped in front of him and led us into the living room. I knew the layout so well I didn't need light to help me find the candles in the china cabinet's silverware drawer. As I walked to the candelabra on the baby grand piano, I also knew to step over the edge of the rug, but Rocco tripped. I reached out and caught him before he fell forward and hit his head against the sharp edge of the glass coffee table.

"Thanks, man," he said.

I lit the candles and the dozen others I kept around the room.

"Romantic," he said.

"Flattering." I repeated what my mother had said when she was having a bad day and wanted the lighting to soften her features. By the time I left for college, the only light she would allow was candlelight.

"Hey, I was just joking." Rocco was flustered. "You're a cool dude, but I like girls . . ."

Before he could continue with his absurd assumption, I explained that my interest in him was purely professional. Of course, acts of physical intimacy were sometimes necessary to fully embody a character. Rocco and I were just beginning our work and a long way from determining if that would be necessary.

I had hoped Rocco could teach me about how those within his profession did their job, but he was back to seeming more boy than man, a hard body on the outside but clearly a slime of insecurities and contradictions on the inside. I was quite certain Rocco would be a source of great frustration to me, and yet the benefits of embodying a character like him would justify all the struggle and pain I'd endure.

"Are you famous?" He stood in front of the floor-to-ceiling built-in bookcase, where my multiple awards were on display. Father had modeled them after the original Antoinette Perry Award, more commonly known as the Tony. The likeness of Miss Perry was on one side of the medallion, and when you swiveled to the other side, there were, of course, the iconic theater symbols, the masks of comedy and tragedy.

Rocco leaned in and read from the base of the award at his eye level: "*Carpenter.*" He read the one to his right: "*Salesman.*" Then the one to its left: "*Fry Cook.*" He reached out, then paused, but I gestured for him to go ahead—it was okay to touch.

He took the Fry Cook award off the shelf. "Heavy." Fry Cook had been a man of girth, 320 pounds. Of course, there was no correlation between the weights of the original character and the awards. The Fry Cook award weighed the same as the Real Estate Agent award, given for my embodiment of a Realtor who'd weighed 160 at most. The awards weighed 3.2 pounds, a mixture of bronze, brass, and a handful of ashes.

I now stood shoulder to shoulder with Rocco.

"You in movies?" Childlike wonder shone through his words.

"*All the world's a stage.*"

He lifted his pencil-thin eyebrow. He clearly didn't get the reference.

"You do any TV?"

"A TV repairman," I said.

"Dude, you crack me up." His laugh was perfection, deep, from the gut, workingman. Rocco was the real deal. I was eager to begin our work.

"Beer?" I asked.

"Sure."

"Domestic or imported?"

"A buzz is a buzz. Cheap stuff's fine." He was rubbing the face of the comic mask like it would bring him luck.

I took the trophy from him. "I hope one day to have one of these engraved *Doorman.*"

Rocco smiled. "Oh, I get it. You want to study me?"

"*With* you," I said. "I think you're a fascinating character."

"You should just have told me that."

"This pleases you?" I had never worked with anyone as enthusiastic at the beginning of our work.

"A friend of mine—crane operator," he said. "DeNiro . . . maybe it was Pacino, or . . . anyway, they paid him just so this actor could hang out with him for a few days and observe him."

"For me to truly embody you, we'd need months," I told him.

"Months?" He was silent. I assumed he was thinking the matter over, but his blank expression made it hard to tell.

Finally, he shrugged. "As long as it's okay with the building manager to have you hanging around. He's got a stick up his ass sometimes."

"We'll be doing our work here," I said.

"Here?" He scanned the apartment, shrugged. "I get Monday and Thursdays off."

"We will be working here every day. You'll live here."

"Ah, sorry, man, I don't think I can make that work. I can't afford to lose my job . . ."

"You won't be going back to your job," I said.

"Does this gig pay that much?"

"It doesn't pay anything."

He recoiled slightly. "Sorry, dude, I'd love to help you out, but volunteer shit's for the retired and the wealthy, and I'm far from both."

There it was, the resistance I had expected. That was okay. I was a master of conflict resolution. "Let me get you that beer," I said. "You got the time?" I looked down at Sal's watch. It had stopped. I tapped it. "May need a new battery."

"My buddies are waiting at the bar. Let's skip the beer."

"Yes, your buddies." I smiled. "First round on me."

"You wanted to get more cash, right?"

"Yes, that's right. Make yourself comfortable." I gestured toward the sitting area.

"Sure."

Every step he took from the award display to the black
leather couch was measured and deliberate. It was clear he
was waiting for me to go into the other room. I enjoyed this
part. I always learned much from how a character acted when
they were attempting to escape.

"I'll go put on something more bar-like and be right
back."

"Sure, dude," he said.

I walked down the hall, and when I was out of his view,
I waited and listened. I could hear Rocco walking over to
the door and jiggling the handle, then banging, followed by
shouting. "What the fuck? The door is locked from the outside. What the fuck!"

Now the anger that clouded all other judgment took
over. On cue, Rocco stomped his way across the apartment,
shouting, "Motherfucker, open the goddamn door." Before
he saw me, I slammed all 3.2 pounds of Fry Cook against his
frontal cortex.

* * *

Our friend Rocco was an easy two hundred pounds. Dead-
weight. With what strength I had and the power of physics, I
moved his body from the floor into the wheelchair I had purchased from a Queens convalescent home to transport characters from one side of the brownstone to the other, where the
work would begin. I'd been in much better shape back then.
I wasn't comic-book-character strong like Luke Cage, the on-
again, off-again love interest of Jessica Jones.

Yes, Linda, darling, I read all your comics. I always took
an interest in what you cared about. The times I pretended
not to care were only because I saw how important it was for
you to have your own things that weren't connected to me.
I let you relish your comic book pages in the privacy of your
bedroom, without knowing that I was doing the same in the
privacy of mine.

I noticed that your detective friend (yes, as I've said, I've
been watching you) is also something you want for yourself. I
understand you didn't want to upset me by telling me about

her. You've spent so much of your life protecting me. I love you, my sweet Linda. But it is my role to protect you. Please know this: my hopes for your happiness transcend my disgust for the police. Be with her. Love her for as long as it will last. It breaks my heart to say this, but it never lasts forever. Never.

As exterminators, we understand how essential it is for our safety that we follow protocols. The same was true in my work with a character, especially at the beginning. Improvision can happen later, but not before a level of trust is established.

I secured Rocco's wrists, forearms, and biceps to the arms of the wheelchair. I had custom-made leather straps for this purpose. In my earlier days, when I used rope, I found it best to tie the arms behind the back.

One must always restrain the neck with a traction device identical to those used by hospitals to stabilize patients with spinal cord injuries. Believe me, it's money well spent. I can't emphasize enough how critical it is to immobilize the head. If the head can move, the spine has wiggle room, and a subject, particularly a flexible one, will manage to get loose. An oversight I made once, but never again. Mistakes, errors in judgment, poor choices, come with the territory. To master the craft, one must be open to failure.

My dear daughter, when I'm no longer around, never forget this: the true genius is not the one born with talent, an overrated and ethereal construct, but the one who learns from his or her mistakes, and thereafter applies the knowledge. This is not only true for the actor but for the writer, the director, the artist, the doctor, the plumber, and even the doorman, like my friend Rocco.

He woke up while I was securing his legs and kicked; got me right in the chin. It hurt, but there was no bleeding; there would be bruising but no scarring. No harm done.

I was encouraged to see he was a survivor. The characters that resisted in the beginning were the ones who challenged and pushed me to the next level. The fighters made me a better actor. The process of breaking someone's will teaches us more about ourselves than twenty years of acting classes or therapy ever could. A lesson my father taught me and words to live by.

Of course, I had to restrain him before he kicked me again and took out an eye. With the help of Fry Cook, I knocked him out again. I know, never strike where the camera will see, but sometimes we must break the rules. Rule number one is the only rule never to be broken—be flexible in body and mind.

I wheeled the restrained Rocco past the kitchen, the master and guest bedrooms, and the bathroom, to the wall. I punched in the code, heard the click, and with a gentle nudge pushed the chair over the lip on the floor, and Rocco entered the room where our work would soon begin.

Father had called this space our special place. We were the only two people who knew it existed. Well, I'm sure Mother had to have known, but she pretended not to. Besides, she didn't have the code, or a clue about what we did and how it was transformative and life changing. Mother's only interest was in her bottles. As long as Father made sure she always had something in reach—gin, vodka, cognac—she had no interest in the groundbreaking work Father and I did. It was in this theater space that Father and I had rehearsed and worked with characters, every weekend and most days after school, as far back as I could remember. Maybe even before I was old enough to talk.

There were actually two rooms, the front one quite spacious, perfect for building whatever a set needed. Tomorrow I would build the set of the Park Avenue lobby. In the prop closet in the back, I had a mini chandelier I could hang overhead. In the back room were a massage chair and sixty-inch-screen television, workingman's pleasures. I thought Rocco would enjoy them. He was of the right age for playing video games. When he came to, I would have to ask him which ones he liked.

Of course, there was a full bathroom, with the Jacuzzi tub.

The space had been fitted with security monitors so Father could see who was outside the room if he needed to. But they'd short-circuited while I was learning wiring with Randolph (never Randy) the electrician. After Mother moved out, there was no one on the other side of the faux wall, so I'd never bothered to get them repaired.

It was better this way, in truth. The work Father and I had done together, and which I continued, could only be done when one severed all connections to the outside world. Distraction was the real threat an actor faced. The ability to focus was what separated the hack from the genius. This reminded me why Rebecca and I could never be together. She was the most distracting force I'd ever known.

It was good to be back at work.

The manual pulley system had been installed before I was born, but it worked like new. I used it to get Rocco from the chair into the bed. I strapped him into a sitting position. With most characters, after a few days, the restraints were no longer necessary. They would settle in, and most found the work rewarding.

I tightened the last restraint and went to the kitchen to prepare some food and a sedative. I knew he would be hungry when he woke. If I needed to have him rest, I couldn't keep hitting him in the head. He already was starting with less intelligence than most characters I had worked with.

I went to the kitchen and climbed on the step stool to reach the cabinet above the refrigerator, where I kept my six Danish cookie tins. One tin stored bandages and antiseptics for wound treatments. Four tins contained various pills within the benzodiazepine family. These pills, Klonopin, Xanax, and Ativan, helped characters experiencing anxiety and/or panic attacks. They promoted sleep, essential to one's well-being and ability to work. The medications were habit forming, but I never needed to use them for that long. The sixth tin stored butter cookies. My favorite. I took the wound-care tin, the Xanax tin, and the cookie tin out and stepped off the stool.

I'd been doing all of my cooking over the past month on a hot plate with Sal, so I wasn't surprised to see the only items in the refrigerator were a half-liter bottle of Gatorade, original flavor, and vials of midazolam, a benzodiazepine with a real kick. The downside to this particular drug was it took twenty minutes to an hour after a character woke before they could remember anything. I was always eager to get straight to work, and such moments helped me practice patience, which was vital for an actor. Often the difference between mediocre and genius came down to the ability to take deep breaths and wait.

Rocco was clearly a tester of patience.

I opened the freezer, where I always had a batch of beef stew on hand. It was the one food Father made when we worked—a meat-and-potato dish for a hungry working-man. While the stew heated in the microwave, I prepared the syringe and food tray with a china place setting.

When I returned, Rocco was struggling to move his arms and legs, reentering consciousness. He moved his eyes down to his leather straps and back up to me. A tear fell from his lashes. I hadn't pegged him for a crier. Criers were so, well, predictable, never clever or challenging. Droning on and on, whimpering, bawling, and begging were their only tools of persuasion.

"What do you want with me?" He was choking the emotion down. At least he was trying not to lose it.

"I want to be you." I put the tray of stew and cookies and Gatorade and midazolam on the bedside table.

"You're going to skin me alive and wear it as a costume." He pushed back against the headrest, trying to get free. He struggled anew, which led to a downpour of tears.

"You're a fan of bad horror movies." I forced a smile, hoping to relax him, but his eyes widened, and it was clear what I'd said had only made him more anxious.

I took the linen napkin from his tray and wiped his face. "Blow," I said. "Your nose."

"I have a daughter," he said. "Her picture's in my wallet." He tilted his head to the right. "In my pocket."

"You said you broke up with your girlfriend because she didn't want children."

"I have a daughter from a girl I dated a bit in high school. She's five. She lives in Rhode Island with her mother. I try to see her when I can, but it's not enough . . ." He went on, rambling, as if incessant chatter were kryptonite to the inevitable. I tuned him out until he said, "Your food smells good."

"The stew," I said.

"Did you make it yourself?"

"My father's recipe." I sat in the leather armchair at the side of his bed, jabbed a fork into a chunk of meat, and brought it to his lips.

He pressed them together, refusing.

"You said it smelled good."

He shook his head.

"Now you don't want it." I could hear my voice rising.

Patience. I had to practice patience.

"I want to feed myself," he said through his teeth. "I'm not a child."

If I unstrapped his feeding hand, he would try to grab my throat and choke me or poke my eyes out.

This was where the fun began.

I unstrapped his right hand. He was a lefty, so this put him at enough of a disadvantage to make it manageable when he tried to attack me.

He took the fork with the chunk of meat, chewed, and swallowed.

"Good, right?"

He nodded, and I put the tray in front of him, holding the syringe in my dominant hand.

The anticipation of waiting to see how the scene would play out was exhilarating.

Rocco finished all but one last piece of meat. He reached for the glass of Gatorade but struggled to bring it to his mouth without spilling.

Time to push the action forward. "Can I trust you?"

"Yes," he lied. He wasn't an idiot. I unstrapped his other hand.

"Thank you." He took a gulp of Gatorade and then put the last bite into his mouth. He only chewed twice before pointing to his throat and waving his arms frantically, signaling choking.

His cheekbones were too relaxed and his eyes had widened overdramatically. I'd seen a number of people choking and this was clearly an act, and a bad performance at that.

I played along. "Let me help you," I said. I got onto the bed and pushed myself between him and the headboard, and before I could emulate the Heimlich, he reached up and, as expected, wrapped his hands around my throat. I gave him twenty seconds of satisfaction, letting him believe he really had a chance of strangling me to death, then jabbed him in the triceps with the syringe. Between that and the one-milligram Ativan pill I'd mixed into his stew, plus the milligram of Ativan I'd put in his Gatorade, it wasn't long before his arms dropped from my throat and he was down for the count. I slid out from behind him. Strapped his arms down again. Sat back in the worn leather armchair that still held the smell of Father's Cuban cigars and the thick notebook in the side pouch. I took out the notebook and flipped through the pages filled with Father's observations of me and then my own character observations until I found one of the few remaining blank pages. I would soon need to buy a new notebook.

A lot can be learned from observing characters while they sleep. Do they sleep on their right or left side? Or in corpse pose, on their backs, arms straight and stiff at their sides? Do they snore or talk in their sleep? Do they have night terrors? Of course, Rocco was restrained, so there wouldn't be a lot of body movement, but I sat and watched and waited for the twitching, the jerking, the struggle to get loose. Even in unconscious states, humans struggle for freedom.

I had observed one hundred characters for thousands of hours, in sleep state, with complete and utter focus, but tonight I couldn't concentrate. Every thought veered to Rebecca, and when I glanced down at the page, the only thing I had written over and over and over was her name: *Rebecca*, never *Becky*. What had I become? A schoolboy with a schoolgirl crush? I was a grown man. I had to forget her. Father had always said, "Women are distractions not to be tolerated."

I tore the page with Rebecca's name from the notebook, crushed it in my fist, and threw it into the garbage can on the other side of the bed. "Two points." I spoke in the fashion of Sal, who remained within me.

I returned to observing. *Character twitched his nose in rapid succession for ten seconds; character stopped breathing for one second . . .*

Rebecca. There she was again. I could see the angle of her chin and how it tilted to the right, something that on any other face would have aggravated me. Symmetry was something on which I placed a great deal of value, but I found her off-center, quirky features endearing. No matter how I tried, I couldn't put her out of my mind. Rocco started to mumble in his sleep, access to the subconscious being invaluable for an actor learning about his character; but instead of moving in closer so I could hear his words, I leaned back and daydreamed of Rebecca.

I had to hear her voice.

Not even working with an interesting character like Rocco could get her out of my head, from under my skin. Her smell still lived in the beds of my fingernails. I had to see her, but it was a risk to leave Rocco unattended. If he woke up, he would probably panic after he remembered where he was, and I needed to assure him that all would be okay.

I reached into Rocco's back pocket, and as he said, there in his wallet was a passport-sized photo of his daughter sitting on Santa Claus's lap and not looking happy.

She looked younger than five. Maybe three. I was struck by how much she resembled Rocco. She had his eyes—the color and shape. What must it be like to have someone walking the earth in your image? *What woman doesn't want children?* he'd said. He'd asked me if I wanted children, and I'd answered no without hesitation.

But now, looking at this photo of the angry little girl on the bored man's lap, I paused. I didn't feel *no*, and I wasn't yet ready for *yes*, but the idea that fatherhood would end my career no longer felt true. I wondered instead if fatherhood might make me the kind of man who could play any part on the deepest of levels. After all, I liked to believe I'd made my father a better man, a better director, a more extraordinary human. Maybe fatherhood would add to my work, my depth.

Why did I feel this way now?

It was more than Rocco's photo of his child.

Rebecca. I had to see her tonight.

She would be the mother of my child.

I placed the photo in the palm of Rocco's hand and wrapped his fingers around it. If he happened to wake before I returned, he would have his daughter's face to comfort him.

* * *

It was now almost three in the morning, and I couldn't find a taxi, so I had no choice but to take the subway.

The only other people sharing the subway car sat across from me, a couple wrapped in an intimate embrace. Drooling on each other, they managed to stay entwined every time the train came to a sudden stop, jolting us forward. Any other time, this would have disgusted me, but on this early morning I wished I had my notebook to record my observations. Over the years, I had done dozens of character studies, but never with two characters at the same time. I wondered if this was what true love looked like.

From across the avenue, I watched Rebecca's building. I could see the older doorman in the lobby, standing at attention. I admired his fortitude. If I went inside, he would, of course, need to call her to get permission for me to go upstairs. There was a high probability she would tell the doorman to send me away. I wouldn't blame her if she did.

My only hope of convincing Rebecca to give me another chance was to see her face-to-face. When she left the building, I could follow her to a more neutral setting. I didn't want to look conspicuous, so I went to the nearest twenty-four-hour coffee shop and bought an orange juice and the *New York Times*, the perfect object to hide behind.

Three buses went by before the doorman, hat in hand, left the building. I waited until he walked several blocks south before crossing the street. No other doorman came to relieve him. Of course . . . that would have been Rocco.

I took the elevator to the twelfth floor. My heart was beating fast, and drops of sweat fell from my brow. I was a man who never sweated, not even in New York's summer heat. And yet here I was, index finger trembling, perspiring heavily, until I gathered the courage to ring the bell. I waited a minute before ringing the second time, then counted to twenty before the third time, and then to ten, until I was leaning on the bell without pause.

She wasn't home. Or she'd sensed it was me and had no intention of opening the door. The newspaper dropped to the floor, and I walked back to the elevator.

I'd stepped inside when I heard her call my name. The doors closed before I could get out.

When the doors opened at the lobby, there she was, my Rebecca.

She had run down twelve flights of stairs for me. Her hair was tangled, her nightshirt stained with sweat. She was a mess, and I had never seen anything so lovely.

She stepped into the elevator and pressed *12*. There were no words exchanged between us until we were in her apartment and she triple-locked the door behind me.

"You want something to drink? NYC tap water?"

I shook my head.

"Eat?"

Again, no.

She took hold of my hand and led me to the bedroom. This time she wanted more than to ask my opinion about colors. She took off her T-shirt and panties and then unbuttoned my shirt. She kissed the hair on my chest and tugged at my nipple with her teeth. I felt aroused, but I wasn't growing hard. I never got hard. And I'd never cared about it until now.

She pushed me onto the bed, slowly unzipped, and quickly pulled my pants down and off, and with great agility and speed she removed my red boxers and flung them across the room. Straddling me, she rubbed her private parts against mine. The largest sensory organ in my body—my skin—was on fire. My groin ached, but still, nothing. I gently pushed her off.

She watched me get dressed. "If you're not into me, why did you come back?"

It took me two deep breaths to understand that she thought I wasn't attracted to her. "I'm very into you," I said.

Her eyes shifted downward, and I instinctively put both hands over my groin. "It doesn't work," I told her. "It's not you."

Her face lit with curiosity, and she started to fire questions at me. To my surprise, I answered every one as honestly as I could.

Hard? Never. Two specialists. Not physical. Psychological. Don't believe in therapy. Won't try it.

By this time, we were both lying on our backs, looking up at the ceiling.

"Life is like living in *The Actor's Nightmare*," she said.

"One of my favorite plays," I said.

"You can't escape reality based on absurdism," she said.

"You were right," I said.

"About what?"

"I am a lot of things."

"What are you today?"

I popped up too fast, and pain shot straight through my lower back. "Ack! I can't move."

"Back spasm." She got up and pushed two pillows under my knees, then went into the bathroom and came out with a prescription bottle.

"I don't take drugs," I said through clenched teeth. The pain was excruciating. Breathing hurt.

"Oh, these are just muscle relaxers. They'll help."

"No drugs."

"If you don't take something, we'll never get you up." Her face flushed, and a vein in her forehead throbbed as she tried to twist open the cap.

"Righty tighty, lefty loosey," I said.

She turned left and removed the cap. She tapped two capsules onto her palm. "They'll help, I promise."

I wanted to trust her, but I couldn't. Not yet. I hadn't taken medication since I was fifteen: pills to stay awake to remember lines, pills to go to sleep.

I tightened my lips and pushed her hand away. The pain cut through me worse than the time Father had stabbed me in the gut.

Rebecca opened my clenched fist and put the two pills in my palm. "It's your choice. I won't make you do anything you don't want to do."

"I need you to answer something." I had to see if I could trust her.

"Ask me anything."

"What gave me away?"

"You mean how did I know you weren't a conductor?"

I tried to nod, but it was too painful.

"I recognized you from a photo that's usually kept here." She knocked on the top of the nightstand. "She takes it with her when she travels. To keep you close."

Rebecca squinted like people do when wanting forgiveness.

The shock and pain I felt almost overwhelmed me. "You knew who I was all this time?" It hurt terribly to breathe, to speak, but I needed to know. "Why didn't you say anything?"

"I thought you were in character for a part you were playing."

I was so relieved to hear that. She understood me. I smiled, then cringed as a fresh bolt of pain struck my back.

"I'm worried about you," she said.

I had never had anyone look after me with such tenderness. With one hand, she held up the back of my head, and with the other she took the pills from my palm, placed them on my tongue, one pill at a time, and held the cup of tap water to my lips. I sipped.

"You were very believable," she said. "You did your research, no doubt. I dated a method actor once, but you take it to a whole other level. I respect that."

I wanted to ask her for notes on my performance, but I couldn't get the words to leave my mouth. The muscle relaxers had already kicked in.

The last thing I remember was Rebecca asking, "Why do you hate your mother?"

LINDA

9

T HE LOBBY DOOR opened to three uniformed cops and Frascon. Her right shoulder pad had shifted to the front of her jacket, creating the illusion of three boobs.

"I have the stuff." I raised the cage.

"No longer needed." Frascon unbuttoned her jacket, exposing her gun.

I looked up at Jess.

"You shot it," Jess said.

"A rookie got to it before I did." Frascon smirked.

"The building manager must have loved that," Jess said.

"Prewar buildings," Frascon and I said in unison.

"No one outside that apartment heard the gunshot," Frascon said.

"Credo knows the details about Mrs. Lyons?" I asked.

"Ms. Donovan, I hope you understand." She sounded like every other frustrated authority figure in my life when they wanted to emphasize that there were protocols to be followed.

"I better pack up our supplies."

"Not yet," Frascon said.

"You didn't tell Credo?"

"This is a possible murder investigation." She smiled at Jess. "Until it's necessary, the public, which includes Mr. Credo, will only be given limited access to the details of this case."

Maybe she didn't hate me after all. "I better return these."

"You're not going back down there," Jess said.

"I don't want to carry a rat cage and rat poison on the subway."

"There's no light. It's too dangerous." It felt good to hear the worry in Jess's voice.

"A rat cage could come in handy on the subway, but probably best not to walk around with poison on your person," Frascon said.

"I'm going with you," Jess said.

"I think she can handle this on her own. You have your own job to do."

Jess hesitated.

"There is one thing you can do for me," I said.

"Anything," Jess said.

I handed her the ring of keys. "Would you give these to Jack, the doorman, for me?"

"You can give them to him yourself when you're back."

"I'm not going off to war," I said. "Jack is going home when his shift ends soon."

* * *

I was getting good at seeing in the dark. I made it to the utility room, returned the cage and rat poison to the top shelf, which was where I had left my phone, and was back on the service elevator without any part of my body going bump in the night. I left the building using the service entrance. Before I could cross the street, I heard my name.

"Donovan." Frascon was standing in front of the building. "You got a second?"

Did I have a choice? I walked over to her.

"Thought you'd want to know forensics will give us something more to go on soon."

"Thanks," I said. Honestly, I didn't want to hear another word about anything that had happened today.

I adjusted the front strap of my backpack.

"When you see your father, please let him know we'd like to speak with him."

"I have your card," I said.

"You got my message?" she asked.

"Have a good night." I forced a smile.

Jack's night-shift replacement opened the door for Frascon to enter. His name tag said *Freddy*.

"Ms. Donovan," he said. I was impressed. He knew who I was even though I'd never met him. Then I remembered the company's name embroidered on my back.

"I have a letter for you." Freddy opened the door for me to enter.

"No can do." I pulled on the front of my coveralls. "Your boss wants me to use the service entrance only."

He moved in closer and whispered in my ear, "He's gone for the day."

I followed him to the front-lobby desk. If it had been Jack, he would have brought it to me. But Jack was an old-school doorman.

Freddy handed me a legal-sized envelope with the management logo and address in the upper right corner and my name neatly handwritten on the front. I was sure it was a letter from Credo telling us our services were no longer required.

"You good?" Freddy asked. "You look a little nauseous."

Suddenly needing fresh air, I stepped quickly out of the building.

While the sun set and the city lights rose on the Upper East Side of Park Avenue, I tore open the envelope. Inside was a check from Credo, payment for our last month's work. I could breathe again.

My phone pinged. A text from Dad.

Sweetie, I dropped by to see if I could change your mind about joining me today to visit your mother. When I arrived, I saw all the activity.

That was Dad's code for lots of cops hanging around.

I thought best not to interrupt your work. Besides, you're an adult and I respect your decision to take care of business. I'm at Port Authority to catch a bus to see your mother. If you have a change of heart, join me. I will be near the cemetery, at our usual place, with the broken hot tub. In all the years we've stayed there, it's not ever worked, but you love the promise of things. I got the last room. Your mom will be so proud to hear you're going to school. She would want this for you. Of course, she'll be worried about how I'll manage without my partner, but I'll reassure her. I'll also tell her you'll try and visit before you leave for California in a few weeks.

I hope everything worked out with your friend.

XOXO Dad

*   *   *

Dad wasn't good about expressing the emotional stuff. He often used my dead mother to tell me what he was feeling.

"I was worried." Jess towered over me. "Glad you're okay." Her smell had morphed from the sweet, citrusy lingerie-chain-store smell to cotton candy soaked in sweat. I found this irresistible.

I clicked my phone off and shoved it in my pocket. "Thanks again for everything," I said.

"Anytime." She paused. I thought she might kiss me again, but instead she flashed her right incisor and walked away. I watched her and mumbled under my breath, *Let her go.* But the farther away she got, the stronger my impulse grew to run after her. I stuck my hand in my pocket and instinctively reached for my phone to call Dad, but instead thought, *Oh hell, why not?*

"Jessica Jones!" I shouted.

She turned around.

"Wait up." I ran to her.

"You need something?"

"I do," I said. "A stiff drink."

"I know a place."

10

M Y TYPICAL MORNING-AFTER routine: Open eyes, look around the room, wonder where I am, see a stranger lying at my side, and wait a minute for the images to flood my brain, for my memories to return—namely, our geographic location and the name belonging to the naked body beside me. Usually before the sun slipped into the sky, I'd find my scattered clothes and wallet and be out the door before the sleeping hottie awoke. If she was already awake, I'd give a work excuse: "Emergency. Roach sighting." No questions asked. No one wanted to linger on roach talk before they had their first cup of coffee, or their second.

This morning was different. The moment I opened my eyes, I knew exactly where I was: in Jess's queen bed with her dozen coordinated throw pillows and her bulldog Sam snoring between us. Last night had been a record for us—five orgasms, all ending with, "Detective Jessica Jones, thank you."

When the afterglow had begun to dim, panic had lit fire to my brain. I knew I had to get out of there. I might have broken her heart, but not having her in my life cracked every vertebra in my spine. Some mornings I couldn't get up and walk. The pain was far from gone, but it was finally bearable. Even if I could believe I was past my commitment issues and I wouldn't run again, I was leaving for college in two weeks. Three thousand miles away. How would we survive that?

"Let me ask you something," she said as I stirred and rose.

I half listened while I searched for my discarded clothing. "Why do people say *on the island* and they mean Long Island, not Staten Island or Manhattan? And why do they say *the city* when they mean Manhattan? Do the other boroughs exist on another geographical plane, or what?"

This distracted me from my impulse to leave. It was the kind of silly yet existential question Jess and I would discuss ad nauseam. I missed that. I no longer wanted to escape. I sat and we talked.

Somewhere between the darkest hours and twilight, I split like an atom and shared with Jess all of my worries and regrets, hopes and fears, in a rush.

It was a mess—I was a mess—but Jess didn't seem to mind. She welcomed every revelation.

"We were broke. You knew that was the excuse I used for not going to college right after high school. You know the truth. I couldn't leave Dad. He needed me. I had been doing his books since high school. Saved us from bankruptcy, twice. He has no concept of business. Big heart. No financial sense. Then even when business got better, we still couldn't afford college—not my dream school, anyway. You applied for that scholarship for me and changed everything."

"You got it?" She wrapped herself around me. "You didn't tell me?" She let go and leaned back.

"In two weeks, I'm off to California."

"That's amazing." She sounded genuinely happy for me. This made me sad. It cut deep. I wanted her to tell me to stay. To give me reasons not to go. She couldn't live without me.

After the sun rose and Sam started to snore, Jess and I fell asleep again in each other's arms.

I could have stayed in bed all day. I leaned over Sam and kissed the corner of Jess's mouth. She rubbed her nose against the pillow, still asleep. Determined to wake her and continue where we had left off hours earlier, I dragged my tongue down her exposed spine, slowing to trace the jagged-edged scar over the spot where her right kidney was, or should be. I wondered about its story, and all the stories that made her. As I reached the inner center of her thigh, my charged phone lit up and vibrated on the nightstand.

Another text from Dad.

Let me know you are alive and okay.

I texted back.

Alive. Okay. Stayed in the city with a friend. Friend?

I found it cute that Dad was being coy with me. He knew exactly who I was with, and I had him to thank for it. I still couldn't believe Dad had known about Jess and he was okay with my being friends with a cop.

"Scarlet Begonias" suddenly shattered the room's silence. It was Dad's favorite Dead song. (Thanks to my mom, who hated the Dead, it hadn't become my name.) It was also my ringtone for Dad. I grabbed my phone and went into the other room. Sam followed.

"You're still in Jersey," I said.

"On the bus. Be at Penn Station in about an hour."

"Dad, when did you clean out the mousetraps?"

"Last night. I told you that, didn't I?"

"If you had, I wouldn't have been so worried about servicing the building today."

"The roach sighting," he said. "Are you sure I didn't tell you I cleared the traps last night? I could have sworn I had."

"Dad, you emptied but didn't replace."

"Of course I did."

"Dad, there was only one trap that I found."

"You know that's something I wouldn't forget," he snapped, something he never did.

"You feeling okay?"

"I'm sorry, Sweetie." His tone was saccharine. Dad was never fake with me.

"You sure you're okay?"

"This trip was more emotional than usual. Just a little drained."

I was to blame for Dad's exhaustion. The anniversary of Mom's death was difficult enough, but when I was with him, I shared the burden. "I'm sorry. I should have been there."

"It's okay." Dad was lying to me. Maybe for the first time in my life.

"I'm worried about you."

"That's not your job. It's my job to worry about you. Okay?"

I nodded, even though he couldn't see me.

"I'm sorry I wasn't there to help you with Mrs. Lyons. The poor woman."

"Someone may have brought the rat in with them and got it to . . ." I paused. I couldn't get the image of Mrs. Lyons out of my head. "Attack her."

"What sick person would do something like that?"

"Whoever it was knows their rats. They used peanut butter to lure it to her."

"Or they Googled a rat's favorite foods," Dad said. "That reminds me. A Detective Frances or something left me a message."

"Detective Frascon," I said. "That's a first."

A long silence followed. I thought the connection dropped.

"Dad, you still there?"

"I was just wondering what you meant."

"What I meant?"

"You said, 'That's a first.'"

"First time I ever had to correct you on someone's name. You never forget a name."

"They do say there's a first for everything."

"She acts tough, but she's cool."

"Who's that?"

"Detective Frascon. You should call her back as soon as you can."

"We're not stupid," Dad said.

"Who said we were stupid?"

"If we killed Mrs. Lyons, why would we bring rats into our own building?"

"Rat, Dad. It was one rat. No one is saying we killed her. They're just gathering information. It's their job."

I would have given anything to take those words back, but it was too late. Dad hung up.

I tried to call him back, but he wasn't accepting. I left five voice messages in a row before he finally texted me.

I'll see you at Epstein's memorial service.

I'd forgotten that was today. I looked down at Sam waiting at my feet. All I wanted to do was spend the day with Jess. She didn't have to be at the precinct until late afternoon unless forensics came through with something earlier.

"Miracles don't happen in New York in August—it's too hot," she'd said.

Her humor was the best kind: it sneaked up on you. Dad would love her, even if she was a cop.

About Epstein . . . he was one of our longtime customers. I had to attend the service. I also had to talk to Dad face-to-face.

I texted back: *See you there.*

Dots showed Dad was texting something. They stopped, then started, then stopped, then started, then stopped. He was clearly uncertain about what he wanted to tell me.

I clicked on my Google calendar. The memorial service wasn't until noon. It was only eight AM. Jess and I still had the morning.

Sam stretched and wagged his tail. I rubbed him under his chin. "I missed you, guy," I said. If only people were so easily pleased. "We can make your mom her favorite breakfast," I told the pooch. "My favorite too."

Sam barked. He liked the idea.

A quick scan of the kitchen revealed that Jess's fridge was filled with her usual "healthy choices."

"Sam, we have a dilemma here. How can I make your mom her favorite, the breakfast of champions—potato and eggs, with just a hint of sautéed sweet red pepper—with none of the ingredients? She has three containers of tofu but not one egg. Three kinds of milk, and not one that comes from a cow or an animal of any kind."

Sam rubbed his head against my bare leg.

I knelt next to him. "You want to go out?" He barked and ran around in circles. "Shush, boy," I said. "Let me get dressed."

Back in the bedroom, Jess was still dead to the world. I couldn't bring myself to wake her to ask where she'd left Sam's leash. I closed the bedroom door slowly behind me, and there was Sam, waiting by the front door. In his mouth was the glow-in-the-dark leash with a cylinder full of poop bags made from recycled material. The apartment keys were on a hook near the door—convenient, but not so close that a thief could reach a hand in from the outside hallway and take them. All of this verified that the woman I'd fucked last night was still as organized and one-step-ahead as always. Her two keys were attached to an I ❤ NY chain. I'd tried to get her to ditch them, but she'd refused. She might as well have tattooed *Tourist* on her cheek.

"Sam, should we leave a note?" I knelt again and gave him another rub under the chin. When I stopped, Sam jumped up for more. "One more rub and we go." I could have sworn he nodded. I rubbed Sam for a good long minute and then found a pen and a monogrammed *JJ* pad in the most organized "junk drawer" ever, and I'd seen thousands (on the job, like Dad, I snooped, but for less virtuous reasons). The pad seemed too pristine for my scrawl, so I left it alone. Instead, I used the back of the box from the extra-large pizza we'd polished off last night: *Walking Sam*. I suppressed the urge to dot the *i* with a heart.

I clipped the leash to Sam's collar and checked the keys to see if they worked. The gold opened the top lock and the silver opened the bottom.

"Where is the key for the door to the building?"

Sam jumped up on his hind legs. He was either answering my question or needed to pee badly. I would have to get Jess to buzz me in when I returned.

Oh well . . .

I locked the door behind us, and we descended five flights of stairs. I couldn't remember climbing all these stairs last night or ever, but then again, I'd usually had a few drinks and a lot of raging hormones to distract me when I came over. By the time we got to the bottom step, I was out of breath. Sam's panting was the only reason I didn't feel like a complete out-of-shape loser, though I suspected Sam was playing it up to make me feel better.

On the street, Sam led the way. He had his route, leaving his mark on every tree and fire hydrant we passed. At the curb in front of a small grocery store called Mom and Pop, Sam took a huge dump. I had no idea what Jess had fed Sam last night, but I was sure it was organic and healthy and nowhere near as tasty as good old-fashioned Alpo, which I had tried on a bet in the third grade.

I attempted to pull out one of the pink, recyclable poop bags from the cylinder, but like a magician's scarf trick, they wouldn't stop coming until the cylinder was empty. Sam pulled on the leash, and I took this as a sign for us to run, but I remembered what Jess had said when we walked Sam before: "There're always witnesses, but people still think they can get away with a poop-and-run."

I tugged, stretched, and pulled at what was now a jumbled mess of pink plastic. I was ready to take my chances on prison when I discovered the perforated edge. I picked up, bagged, and tied, then dropped it in a nearby trash can filled with other bright-pink and blue and a few orange poop bags. "Ready to go home, Sam?" He pulled me to the door of the Mom and Pop grocery. "Sorry, dogs can't shop."

A tall young suit came out with two matching fluff balls on leashes, jumping up on their hind legs and rapidly moving their tiny mouths at Sam, whose attention was on the tall, lean, and sleek dog that exited behind them. Its human, short and pudgy, and I exchanged half smiles as our dogs sniffed each other's butts. I always felt uncomfortable in these situations. Should I introduce myself or wait for the other owner to? Ask the dog's name? I despised dog-owner chit-chat: *I think they like each other*, or *Looks like Sam made a friend*. Exactly the kind of forced exchange that made me not want children. Before I could figure out what to say, the sleek dog pulled its owner in the direction of a well-groomed, purple-bowed poodle.

It looked like dogs could go shopping here.

I was probably projecting, but Sam looked sad. "Come on, boy, let's get some stuff to make your mom breakfast. And maybe she'll let you eat some too. I know you love eggs."

Inside, Sam's cropped tail wiggled back and forth. "Morning, Sam." I didn't recognize the woman behind the counter. She pointed to the sanitizer dispenser by the entrance. I assumed this was meant for me.

It squirted the fancy foam, not the sticky liquid kind. By the time I'd finished rubbing my hands together, the woman, around my age, was out from behind the counter, kneeling in front of Sam. As she scratched under his chin, I saw she had a tiny red flower tatted above the inside of her wrist.

"A begonia," I said.

"You know flowers."

"The Dead."

"You're one of those," she said.

"My father's a big fan," I said. "Favorite song."

"It's also a symbol." She paused. Clearly, she wanted me to ask.

"For what?"

"Beware. Be on guard. Bad shit, bad people, can walk through that door at any moment."

"Where can I find the eggs?" I asked.

"You're a friend of Jess?"

I hesitated.

"Dog thief?"

"You know Jess," I said.

"I've only been working here a month, but we've gotten close."

"Eggs," I said.

"Eggs are in the in the fridge to your right."

"Thanks." Sam followed me to the back, where I found the eggs—farm raised, organic, or normal. I went with the rip-off organics. Jess was worth it. The onions were sold loose, but the potatoes were available only in five-pound bags. A lot more potatoes than I needed for breakfast, but I could mash them or make potato croquettes and chicken cutlets for dinner.

I paused. Jess had been the first woman I didn't want to leave right after we fucked, and after our first night I had made her a home-cooked dinner. Here we were, back together for only one night, and I was right back where I'd started, planning and making home-cooked meals for her and loving every minute of it.

Sam pushed his head against the back of my leg. Screw it. I picked up the bag of potatoes and two bell peppers and went to the register.

Outside, I scratched Sam under his chin. "Now let's go make your mom some eggs and potatoes." He barked twice in agreement.

Back at Jess's apartment building, before I had my phone out to call her to come down and let Sam and me inside, a man with gray hair exited the building. He held the door open for us.

"Thanks," I said.

"My pleasure," he said. "How are we doing today, Sam, my buddy?" He bent and patted Sam on the head.

"You get around, guy," I told Sam, before he led the way up the stairs.

Jess met us at the top. She was wearing a blue tank top and shorts and trainers that cost more than what I spent in six months on clothes.

"You going for a run?"

"What do you have there?" Jess peeked in the grocery bag.

"Breakfast," I said.

"You know I don't usually eat breakfast."

"This is my specialty."

"Potato and eggs!" She couldn't have sounded more excited if I had given her a diamond ring. With Sam at my side, Jess led me to the kitchen table. There was a note on the fancy pad, with handwriting almost as ugly as mine, taped over the message I'd left on the pizza box. *Thanks for walking Sam. Last night was fun.*

Fun? That was a too-familiar line. The polite blowoff. I'd used it more times than I cared to remember.

I dropped the groceries on the table.

"That's a lot of potatoes."

"Return them to your friend." I pushed by her and opened the front door. Sam barked. Jess didn't say a word to stop me. This time I ran down those five flights of stairs. I had to get outside before I suffocated.

11

I CIRCLED JESS'S BLOCK for over an hour. I didn't know what I was hoping for. Yes, I did. I thought if she saw me, she'd come running to me and beg me to forgive her for messing up my thoughtful breakfast plans and ask if we could get coffee or go back to her place.

I was in front of her building when my cell rang. Hopeful it was her, I fumbled it onto the cement. I picked it up, and the glass wasn't cracked, but my heart splintered when I listened to the voice mail. It was the doctor's office reminding me of my appointment tomorrow for my physical, which I needed along with proof of my vaccinations to be allowed to start classes at USC.

"Please remember to fast at least twelve hours before your appointment."

No problem. The way I felt, I didn't care if I ever ate again. I was everything I despised in a woman: a delusional, dramatic, desperate, love-sick walking cliché. I really couldn't blame Jess for wanting me out of her apartment.

There was also a text from Dad.

Your black suit is dry cleaned and hanging in your closet.

I'd never make it to the Bronx and back before the start of the memorial service. If I showed up dressed in this old T-shirt and jeans, with holes from wear, not style, Dad would have a silent fit. And he'd be right. It was a sign of disrespect to dress inappropriately. I had no choice but to use the credit card I carried for emergencies and buy clothes.

I Googled stores, but the closest reasonably priced store was a Gap, and that was twenty blocks away. There were only high-end, overpriced boutiques in this neighborhood. I was about to give up and pay my respects in shame when I saw a clothing store with a *Summer Sale* sign in the window.

"May I help you?" The saleswoman, dressed in a chic bright-yellow sunflower-patterned miniskirt and a sky-blue sleeveless silk top, exuded the energy of a can of soda opened after it's been shaken hard. I had the feeling she wasn't going to stop bubbling over until I bought something, but at least she didn't assume from my ragged appearance that I couldn't afford this place, even if I couldn't.

"I need something for a memorial service that starts very soon."

"I'm sorry for your loss," she said, and before I could respond, she had me and the only thing close to appropriate in my size, a dark-blue cocktail dress, in the dressing room.

I barely had my jeans off when she was knocking at the door. "How we doing in there? Need any help?"

"I'm fine," I shouted, hoping she wasn't going to burst through the door and dress me herself.

When I came out, she posed me in front of a three-sided floor-length mirror.

"You look beautiful," she said.

I look weird, I thought. I hadn't worn a dress since my high school graduation. Dad didn't like me in dresses. He claimed I didn't look comfortable wearing them, but I knew he was the one who felt uneasy. I think I reminded him of his mother, who he'd once told me would never leave the house without her makeup and heels. I was more of a fitted-suit or T-and-jeans-under-coveralls kind of girl.

Which reminded me: I'd forgotten my coveralls at Jess's apartment. I had an excuse to call her when I was ready.

"It's a little short." I pulled at the hem. "A little tight." I grabbed at the waist. "You sure you don't have any black slacks?"

"Short is the style, and the fit is flattering. You have great legs. Why would you hide them?"

"I guess I'll take it." The clock was ticking. I didn't have a choice.

She had my clothes in her arms. "I assume you'll be wearing it out? Let me bag these and bring you the perfect shoes. A size eight, I'm guessing?"

"I don't need shoes."

"You want to wear those?" She rolled her eyes down to my work boots. It was a look, but probably not for the memorial service.

I stumbled out of there in a navy-blue sleeveless cocktail dress and an open-toed wedge, which the saleswoman had tried to convince me wasn't a heel, not a real heel.

It turned out the sale wasn't a real sale and maxed out the $800 limit on my emergency credit card.

I couldn't find a cab, and my Uber account, which I only used in emergencies, was connected to the credit card.

In my not-really-wedges, not-really heels, not-really-comfortable shoes, I walked twelve blocks to the memorial service, bumping into strangers along the way, because instead of having my eyes straight ahead, they were fixed on the phone in my hand (no pockets in the dress) as I willed Jess Jones to call or text me.

Almost every seat was taken when I got there. Mr. Epstein was a popular man, always good to his customers, and he treated Dad and me like people, not hired help.

The closed casket made me uncomfortable. Something about needing to see it to believe it.

Dad was in his usual spot, two rows behind the grieving family. Too close is presumptuous, and too far is rude, went his philosophy. You don't want to impose, and you don't want to look like you're planning a quick exit. His ponytail was neat, and he was wearing his one good suit. He looked good.

As I looked for an unobtrusive seat, Dad glanced over his shoulder and spotted me. He waved me toward him and stepped into the aisle. I put my phone on silent and took the chair one seat in.

He eyed my shopping bag and whispered, "I see you went shopping."

"I needed something appropriate to wear."

"You have a good time with your friend?"

Before I had a chance to respond, the rabbi walked up to the podium. He started his sermon with a joke. "Mr. Epstein would thank us all for coming, but he'd be wanting to know who's minding the store."

It was nice to see Dad laugh. It had been too long. He took hold of my hand, and I could feel his love, which felt consolatory. I loved Jess, a lot, and wished she'd been into me as much as I thought she was. Yesterday in the basement, acting all vulnerable, and then last night—I supposed it was all payback for the way I had treated her. Well played, Jess. Well played.

The service was over in less than an hour, and after the rabbi and the family left the room, we were free to leave too. In the lobby, Dad and I signed the guest book. He took one of the memorial cards and handed one to me. It had a picture of Mr. Epstein and a poem written by his granddaughter. I liked how it was so personal, and not the generic saint on one side and prayer on the other that the Catholics gave out.

Dad walked ahead to find the family, and I put the card back on the pile. I had enough death cards for several life-times, and all I could think was that it was more stuff to store or recycle when I left for school. Dad claimed he was going to keep my room exactly as I'd left it for when I came home for breaks, but I hoped he'd turn it into a home gym or a meditation room or anything that was for himself.

Outside, after we offered our condolences to the family, Dad and I walked a few blocks west to another of our regular customers—Dad's favorite diner. He preferred to eat where he sprayed. The free food was great, but knowing the place was pest-free was everything.

ACT III

I WOKE FROM THE muscle-relaxer meds feeling weak and disoriented. As I struggled to separate my drug-fueled nightmares from reality, I heard singing coming from the other room.

The voice was too off-key to be a dream. What time was it? I wondered.

Then I remembered: Rocco. I had to get back to him. If he was awake, he would be hungry and stressed beyond belief. But I couldn't move my neck. In fact, I felt restrained from the neck up. Panic and pleasure pulsated through my body. Rebecca was holding me captive? Was it to mentor me? Or study me?

I had never been on the receiving end of the process and wanted to experience it with Rebecca. But Rocco . . . I had to get back to him. I hoped he wouldn't be too disappointed when I told him we couldn't begin our work together. Something better, more glorious, an opportunity of a lifetime was in my reach. I wouldn't use those words, of course. I would say something more sensitive. I would never want to make him, or anyone, feel rejected. That would be cruel and inhumane.

"You're awake." I heard Rebecca, but I couldn't turn my head to see her. She pulled a chair up to the side of the bed and sat with a bowl and spoon in hand.

"Do you like chicken rice soup?"

"Homemade?"

She chuckled. "Somebody's home." With a smile, she began spooning soup into my mouth, alternating between chicken, broth, and rice. When we were halfway done, she asked, "Ready to try and get up?"

My legs, my arms, felt heavy, but they weren't strapped or tied down. I could shift my hips and twist my waist and raise my arms and kick my legs. My neck . . . not so much.

"I'm going to remove the neck brace, but you need to move very slowly. Promise?"

"I promise."

I wondered if this was how my characters felt the first time I removed their restraints. Titillated by the possibilities of what might happen next.

She gingerly lifted my head and removed the brace.

I turned my head to the right and left and back to center.

"How do you feel?"

"Exhilarated," I said.

"I told you those muscle relaxers would do the trick."

Drugs. Mother. Her muscle relaxers. Her apartment, her bed . . . and her protégé Rebecca.

"How long have you known your patron?"

"Your mother?"

"Don't call her that," I said.

"What happened between the two of you?"

I could have told her what a wretched woman Mother was, but there are some truths one must learn for oneself.

"What time is it?" I asked.

"Eight," she said.

"Morning?"

"Evening."

I quickly calculated the number of hours I'd been away from Rocco. I'd left him at three in the morning. He'd spent seventeen hours with no food, water, and no insulin!

"I have to go." I jolted out of bed, and felt so light-headed I had to grab hold of the back of Rebecca's chair to keep myself from falling over.

She stood and wrapped her arm around my waist. "Take it easy. You can't go from zero to a hundred."

"I have to get home."

"Don't tell me you're married."

I couldn't tell if this was a serious question or an attempt at humor.

"I left . . ."

"The stove on?"

"My cat. I left my cat."

"Your cat? Oh God. I didn't know you had a cat."

Seemingly distressed, she raced to the closet, took my shirt and pants from a hanger, and brought them to me. Then she started to dress me, but she moved so quickly that she was putting my buttons in the wrong holes. I would have stopped her, but she was quite intent on helping.

"I'm so sorry," she said. "I didn't even think—"

I took both her hands into mine. "It's fine. He's probably hungry, but he'll be okay. Seventeen hours isn't the end of the world."

She raised her head from my chest, where she had mismatched another button and hole. Her eyes targeted mine, and she spoke in a hesitant but grave voice. "It's been six days."

She'd kept me drugged for six days? Her hostage after all? I was horrified and impressed, but why was she letting me go now?

"The doctor said not to move you."

"Doctor? What doctor?"

"You were waking up in terrible pain. I wanted to call a doctor, but you insisted you only needed rest, and . . . well, I'm not a fan of doctors myself, but after two days I got scared, and I called the doctor your mother uses to treat her back." She showed me the bottle on the nightstand. I remembered the pills well. Mother always had some condition for which her private doctors prescribed medication without question.

"Along with the muscle relaxers, the doctor said to give you these painkillers. He said you'd be okay in a few days, a week tops."

I pushed her out of the way, knocking over the chair. With my shirt misaligned and not tucked, and no belt because I had no idea where it was and no time to find it, I rushed to the door. I was fumbling with the second lock when Rebecca came up behind me. "I'm going with you."

There was no time to argue, and I had no interest in stopping her. With six days having passed, I knew what I'd find when I got to the brownstone, and I wanted Rebecca to share the moment with me. There wasn't anything more raw or real than to be in the presence of death and decay. Rebecca was an artist. She would understand.

We hailed a cab, and the only words exchanged were between the driver and me.

Inside, the brownstone gathered enough natural light for us to see.

Rebecca went right to making lip-smacking sounds of the kind meant to summon animals to you. "God, let him be okay," she said. "What's his name?"

"Rocco."

"Rocco?" Smack-smack. "Rocco?" Smack-smack.

While Rebecca searched under the couches and chairs and even under the rugs, I walked over to the sealed room. I had every intention of entering the passcode into the hidden keypad and inviting Rebecca to come inside with me. It would be a bit of a shock to her system at first. The odor would be not of this world, but of that other place where we reside when crossing over.

"Kinky." Rebecca came up behind me, holding a leather strap. I kept extras around in case a character needed additional restraints, or in the rare instance that a strap broke. "Is this why I didn't do it for you?"

"Excuse me?"

"If you're into bondage, it's not off the table."

Bondage? "Are you implying that I partake in sadomasochism?"

"It's nothing for you to be embarrassed about."

"I think you should leave." My voice was tight, contained, but I knew if she didn't walk out now, I would start yelling, and I couldn't tolerate a scene at that moment. I needed to confirm my character's state.

Rebecca didn't move a muscle at first. Not even an eyelid. Then she stormed off, slamming the front door behind her.

I smelled Rocco before I saw him.

He was bloated and blue. From the contorted position of his body, it was clear he'd struggled to get loose. He had bitten right through his tongue and bottom lip. He'd thought I had abandoned him.

Abandonment, the cruelest act of all.

I fell into the leather chair by his side, picked up my notebook and pencil, inhaled deeply, and wrote, *Rocco. Forgive me.* And then I wept.

*   *   *

With a job this straightforward, bodily fluids and waste contained to one area, no breakage, it should have been a simple disposal job. But today, every step felt as if I were treading wet cement. It was all I could do not to sink. I told myself it was the aftereffects of the drugs.

The sun had risen, and the shell disposal still wasn't complete. We'd used crematoriums in our work for generations, but you can imagine what a chore it had been to transport the shells from the workroom to the basement. My father, your grandfather, a genius, had developed a system that was more efficient and practically flawless.

In the workroom he had installed a door, the height of an average minifridge but wide enough to fit a grown character with bulk. The same lever and pulley used to lift and transport the incapacitated character was used to move its shell to said door, opening to a chute my father had engineered based on those found in NYC buildings to transport garbage to basement compactors or furnaces, though this one was wide enough to fit a six-by-three-foot shell.

The next part of the system is where my father's genius really shines. The shell, when properly lubricated, slides easily down to a conveyor belt, which will automatically move the shell through the crematorium's open doors, incinerating it. Flesh, bone, and other human matter turn into ashes and bone fragments, from which, at a later date, I would take a handful to my guy in Queens, and he would craft it into another one of my trophies.

But I had much to do before I got to Queens.

Like I've said, it was a flawless system, usually. This morning the shell got stuck at the top of the chute. I pushed and pushed, for naught. I couldn't get it to go down. "Why is this happening?" I shouted. Shells twice the weight and width had slid down without interruption. Where had I gone wrong?

I retrieved Father's manual from where it had been sewn into the seat of the leather chair. Father had trained me so well I had never before needed to refer to it. It was leather bound, of course. It still smelled of Father's cigars, and when I inhaled the pages, I caught a whiff of petroleum.

That's when I lost it. I punched the sides of my head, screaming, "Stupid! Stupid!" I had forgotten to grease the outside of the shell. Father had so often warned me how, without an abundant amount of lubrication, body parts could get stuck on a screw or protruding piece of metal in the chute. Botching this step had been so worrisome to me that I'd sometimes made a character bathe in motor oil before ending our partnership.

After an hour and twenty minutes of pulling with my arms, using my legs for leverage, I got the shell out of the chute, oiled it well, and sent it on its way.

I collapsed to the floor. Not from exhaustion. Not from pain. (My back muscles seemed to have benefited greatly from Rebecca's over-the-top treatment.)

It was despair I felt. Bone-crushing despair. I had never known regret until now.

Why was this happening? No character in all my years of work had made me feel this gut-wrenchingly ill. Not even Sal, and we had just started to make a breakthrough when he had to go.

Yes, it was regrettable that Rocco had been alone in the end. How lost he must have felt in those last moments. Abandoned.

Still, the burning I felt in the marrow of my bones confused me. What made this character so special?

I pulled my knees into my chest, dropped my head down, and the answer came, as clear as day: *Rebecca.*

This was about her. She had kept me hostage for days. She said she hadn't known about Rocco, my alleged cat. But what if she had known about Rocco the man, and she was testing my limits? Had she forced me into this deep despair to see if I would swim or drown? Your grandfather would break me into minuscule particles so he could rebuild me his own way, and he did so again and again. But this despair felt so different . . .

I was mourning, grieving, because of Rebecca.

I needed it to stop. All of these feelings, biological responses, crashing against my core, trying to break in and destroy me, had to stop, now.

For this to happen, I needed to find my way back to her, and to do that I needed to do what Father did when he needed to recharge. I sealed my workroom, left the brownstone, and at the southeast corner of the street, I stepped into a group of pedestrians crossing the street, pulled out my pen, and stabbed it into my neck, hard. Then I did it again. And again. Until I lost consciousness.

* * *

There were no witnesses to my stabbing. Father always said if you want to go unnoticed, stand in the middle of a crowd. When the police questioned me at the hospital, I told them I hadn't seen the attacker. They found it curious that a pen was used in my assault.

Luckily, there was no permanent damage to my vocal cords.

After two days in the ER, I was admitted to the psychiatric ward for observation. They informed me that my wounds appeared to be self-inflicted. I had no memory of this until much later. But the time I spent recovering gave me the blessing of living in a world without outside distractions; not having to hear people drone on and on inanely was wonderful. But the most remarkable thing was the clarity I found. Without the craziness of the world interrupting my every thought, I could finally hear myself think. It was during this time that I realized what a great disservice I had done to Rebecca. Her thinking I was into bondage was not so out of the question, given the evidence she'd found. And even so, it hadn't sent her running. She'd cared enough to stay and was willing to do what she thought I wanted. She wanted to make me happy, and in return, I'd sent her away. I didn't know if she had tried to contact me or if she even wanted to see me. I had been so unkind to her the last time we were together. I couldn't blame her if she never wanted to see me again. But on the slim chance that she did, I had to go and find her.

* * *

On the day I was released, I took a cab to Park Avenue.

The doorman was Jack, a pro even back then. We had only met once, but he remembered me.

I explained about my accident and told him I'd been out of commission for weeks.

He said Rebecca was no longer apartment-sitting. She'd left a week ago and there was no forwarding address. The owner—your grandmother, the mother I pretended, acted, wanted to believe with all my heart was not my mother—was still away and would be gone for several more months. I thanked him and took a yellow cab to my brownstone.

The cab ride was the longest ride of my life. Cab rides are always endless when there's no hope left. And I had none.

I let myself into the brownstone and climbed the stairs to the main floor and saw a light coming from under the door. Was someone inside? How was that possible?

I opened the door and almost fell over with joy. Sitting on the couch, with all of my Tonys resting at her feet and reading the *New York Times*, was my Rebecca.

I might have thought she was a mirage had she not been reading the paper—not even the Sunday edition but the regular daily edition. There was no way that in any fantasy of mine, Rebecca would be engaged with that error-riddled rag. She was real and she was here. *New York Times* or not, I had never been happier to see anyone. I had never known happiness until that moment.

In no rush to leave this miraculous moment behind, I waited for her to look up and notice me. Everything she did—twitching her nose, scrunching her brow, pursing her lips—was delightful. In my research on the human condition, I'd read dozens of studies on attraction. What makes two people connect or not connect? Until now it had been an intellectual pursuit. Now it was clear to me the answer wouldn't be found in a journal or an article or some PhD dissertation. It wouldn't even be found in art. The answer could only be found through personal experience: a cliché known as chemistry.

I also saw that Rebecca had transformed the brownstone. This room was different, airy and cheerful. Live flowers in several vases. The only thing I ever remembered my parents having in common was their disgust for cut flowers, which they considered a reminder that beauty is short-lived. ("We have mirrors for that," Mother often said.) I used to agree with them, but today I could see the yellow in the sunflowers and smell the lilacs in the air. It all made me smile. Giggle.

"You're back!" She dropped the paper and jumped off the couch, knocking over several of my awards, but I didn't care. "An accident?" She pointed to the bandage on my neck.

I nodded yes, and she took my hand. Stepping over the dozens of awards she had surrounding her, she led me to the couch. We sat with no space between us, and yet I didn't feel like I would suffocate.

"You're here. Why?" I asked. I needed her to explain. And she did.

For weeks she'd tried to call me to apologize, a dozen, two dozen times, but the calls had gone straight to voice mail until the machine was full. She knew if she was ever going to make things right, she would have to see me face-to-face.

Three days ago, she'd found the courage to knock on my door, but there was no answer. She turned the knob, and the door opened.

I'd left the door open? I must have been more distracted than I thought.

If the door was unlocked, she reasoned, then I had to be home. I wasn't, and so she waited. I didn't come back that night, and by the morning she was certain something bad had happened to me. She called every hospital in the area, but no one had been admitted under my stage or birth name. She frantically took the awards off the shelf, hoping there would be a name, or a clue, as to how to find me. The named professions—carpenter, plumber, airline attendant, and so forth—gave her nothing to go on.

"I'm sorry, but I was so desperate, I called Europe." Mother.

"She told you to keep your distance," I said.

"To stay far away," Rebecca added. "But I made it clear to her that I didn't appreciate threats, and she hung up, or the line went dead. Either way, I didn't call her back. I never want to speak to that woman again."

Rebecca had chosen me over Mother.

"What happened?" She gently touched the bandage around my throat.

When I didn't respond, she didn't push me for an answer. She wrapped her arms around me and I melted into her, the cliché of clichés, but when our foreheads touched, I remembered the entangled couple on the subway the night I'd left my work to see Rebecca and make things right. Now I was sure I had witnessed love.

"I'm sorry for that day," she whispered in my ear. "I have a big mouth."

I pulled my head back and traced her lips with my middle finger. I was in desperate need of a manicure. "Beautiful." I had to strain to say this out loud.

And she kissed me. I kissed her back for all the time we'd lost, and for what felt like no time at all, not enough time.

"I blew a fuse," she said.

"Fuse?"

"Hair dryer and microwave. Too much stress on these old buildings with a-hundred-and-ten voltage. I went to the basement to look for the fuse box, and . . ." She leaned toward me, as if to confide. "I know your secret."

I immediately assumed she'd found the box of ashes and bone shards from Rocco's shell. I could tell her they were my father's remains, or those of our pit bull Joey. I'd never discovered what Father did with the pup's shell after I found him dead on the kitchen floor.

"He had a good life," Mother had said, before she broke down and cried. Yet she never shed a tear for Father. And I'm sure she wouldn't have cried if it had been me lying by my bowl of half-eaten table scraps.

I needed to respond to Rebecca about her discovery. I knew that a relationship founded on lies was doomed. I picked up the pen and notebook. I was ready to tell her all about my work, but I hesitated, only because I wasn't sure where to start. Did I go all the way back to the The Knife?

Father said they'd called him this because of his sharp business sense. In the early years of the last century, he'd seen a need for discretionary disposal, and in several of his town-houses, he'd installed large furnaces, crematorium chambers, to meet the demand.

The Knife never married and had no children. He took on an apprentice. Your great-great-grandfather at the age of eleven.

Father never knew exactly why his grandfather had chosen to work for The Knife, but he supposed it wasn't important to the story; what was relevant was that your great-great-grandfather inherited The Knife's business and his townhouses. By the time Father was born, this was the only brownstone our family hadn't sold off and the original business had gone bankrupt, so to speak. My grandfather, a thespian of the people, had his own vision and had upgraded to what was a state-of-the-art crematorium at the time. He directed my father, who then directed me, not only in the method of the work but in how to use and maintain the tools of our trade. Father always said, "There are a dozen actors for every role, but the one who knows how to build a stage is the one who will get the part."

Before I could write any of this on the page, Rebecca took the pen from me.

"A crematorium," she said, revealing what she'd discovered. "Wonderful."

I felt half the weight of my family history fall from my shoulders. We would share it and the work together. I was so overwhelmed with joy and relief, I did something I had never before done: I initiated a hug.

"Does it still work?" she said near my ear. I let her go, leaned back, and nodded.

"I can use it?"

I nodded. *Yes, yes, yes.*

"You'll show me."

"Of course," I squeaked out.

"This place was once an underground funeral home? The mob supposedly had secret crematoriums to get rid of people after they whacked them."

Mob? Whacked? Once she said it, it did make sense: The Knife could well have been involved in organized crime. And that meant my great-grandfather, your great-great-grandfather, had also been involved by default. But my father and his father were—

I picked up the pen and pad and, in all caps, wrote: *ARTISTS.*

"I know," she said. "Those things get as hot as eighteen hundred degrees Fahrenheit. It's the low end of the temperature of a kiln. I bet I can still use it to fire my own sculptures. I do some metal, but most of my work is with clay."

Oh. I was disappointed. She didn't understand my work. She was thinking only about her work, her art. But that smile, with her right incisor exposed, was the widest, most sincere smile I had ever seen. And it was all because of me. That felt nice.

"You hungry?" she asked.

I was starved. I hadn't had much of an appetite these past few weeks, and it was a good thing, because the rehab center's food was inedible.

VERY, I wrote under *ARTISTS.*

Rebecca took my hand and led me to my bed, which soon became our bed.

*   *   *

Rebecca was an amazing cook.

Our first meal together, she made steak, cooked to perfection. Rare but not bloody. Her seared garlic-mashed potatoes were matched by no other. As we ate apple crisp that she'd made for the first time from a recipe she'd found in a women's magazine, it tasted like it had been passed down generation to generation.

We made plans.

Rebecca insisted she wanted nothing to do with her former patron. Nor did she need, or want, details about my fraught relationship with Mother. She took it on faith that, for a son to sever all ties with the woman who had birthed him, reprehensible acts must have been committed against him.

Still, she needed to know the sacrifice she was making by choosing me. I told her about Mother's will and the fortune she would be losing. I was comfortable financially, but I couldn't offer the kind of wealth and security Mother promised.

Rebecca turned her back on all of it. For me.

"It's not only because of you," she said. "I can't create under the pressure and expectations she created."

I was surprised, maybe even jealous, to hear this. Mother had never taken an interest in my life's work. She'd left it all to Father, and when he died, there was no one who cared if I survived or thrived as an artist. But none of that mattered now.

I proposed she move in with me and she could do her art here, when and if she wanted. She said she could set up a small studio in the guest room, but I told her no.

"The best light is in the living room." I boxed up all of my awards and in their place filled the shelves with all the art supplies she could ever want.

She painted, and sketched, and I posed for her. When she was ready to sculpt, I would fire her pieces in the crematorium, giving them everlasting life.

Someday I would train her, as my father had trained me, how to use the crematorium. Until that day, she was the master and I was her loyal subject.

And so Rebecca stayed, and this was where our love story really began.

Rebecca and I took long walks through the parks of New York City: Central Park, Morningside Park, Pelham Bay Park in the Bronx. Our favorite thing to do was to watch the children play on the swing sets, or on what Rebecca called the monkey bars. Of course, I had seen these contraptions before, but Father said they were too dangerous, and I had a career to protect. Every time Rebecca and I watched children climb to the top of that ten-foot structure, the oxygen caught in my throat and Rebecca would have to remind me to breathe. "Kids are flexible, durable. Don't worry."

I knew she would make a good mother, a situation-comedy mom, the kind that made you laugh and solved all your problems in twenty-two minutes.

When we weren't walking the parks of the city, we were at home cooking and reading and giving each other foot rubs, and she showed me ways to please her in the bedroom until I no longer felt like that part of me was broken.

Rebecca sketched and painted and created. We were happy.

LINDA

CHAPTER

12

Carmen's Diner had long been Dad's and my "special place." We'd drink refill after refill of coffee, black for me, whole milk for Dad, none of that skim or 2 percent crap, and we'd talk about the business and all the clients I wanted to strangle. For his part, Dad would offer some overly forgiving reason why they weren't assholes, simply misunderstood. Betty, the waitress that time hadn't forgotten, came to serve us, with her bright-red lipstick and powder-white hair coiffed in a high bouffant. She'd been a dancer in her day, even a Rockette for a few years in the late sixties. She greeted us wearing her light-pink waitress uniform, short enough to expose the longest legs on any woman, or man, I had ever seen before meeting Jess.

Betty owned the diner, having bought the place from Martha, her boss until she retired. Martha had named the place Carmen's after her favorite film star, Carmen Miranda, who'd ordered a tuna on rye the one and only time she'd eaten here, over seventy years ago. Her table was always reserved for her with an autographed, framed picture hanging on the wall. After Martha left, Betty kept the shrine, and even when a line ran out the door, the booth remained empty.

Betty had never stopped waiting tables, which she swore was her secret to running a successful business. Today she gave Dad a longer-than-appropriate hug, knowing that a suit meant someone had died. She'd crushed on Dad ever since, as she described it, Dad had saved her life. Dad said he was only doing his job, but the exterminators she'd used at the diner before us were ripping her off using "stinky water"— cheap, diluted pesticide with an added odor to make it smell but not kill. Betty's health inspection rating had dropped to a C, and she was losing business. Dad had her rating back up to an A after two visits. He'd saved her business, which for Betty was her life. I'd encouraged Dad to ask her out, but he'd never been interested in romancing anyone alive.

Betty led us to our booth, the best booth in the place.

After Carmen's, of course.

Dad always sat on the side facing the door. For years, Betty had thought he was a war veteran or in the Mafia. When she discovered neither was true, that instead he did it to protect me, she'd told me in front of Dad, "You're your father's heart."

"My kidney and every other vital organ too," Dad had laughed.

Now she turned over our coffee cups and poured. "It's nice to see you in something besides work clothes."

"She has a nice suit at home," Dad said.

Betty rested the coffeepot on the table, slipped her hand down the back of my dress, and checked the label. "One of the best." She smiled, exposing red lipstick on her teeth. "Don't you return it," she warned with a smile. She must have seen the hidden price tag. "Doesn't your daughter look too gorgeous?"

Dad kept his eyes on the menu he had long ago committed to memory.

Betty leaned into me but spoke loud enough for Dad and every other person in the place to hear. "Fathers never want their daughters to look sexy."

"The special," Dad said loudly. "I'll have the special."

"It's liver and onions today," she said.

"Perfect."

"For the sexy lady?" She gave Dad a sidelong glance. She loved pushing his buttons.

"A cup of split pea."

"You have to eat more than that," Dad said. "Bring her a burger with a fried egg too."

"Just the soup," I said.

"Bring her the burger," Dad said.

"Betty, just the soup."

"The burger." Dad's smile remained warm, but his eyes were bone-chillingly cold.

"I bring the soup first, and if you're still hungry, we bring the burger." Betty walked away before Dad or I could repeat another word.

"It was a nice service," he said. "We should do one for your mother."

"Uh, she died twenty-five years ago."

"I always felt bad she never had a proper service."

"But she has no family," I said.

"What are we?"

"You want to have a memorial service with just you and me?"

"We can invite some of the neighbors and family, like Betty—"

"They didn't know Mom," I said.

"They know us."

I'd said it before, and I would say it again: there's no arguing with Dad when his mind is made up.

"Sure, Dad," I said. "We can have a service."

"We can do it in the fall. Your mother's favorite season."

"I'll be in California," I reminded him.

He tore open a pair of sugar packs. "You can invite your girlfriend."

"My girlfriend?"

"Whatever you call this woman," Dad said. "You care about her."

"That's why you look so beautiful." Betty had returned with Dad's special and my soup. "You're in love. Finally."

"I'm leaving. Long-distance never works," I said, feeling trapped in the cramped booth.

"Love knows no time or distance," Betty said.

Dad sugared his coffee with both bags, which was unusual. Usually, he stayed away from sugar and called it poison.

My cell rang. It was Jess.

"Your friend?" Dad asked.

"Answer it," Betty said.

Dad lifted his chin in agreement.

I picked up. "Hi, Jess. Give me a minute." Dad let me out of the booth. "I'll be right back," I told them, and stepped outside into a cacophony of street noise. I had to put my hand over my ear to hear what she was saying.

"Where am I?" I repeated what I thought I'd heard Jess say. "West Side."

"You forgot your coveralls."

I went right for the earlobe, tugging as hard as I could without causing damage. I was disappointed, upset. I thought she'd called to tell me she wanted to see me, that she missed me already. She just wanted my dirty work clothes out of her apartment.

"Don't worry, trash 'em. I have others," I lied. My only other pair had worn out and been cut up for rags.

"I can bring them to you," she said.

My heart pounded louder than the traffic.

"It's all right . . . ," I began.

"Uber. It'll take fifteen minutes. Address?"

She wanted to come to me, and I wanted to see her. I looked in the diner's window. Dad and Betty were talking. I often wondered what they discussed when I wasn't around.

I weighed my options and decided this wasn't a good time for Jess and Dad to meet.

"I can pick them up at the precinct," I said.

"Linda, did I do something to offend you?"

The noise and my nerves were unbearable. "Give me a second." I went back inside and found an empty stall in the bathroom. I lowered the lid and sat down. "You didn't offend me."

"The way you rushed off. You were clearly upset."

"I didn't want to overstay my welcome."

"I was looking forward to having breakfast with you."
She sounded sweet and sincere.

"I'd like that sometime."

"I'm hungry now. Have you eaten?"

"I'm at a diner, and I already ordered."

"What diner?"

"Carmen's, on Seventy-Second," I let slip. But my relief
was palpable. I guessed I could live with Dad meeting her.
They had already talked on the phone.

"Betty's the coolest."

"You know the place?"

"It's a regular cop hangout."

Quickly, I reconsidered. I had to prepare Dad before
they met. He was dealing with a lot, between my mother's
death anniversary and my leaving for college soon, and two
of his customers dying so close together, and one in such a
gruesome, cruel way. I was dealing with a lot too. When and
if they met, I wanted it to be under happy circumstances.

"Why don't I take my food to go and bring you something. You're still home?"

"All day," she said. "Get me the special."

"It's liver and onions," I warned.

"I like living on the edge."

"One special coming your way."

"See you soon." She hung up.

* * *

Not long after, Betty and I were in the bathroom, washing
our hands side by side. She smiled at the mirror. "Why don't
people tell you when you have lipstick . . ." She rubbed her
middle finger across the top of her teeth.

"I didn't notice." I pumped the soap twice.

Betty's eyes scanned the length of my reflection, then she
changed the subject.

"Tell me . . . why don't you want your father to meet
this girl?"

I turned on the water and recited the alphabet song in
my head. Two times through was enough to kill the germs,

but I was on the fourth round when Betty handed me a paper towel.

I shut the water off and dried my hands.

"She knows you," I said. "Jessica Jones."

"The detective. Tall. Not too thin. Strong. She comes here with the older one."

Detective Frascon was still probably ten years younger than Betty, but I kept this to myself.

"The one with the bad fashion," she added. "Shoulder pads." She shuddered. "When they died in the eighties, they should have buried 'em all."

"Jess . . . Detective Jones says you're cool, which you are. She wants me to bring her the special."

"They come for the food, but they return for my charming personality," Betty said with a laugh.

"I don't think it's going to work out between us," I said, realizing how nice it was to have someone I could share anything about Jess with.

Betty wiped her hands and pitched the paper towel into the basket. Great shot. "Your father doesn't like the police, but there's a deeper truth."

"He blames them for my mother's death."

"They didn't shoot her, did they?"

"After he got the call from the hospital telling him my mother had left with me, he feared she'd harm herself. Postpartum, he said. He was working a site in Brooklyn and knew he wouldn't be able to get to her before it was too late. He begged the police to go to their home."

"They didn't go?"

"Not soon enough."

Betty was silent for a few seconds.

"Your father wants you to be happy."

I wouldn't have believed her yesterday, but after discovering Dad had known about Jess all this time, I knew she was right. I hugged Betty tight. "Thank you."

"For what? I did nothing. So, one special to go, and I'll wrap your soup and throw in a burger. The burger's on me. For love."

13

I FOLLOWED BETTY BACK to our booth. Dad had two more sugar packets in hand, but he wasn't alone. Standing over him was Detective Frascon.

"Detective," Betty said. "Your usual?"

"Police business," she said.

"Sounds very official."

"She's here for me," Dad said.

"Ms. Donovan." Frascon angled her neck in my direction, eyeing my attire. "Exterminator's gala?"

"We just came from a funeral," I answered for him.

Dad didn't have to shake his head for me to know he was disappointed. I'd broken the cardinal rule: never say more than you have to.

"Your father's a hard man to reach."

I sat down next to him, taking the outside seat for once. "I told you he was out of town."

"He's here now," she said.

Dad simply stared into his coffee mug. I wanted to shout, *Say something!* His silence and zombie-like expression alone made him appear guilty.

"You have more questions for us?" I asked.

"I have a few questions for your father."

Dad dropped the sugar packs and looked up. "Fire away, Detective."

"Mr. Donovan, it would be much appreciated if you would come with me to the precinct."

"Is my father under arrest?" I stood, banging my knee against the table. I tried not to wince but failed.

"Sure," Dad said, standing, but I refused to move out of his way. I needed to protect him, from what I wasn't sure. "It's okay." Dad put his hand on my shoulder. "The detective has a job to do. I'm happy to help."

"I'm coming with you."

"You take care of business, and I'll see you soon." Dad kissed me on the forehead.

It seemed like he was trying to tell me something, but what, I hadn't a clue. I stepped out of his way.

He and Frascon walked out of the diner as Betty returned, a brown paper bag in her hand.

"They left," I told her. I thought I might cry.

"Always such a rush, these police. Like they're firemen. Any idea what's going on?"

"Yesterday, I found one of our customers dead."

"So now your father's a murderer?"

I was dumbfounded, speechless for a moment.

"The man I know is no killer," said Betty.

"Of course he's not."

"Then why are you worried?"

"A lot of innocent people go to prison."

Detective Frascon and Dad were back. "Dad?" I went to him.

"Need to see a man about a horse." Dad headed for the bathroom.

Betty approached us, curious, and tried starting some chitchat, but the detective wasn't having it. She tapped her foot impatiently, ignoring Betty while keeping an eye on me.

I watched her for a minute, then decided to go with the direct approach. "Rita, is my father in trouble?"

Frascon still didn't respond; instead, she looked down at the nondigital, not-smart watch on her wrist. Man, she really was from a different time.

"Damn it!" she said suddenly, pushing past me and rushing for the restrooms. Before I had time to process what was happening, she was back and running toward the front door. "He's in trouble now," she said as she rushed out of the diner. Stunned, I looked at Betty, who looked back at me. I went outside, looking for Frascon, but she was nowhere in sight.

I walked back inside, feeling cold and numb as though I'd entered a state of shock, and found Betty cleaning our table. Dad had hardly touched the liver and onions.

For once, Betty seemed to know better than to comment on our business. She simply inclined her head toward the booth seat where I'd left my cell and the boutique bag with my old jeans and T-shirt.

"Betty . . . I . . ." Words failed me.

"Come," she said, and I followed her into the men's room. The window was wide open and the room empty.

Still saying nothing, Betty hooked her arm through mine and walked us out of earshot of the few tables with customers. "You have a problem," she said in a low voice.

"You're telling me. My father just ran from the police!"

"It's worse," she confided. "Your girlfriend's a rat."

Oh God. Betty was right. Jess must have called Frascon right after we spoke. How else would she have known to find Dad here? I'd been worked . . . manipulated. Picturing Jess, I felt anger burning in my chest. But I also knew this was my fault.

"I should have listened to him," I said out loud. "Never trust the police."

"The heart isn't the smartest organ," Betty said. "But it keeps us alive."

"They'll think he's guilty because he ran. They won't understand it's because he blames them, hates them, because of my mother's death. What am I going to do?"

Betty unhooked her arm from mine. "Come." I followed her to the takeaway window. "Pickup to go for Donovan," she called out.

A young man handed her a brown paper bag. She faced me and said, "Your special."

I pushed it away. "You want me to bring her lunch?"

"You want to help your father?"

"Of course."

"You and the detective were intimate?"

I felt my pores burn with embarrassment. "We were together for a while," I admitted.

"Bring her the food."

"Liver and onions is going to help my father?"

"She has a job to do, but she also has feelings for you. Not just in a sex way."

I didn't question Betty's take on this. She knew people. She could tell you a person's life story from the way they held their forks.

"But she's a cop first," I pointed out.

"A cop who will listen to you. You bring her the food as planned and act all worried about your father."

"I am worried!"

"Right, so you won't have to act. But play it up. Turn on the waterworks if you need to. Get her to feel sorry for your predicament. The loving single father who raised you is missing."

"He ran away, Betty, like he's guilty."

"You know he's innocent."

I nodded.

"Play on her sympathy, and knowingly or unknowingly, she'll give you something. Information we can use to help your father. It doesn't matter what she thinks about your dad. It's what she feels about you."

My stomach hurt thinking about last night and how all that had felt possible was now lost again.

"If they had any real evidence, your dad would have been cuffed and arrested. Right now, they have questions."

"Half her face was gone. A rat, Betty."

"God have mercy on her soul." Betty crossed herself.

"She had peanut butter on her," I said.

Betty was pacing like an old-timey detective. "This woman had enemies. The question is who?"

Hearing this, I had a terrible feeling. "What if they try to blame Dad?"

Betty laughed. "Your father closes his eyes when he sprays for roaches."

Does he? I'd never noticed.

"Not because he's squeamish," she continued. "Because he can't bear to watch anything suffer." She reached out and touched my cheek. "Darling, your father is not a stupid man. Why would he ever bring a rat into his own place of work?"

"That's what Dad said."

"You make them understand why your father ran away. And all will be okay."

I felt a spark of hope.

I pulled Betty to me and, with the liver and onions between us, hugged her tight like she was going away for a long time. She was the only other living person who knew my father the way I did. A man who couldn't even watch a roach suffer.

Betty patted me on the back as my phone pinged. I stepped away. She raised her eyebrows inquiringly as I checked the message.

"A text. From Jess," I said. "She's asking for a rain check. She has to go to the precinct for a work thing."

"You better get to the station." Betty walked out of the diner, and I followed. "Not a cloud in the sky," she said, staring up.

"Not a cloud," I said.

"Good luck, honey." She handed me the greasy bag of liver and onions, with a burger on the side. "I'm here if you need me."

14

I ARRIVED AT THE precinct with a stabbing pain in my feet from the wedge heels and their lack of arch support. The uniformed officer behind the desk looked up and asked, "What's that smell?"

"Lunch for Jess . . . Detective Jones."

He pointed to a large dry-erase board behind him with three columns. *Name. In. Out.* Detective Jessica Jones had a magnetic dot in the *Out* column.

"Would you mind checking?"

Leaning back to maintain an arm's distance, the sergeant glared at me over his computer. "I see everyone who comes in and out, and she's not in."

"Maybe you were getting something to drink when she came in?" I lifted my chin to the coffee and half-eaten chocolate chip muffin on his desk.

"If it'll get you and that stink out of here . . ." He picked up the phone and dialed what I assumed was her extension.

I could hear the ringing through the receiver, and on the fifth ring he hung up. "She's not in."

"Maybe she's using the restroom—"

"If you want to leave a message . . ." He put a pad and pen in front of me.

"I'll text her."

"If you have her cell, why are you wasting my time?"

I texted: *At the front desk. Brought lunch.*

She texted back instantly. *Leave now.*

"Any luck?" the desk cop asked.

Another text arrived: *Meet me at my place in an hour.*

Dazed, I looked up at the sergeant. "Must've gotten my signals crossed. Thanks."

I quickly exited the precinct, but my aching feet had barely hit the pavement when Detective Frascon approached me from behind. "Ms. Donovan."

I considered running, but one runner in the family was probably enough. Besides, in these shoes I wouldn't get far.

"Your father," she said.

"You found him?" I could hear the desperation in my voice.

She shook her head. "Vanished. Patrol car checked your apartment, but nobody's home."

"He's innocent," I blurted, as if that would settle matters.

"Let's talk." She opened the door to the precinct and ushered me in ahead of her.

Jess had told me to leave, but what choice did I have? I went back inside and followed the detective deeper into the building.

"Just a few questions," Frascon said as she opened the door with an adhesive sign on it: *Interview Room 2.* She asked me to take a seat and if I wanted water or a coffee. I told her I was fine, and she left.

The room was straight out of one of Dad's cop-drama shows. Puke-green walls, gray cement floor, six-by-six brown folding table with two white plastic chairs for the interrogators on one side and one white plastic chair for the interrogated—that was me—on the opposite side. Missing was the mirror-mirror-on-the-wall to show who's the guiltiest of them all. I did see a camera attached to the ceiling, pointing at my seat.

The stink—generic cleaning fluid combined with egg salad left in the sun too long—reminded me that this was no TV set. I was no actor. This was real life, my life, and they were looking at me as an accessory to a crime.

The door opened. It was Jess. She looked tired. I wondered if it was because of me and the time we'd spent together last night. Or was it the guilt she felt over stabbing me in the back to trap my father?

"Enjoy." I shoved lunch across the table.

She glanced up at the camera and said, "What do I owe you?"

"Nothing."

"Cops can't take gifts." She gave me what was clearly a fake smile and took a blank check from her wallet. "I don't have cash," she explained.

"Seriously, I don't want your money."

"I insist." She filled out the check and handed it to me. "Did I spell your name correctly?"

In the payee line, she had written, *Say nothing. Ask for a lawyer.*

The door opened. Frascon was back. She took the seat next to Jess as I dropped the check in my boutique bag.

She sniffed. "What's that smell?"

"Lunch," I said.

"Why don't you put that in the fridge," she told Jess. "It's stinking up the place."

Before Jess stepped out of the room, she pulled at her earlobe meaningfully. I appreciated the reminder but still didn't trust her.

"Are you sure you don't want a coffee? Something from the vending machine?" Frascon smiled. "We have the good brand of Cheez Doodles."

I didn't know one brand of salty snack from another, but her wrinkled brow was a sign she wanted my cooperation. She needed me.

"Your father running doesn't look good for him."

"You have to understand his history with the police—"

"Your mother's death," she said knowingly.

Was there anything Jess hadn't told her partner? Had she shared how many times I came last night?

"This is a hard time for him right now. I'm going away to college."

"Empty-nest syndrome is not an excuse for running away from the police."

In my peripheral vision, the camera shifted down. I might have imagined it, but it reminded me that others were watching, no doubt including Jess. Why else would she be gone so long?

"How often do you service the Park building?"

"Every week," I said. I was sure she already knew this.

"Yesterday was your scheduled time?"

"That's why I was there," I said.

"Your father wasn't," she said.

"You already know why he wasn't there."

"That's right," she said. "Your mother's anniversary."

I didn't say anything.

She continued. "The night doorman confirmed the night before last, as he was clocking into the building, a man fitting your father's description was leaving through the service entrance."

"Dad was there checking on the mousetraps, since he knew we were going to see my mother the next day."

"If your father was just there the night before, why did you come the next morning? Did you not know he was there?"

I hesitated and then lied. "Of course I knew."

"You failed to mention this to me and Detective Jones?"

"I don't know. I wasn't thinking about it. I was there because of the roach situation, not the mice."

Frascon leaned across the table. "Why did your father run?"

"I'm all he's had since my mother died, and I'm leaving him," I said, louder than I'd intended.

Frascon leaned back and folded her arms. She stared at me in silence—a tactic to get me to crack. If ever something I'd said would be used against me or my father, it would be now. This seemed like the right time to take Jess's advice. But then again, if I asked for a lawyer, it would only confirm I was hiding something.

Jess entered the room with a Diet Pepsi and a Styrofoam cup of coffee. "Your father's DNA was found on the body."

"Thank you!" Frascon snatched the coffee from Jess's hands.

Clearly, she hadn't wanted Jess to share that fact with me. "What is this, CSI?" I asked. "You couldn't have sequenced my father's DNA and run it through your database this fast."

"We could if we matched it against a sample from another source," Frascon said.

"What source?"

"We had a warrant," Jess said.

"Wait. You said you went to our place to find my dad? Are you saying you searched it as well?"

Jess didn't answer. She didn't have to. She wasn't trying to help me. She had been setting me up, but for what I wasn't sure.

"My DNA was in both apartments too. How do you know it wasn't mine you found on the body?"

"It's sweet that you would be willing to take the fall for your father," Frascon said. "I doubt you wear men's extra-large briefs."

"You went through our dirty laundry?"

"Good place to get DNA."

I reached across the table and snatched the Diet Pepsi out of Jess's hand. "That doesn't mean he killed her." I twisted the cap off.

"We still haven't confirmed she was murdered." Jess shifted her eyes downward.

I was sure she could feel the heat from Frascon's piercing glare. If looks could burn, Jess would have a hole straight through her cerebral cortex.

"Then why am I here?"

"Until we get the autopsy report, homicide can't be ruled out, but we asked you here today about another matter."

Please, what more can there be? "What is it?" I demanded. "Jess, please."

"I can take it from here, Detective," Frascon said. It was clear from her tone and the dent her thumb had gouged into the Styrofoam cup that she was close to losing her shit. Maybe this wasn't an act and Jess was trying to help me. If she was setting me up, why would she have warned me to keep my mouth shut and get a lawyer? I waited for Jess to elaborate, but she sat silent, her eyes focused on the bottle cap trapped between my thumb and fingers.

Frascon pushed a paper in front of me. It was some sort of financial statement. "This was found in Mrs. Lyons's wall safe with several other documents."

"What exactly am I looking at?"

Frascon knocked her knuckles against a line on the paper that read *Beneficiary.*

"*Foster John Bennett, Junior,*" I read out loud.

"The son—estranged, it would appear—of the late Foster John Bennett, Senior and recently deceased Mrs. Marilynn Christine Lyons."

I glanced back down at the financial document. "This Foster Junior inherits twenty and a half million dollars from his mother's estate."

"Half her estate. The rest goes to charity and an endowed scholarship."

"Why aren't you talking to Foster Bennett, then? Seems to me he's the one with the motive."

"We're hoping you can help us find him."

"What? I don't even know this guy."

Frascon gave a slight nod to Jess and slid two more documents at me—photocopies of affidavits for legal name changes. "These were on file at the county clerk's office."

The first was for the legal name change of Mr. Foster John Bennett, Jr. to Anthony Michael Donovan.

Dad?

The second was for the legal name change of said minor, Linda Rebecca Bennett, to Linda Rebecca Donovan.

Me?

"You're kidding me." I slid the documents back at Jess. "You want me to believe my father is the heir to some rich woman's estate? Those documents don't even look real. Where's the notary seal?"

Jess whispered, "It's there," and my ears almost bled.

"Whatever move you're trying to pull"—I waved my half-empty bottle between them—"it's bullshit."

"Foster John Bennett, Junior," Frascon said, "was your father's name before he legally changed it in 1995."

"You would have been a year old," Jess said. "The documents are real."

"That would make Mrs. Lyons my grandmother?" I stood and leaned over the table, looking straight into Jess's eyes. "That's not possible. My father said my grandmother died in a car accident when he was a child. His father raised him."

Frascon came around the table, put a hand on my shoulder, and guided me back into my chair.

I shrugged her hand off.

Frascon returned to her seat across from me.

"Mrs. Lyons is your biological grandmother," Jess said.

"Do you know my father wanted me to have grandparents, family, so much that he took me to a nursing home in Queens to visit this elderly woman? I think she was a former customer of Dad's. She had no family. Nonna—I thought that was her name. I didn't know it was *grandmother* in Italian. She would talk to Dad and me about her life in Italy and her dead husband and son, who sometimes she confused Dad with. The nurses would remind me every time I went to visit that Nonna suffered from dementia and I shouldn't take it personally if she acted mean or indifferent, but she was always kind to me. She asked me questions about school and the music I liked, and we both loved sitcoms; her favorite was *How I Met Your Mother*. She always was kind and interested.

"After one of our visits, I told Dad I wished I had a grandmother like Nonna, and he said I could adopt her. So we did. He had me sign papers that were pretend, but I believed they were real. Every time we said good-bye, she kissed me on both cheeks and said, 'You're all right in my book, kid'— a line from some old-time movie. I loved it. I loved her."

"You stopped visiting her why?" Jess asked.

"She died in her sleep. I was twelve. We couldn't afford it—I know that now—but Dad found the money to make sure she had a proper funeral."

"That must have been hard," Jess said.

"What a gift to have had a grandmother at all. That's love," I said. "Why would my father go through all of that if I had a living grandmother?"

Frascon fanned out half a dozen eight-by-ten headshots of older women. "Any look familiar?"

I picked up one, and it was all I could do not to kiss it. I hadn't realized how much I missed her until I saw her photo. Dad wouldn't let me keep any pictures of her in the apartment; he thought it was better to remember her in our hearts. The only photos he had of anyone from his past were of my mother, in that album he pulled out only once a year.

"Lisa Broconi," Jess said. "Widowed young. One child. A son, never married. The son was in his thirties when his body was found at Grand Central Terminal in an abandoned utility room along the subway."

"You're going to blame that on my father too?"

"It was back in my rookie days," Frascon said. "Grand Central was my beat. Most of the crimes were pickpockets and vagrancy. Boring shit. Of course, on my day off they find a decaying body in a secret room, hidden along the tracks of the seven, or was it the six train? Those are the breaks." Her matter-of-fact take was disturbing, but it made sense for a homicide detective.

Jess took the photo from me, and pointing to the name printed on the back, she asked, "This place sound familiar?"

"Castle Living," I read out loud. "Yeah. That's the place she lived. I remember 'cause Dad would joke about the Castle being in Queens, and I thought we had to go over a moat to get there."

"Your father did more than pay for her funeral," Jess said. "Seemed to be more of a benefactor sort of relationship."

Frascon added. "He paid for her to live at the residential home."

"We didn't have that kind of money. We don't." It would have been easier for me to believe Dad had fornicated with fake Grandma than it was to believe he'd financially provided for her. Maybe he'd had more money when I was younger?

"We confirmed with the management company," Jess said. "A trust was set up through Mrs. Lyons's attorney to pay for all of Mrs. Broconi's living expenses until she passed."

"The money that took care of 'Nonna' came from your biological grandmother," Frascon concluded.

"Why?" I asked, but they both knew I didn't expect or want an answer.

I stood, then sat, then stood and sat again, mind spinning. Finally, I asked the detectives, "What did Mrs. Lyons do to my father?"

"I don't follow," Frascon said.

"For my father to have broken all ties with his mother, she must have abused him. Family is everything to Dad."

"We don't have evidence she did anything to him." Jess's tone contradicted her statement. She was thinking the same thing I was. Mrs. Lyons had abused my father. Why else would he have changed his name and gone to such lengths to keep the truth from me? I barely knew anything about Dad's past, though I'd always sensed there was a lot of pain he was hiding from me. The only thing he'd ever said about his mother was that it was she who'd put his father in an early grave. He'd only said this once.

"You don't change your name and disassociate from your mother if she didn't hurt you, beat you, or sexually abuse you. I don't know the specifics, but whatever she did to Dad, it cut him to his core." Neither of them said a word. "She knew I existed? She never even tried to see me."

"She saw you." Jess slid across the table a purse-sized photo album, the kind that parents who work too many hours carry with them everywhere. Flipping through it, I saw what looked like classic stalker photo moments from my early life, shot from a distance and out of focus: The little girl waving on her first day of kindergarten. Adolescent me playing the trumpet in her eighth-grade concert.

"This belonged to Mrs. Lyons?"

Both detectives nodded. Jessica's expression looked pained.

"She's been watching me all my life?"

Jess's whispered "Yes" was what made me break down. Before I knew it, tears were pouring so fast that everything literally became a blur.

"It's clear your father hated his mother," Frascon said, as she handed me a tissue.

I refused it, feeling a fresh wave of pain as I realized what I'd done. I no longer could, or wanted to, stop myself, so I reached up and pulled my right earlobe and then my left, harder than ever, making both Jess and Frascon wince. Yes, it was painful, but it hurt far less than what I realized I had done. I'd given them more ammunition to use against my father. I'd played right into their paint-by-number picture of who my father was: a man who hated his mother and who would gain financially from her death. They had a doorman confirming Dad had been there the night Mrs. Lyons was killed. I couldn't confirm if he was home or not that night. I remember I had gone to bed early.

I shook my head, trying to reset my thoughts. Jess and Frascon were getting into my head. Making me doubt the one person who had loved me unconditionally and taken care of me. No, my father wasn't a killer. He was a total soft touch; Betty'd said the same. He closed his eyes when he sprayed for roaches because he couldn't stand to see any creature suffer.

But this wasn't any creature, said a hard voice in my head. This was a woman who'd destroyed him in a way only a mother could, alive or dead.

"My father is not a killer," I managed through my tears.

Frascon stood and rested both hands on the table. "I get it. He's your father. Daughters are easily blinded from the truth until the day comes when they can't turn away from it any longer." She reached across the table and touched my thumb. I jerked my hand away. If she was trying to comfort me, for fake or for real, I wanted no part it.

"I've been where you are," she said. "I thought my father was a saint. My mother was the bitch and it was all her fault. She was shielding me from the truth. My father was a lying scumbag who fucked every woman that came his way . . ."

Jess put her hand on Frascon's arm in a gesture of sympathy or warning, I couldn't tell. Either way, this didn't bode well for Dad.

Frascon took a deep breath, sat down, and went straight back into cop mode. "Where were you the night Mrs. Lyons was murdered?"

I knew the words I used next would matter more than anything I'd said before in my life. A stray syllable, the wrong emphasis on a phrase, could incriminate me. Or substantiate Detective Frascon's theory about my father's guilt, or about my covering up for his crime, a crime I still prayed he hadn't committed. I had no evidence to refute their DNA samples, no witness or alibi for my father, no way to contradict the doorman's testimony. In fact, everything pointed to his guilt. They even had a motive: Mrs. Lyons was the mother he'd hated, resented so much that he'd legally changed his name and mine. He wanted nothing to do with her, and then he'd killed her, probably, and let a rat feed on her body. God. None of this was possible. This wasn't my father, Anthony Donovan.

"I want a lawyer," I said.

"You haven't been charged," Frascon said, intentionally omitting *yet*.

"Charge me and let me see my lawyer, or I'm out of here now."

I counted in my head to three, picked up my boutique bag, and without looking back, walked out of Interview Room 2. I didn't stop until a block away from the precinct, where I bent over and vomited over the front of my dress and wedge heels.

ACT IV

THE FIRST TIME in weeks that Rebecca had left the house without me, I entered the saferoom and was overwhelmed by the smells of my life before Rebecca. The blessing, and the curse, of the space was the ventilation system, as it allowed air in for one to breathe, but the intake hung over the dumpster in the alley, with its rotting produce and other decaying matter. The garbage provided the neighbors with the explanation they needed for the misunderstood odors they found so offensive. But that day, the room's aroma smelled nothing like the trash outside. I opened the door to the chute and almost fell on my behind. The smell was coming from inside the chute.

I had disposed of the shell. The cremation had been completed. All that was left was to make the trophy, but seeing my guy in Queens meant time away from my Rebecca. Awards and the work didn't matter more than she. Father had been right again: a relationship with a woman would get in the way of my work. But Father had never prepared me for how little that would matter when I met my perfect partner.

I shined a flashlight down the chute. If a piece, a finger, a toe, of the shell had broken off and gotten stuck, that would be the reason for the intensity of the odor. I couldn't see anything, but the whole length of the chute was never visible.

I sat in the leather armchair, struggling with the question of whether or not to eliminate what I clearly saw was a sign from God—not the formless entity that commits senseless acts of violence, but a God that bestows purpose and meaning upon our lives. My God. My Father.

I don't know how long I sat there, drenched in memories of all the years of work I had done with Father, and later on my own, in this space . . . all the characters I had studied and become.

Then I thought of Rebecca and the night I had almost shared this sacred part of me with her, and though I still believed she would have understood my process, embraced my journey as an artist, I no longer wanted any of my former life to overshadow the present that she and I shared.

These past months I had spent with Rebecca meant more to me than my own life. This woman, with her ordinary face and extraordinary crooked smile, embodied all the answers I had been searching for. If I wanted a future where truth and beauty were promised, I had to seal away the past for good.

I grabbed from under the bathroom sink a two-gallon bottle of bleach and a half-emptied container of disinfectant and brought them to the room. My plan was to pour both chemical solutions down the chute, but then I read the label: *Kills 99.9 percent of bacteria from most surfaces.* The resilience of the .01 percent stopped me in my tracks. Before I could continue, I heard the doorbell.

I quickly exited the saferoom, closed the faux wall, returned the cleaners under the bathroom sink, and discarded my pungent clothes into the hamper. Then I threw on a bathrobe, ran to the front door, and called, "Who is it?"

"Hon, it's me."

"Rebecca." I had never been more thrilled to hear anyone's voice.

"Open the door. I forgot my key," she said.

* * *

After I shaved and showered, I dressed in the one suit I owned, and that night at a lovely bistro specializing in bouillabaisse, I proposed. Rebecca ordered the flourless chocolate cake, a conundrum of a dessert (how could there be cake with no flour?). I ordered a lifetime of happiness. We laughed over my being intentionally corny, and she said *yes, yes, yes*.

The next day we walked to City Hall and applied for a marriage license. Soon after, we became husband and wife.

At that point, I thought if I never embodied another character, it would be okay with me. My work was complete, almost. The only role besides Rebecca's husband I had any interest in playing was the role of a father, the father to our child.

We both agreed to start a family right away.

Growing up without a lot, and having had even less over the years, Rebecca had struggled as an artist and constantly worried about spending money. So, before we sought professional help, we tried doing it ourselves, the whole turkey baster thing. When that didn't work, I insisted we go to the best infertility clinic in the city. We succeeded on the first try. It was a miracle. Rebecca was pregnant.

My sweet daughter, I know hearing the details of how your existence came to be may be somewhat uncomfortable for you. Embarrassing, perhaps. Please understand my intention is only for you to know how very much you were wanted. You didn't happen by circumstance, a broken condom, or too many libations.

No, you were planned.

*　*　*

One morning at the beginning of Rebecca's third trimester, I went out to get us bagels. Not my favorite of foods—too doughy—but your mother loved the "everything" kind: covered in poppy seeds, garlic, onion, sesame seeds, with a shmear of the spread that the ignorant call cheese. Despite my feeling that "everything" equated to nothing distinctive in taste, I ordered one for myself too. I wanted to learn to love everything she loved.

When I returned, Rebecca said, "You got bagels," and kissed my right cheek. She peeked inside the bag.

"Everything!" She placed my hand on her abdomen. "You made the baby so happy."

Something moved. I pulled my hand back.

Rebecca returned my clenched fist to where the movement was. "The baby. She's kicking. That's a good thing."

Normally, pleasing her thrilled me, but before I could bask in her delight, she touched her nose, let out a deep breath, and explained there was a faint odor that was driving her crazy. I told her I hadn't smelled anything. She apologized, then explained how pregnant women often experience a heightened sense of smell. The bile in my stomach began to boil, but there was no reason to panic. All I had to do was wait for Rebecca to nap, and then I would sneak into the room and pour the bleach and the all-but-.01-percent disinfectant down the chute.

"I'll take care of it," I said.

"I have someone here now."

"Where?" I asked.

She pointed in the direction of the saferoom. I strode down the hallway with Rebecca waddling behind. There, tapping around the faux wall, the gateway to my past, was a short muscular man wearing gray overalls, *Donovan Exterminating* embroidered in red on the back, a metal tank resting on the floor at his side.

"What's happening here?" I asked.

"Anthony Donovan." The exterminator turned to me and extended his hand. His grip was firm but dishonest, and I was intrigued.

Rebecca explained they'd met at the dumpster in the back alley this morning. She was throwing out our kitchen garbage and he was emptying mousetraps. Inspired by unpleasant odors, the odd smell in our house entered into the conversation. He told her about our neighbors' mice situation and offered the possibility that one may have crawled into our vent and died.

"I think I figured out where the vent leads to." He knocked on the paneling. "Hollow. Sounds like there's an open space on the other side."

"A room?" Rebecca asked.

I wasn't ready to talk about it, but I didn't want to lie, so I said nothing.

"A panic room," Donovan said.

"Panic?" Rebecca said.

"Safe," I said.

"That's right," Donovan Exterminating said. "Saferoom is another name folks use. I've serviced lots of places that have them."

"I don't understand." Rebecca looked at me.

Donovan answered, "The rooms are set up for people to hide in case of a home invasion or robbery, or in the days of Prohibition, to avoid the police. They usually have monitors so they can watch people on the outside." He looked up at our ceiling and in the far corner pointed to the wall plate that I'd used to cover the exposed wires. "There was probably a camera there at some point."

The man was observant.

"How do you get in?" Rebecca was sliding her hands around the faux wall.

"There's usually a hidden keypad," he said.

I had to get him out of here before he found it, and there was no subtle way to do this.

"Get out, now."

"Excuse me?" he and Rebecca said in unison.

I picked up his metal tank and rushed to the front door, but before I could throw the tank down the stairs, Rebecca grabbed it and handed it to Donovan Exterminating.

I took a fifty from my wallet, but he was down the stairs and out our front door before I could give it to him.

Rebecca pushed past me and back to the faux wall, but before I could stop her, she tapped on the right spot and the hinged cover opened, revealing the keypad.

"Code, please," she said.

*   *   *

I could see Rebecca was upset, but showing her the room like this meant delving into a history I wasn't yet prepared to share. Still, I didn't want to lie to her.

I knew our relationship had started with my pretending to be someone I wasn't. That was acting, not lying. During the past year we'd been married—it was three weeks until our anniversary—I hadn't played any other part. I hadn't been anyone but me.

From the way she twitched her nose while her eyes fixated on my mouth, I knew she wasn't going to let this go until I gave her an explanation.

"This was Father's room." It wasn't a lie.

"Your father had a panic room?"

"A saferoom," I said. "Really, a workroom." I pressed my cheek against the wall, as if I could somehow feel what I had thought was forgotten until now. "We spent a fair amount of time together here. I was the only other person he shared the code with."

"Did you play with model trains?" Rebecca referred to our inside joke, our origin story, in which I was the train conductor and she a stranger who had no idea who I was.

The memory of my time with Sal and all the work I'd done over the years caused a twinge in my chest.

"I love you," I said, to fill the space between us.

"Show me," she said.

I took several steps back. I didn't want to remember anymore. I didn't want to see or feel it, the yearning, the passion, the obsession I'd once had. But I couldn't stop it. I couldn't shut up.

"This is where my father taught me everything he knew. All of his dreams and hopes for me to one day be a great actor."

"A stage father," she said, with clear disdain and pity in her voice.

"He was a director," I corrected her, and no matter how hard I tried to stop, the images, the words kept coming. "He kept me here for hours and hours, away from the outside world, training me to do the work, to be the work. He sacrificed everything for me, and because of that woman, he died before he could see me play the greatest role of a lifetime."

"I've never seen you cry before." Rebecca reached out to wipe my tears away.

I flinched and repeated, "He sacrificed it all."

Never let a woman see your pain; she'll use it against you. It was as if Father stood at my side, speaking truth into my ear. Rebecca saw it. All of it. The weakness. What had I done? How could I have been so stupid? Pathetic. Crying real tears. She would leave me for someone who deserved the part of her husband, father to her child.

I rushed out of the house, hoping Rebecca would call after me to stay, to not leave her, but she didn't.

A block away, I ran into him: Anthony Donovan of Donovan Exterminating.

* * *

Donovan put his metal tank in the back of a van with his logo embossed on the side and a giant rubber rat stationed on top. I came up behind him, and he jumped.

"Did I startle you?" I asked, knowing I had.

"No problem," he said.

"I wanted to give you something for your trouble." I pulled the fifty again from my wallet.

He turned his back, a sign that he didn't want my money. "Just trying to help your wife out. Didn't mean to cause any problems."

"Sensitive matters," I said.

He raised his hand to my face. "No need to explain. I get it."

"What's that?"

"A man needs his private space to do his thing."

I wasn't sure what he thought my thing was, but from the way he raised his eyebrows, I assumed it was sexual in nature. I would have corrected him had my attention not been diverted by a metal box in the back of his van reflecting the setting sun.

"Is that some sort of trap?" I asked.

"Catch and release."

"For rats?"

"Rats? You don't catch a rat." He chuffed, as if that were a universally known fact.

"Isn't it your job to handle all vermin?"

"Buddy, I'm saying you don't catch a rat. You kill a rat." He stood taller, and his whole body bloated with pride. "They're sophisticated and have a complex hierarchy. They also can eat straight through your walls. Any exterminator who tries to sell you on some bullshit about how he's trapping and freeing those poor rodents is scamming you, or stupid."

"Fascinating," I said.

"Their teeth keep growing, so if they don't keep chewing, those fangs'll grow right out of their skulls."

"What's this?" I picked up a block of what looked like pressed cardboard.

"Careful." He took the block back from me. "That's poison."

"How long have you been in the business?"

"Fifteen years." He slammed shut the van's rear doors. "I came to this country soon after secondary school to stay with my uncle, who lived in the Bronx."

I assumed from the company's name, Donovan, that he'd come from Ireland. "I don't detect an accent."

"I taught myself to lose it," he said.

"You're self-taught?" I was intrigued.

"I'm good at accents," he said with a heavy Irish brogue. "I can put them on or take them off." This time he used an Italian accent. Southern Italy, if I wasn't mistaken.

"You're very good," I said.

"People think it's about imitation, but the key is becoming the person who'd speak with that particular pattern of speech. You know?"

"Are you an actor?"

He smiled shyly. I felt like I had caught him with his pants down.

"There was a time I dreamed of being on Broadway," he admitted.

It was like he'd smashed his metal tank against my skull. I was blown away. It was the first time I'd felt something missing inside me since I'd given up my work almost a year ago. A workingman who'd trained himself to act, to imitate accents, to become the people he embodied.

"So you're Irish?"

"This name?" He tapped the side of the van. "Nah. The only man who'd give me a job was Mr. John Donovan, or as he liked to be called, the Fat Man."

"Fat man?"

He lifted his pinkie to my face. "So thin. Like a string bean."

"Ironic," I said.

He gave me a strange look. "You know, that's how nicknames work. A fat man's called skinny, and a skinny man's called—"

"Fatty," I said.

"Exactly," he said.

"What's your nickname?" I asked.

"Just Anthony."

"Just Anthony. Really?"

"Yep. Where I'm from, there were tons of Anthonys, and every one of 'em had a nickname, so by the time I was born, there was no one left called Anthony."

"Which is why you're Just Anthony."

"Yep, but actually I'm as Italian as pasta primavera. Anyway, when Donovan retired, I bought the business from him and kept his name out of respect. Also, it has a nicer ring than Just Anthony."

I disagreed. I liked Just Anthony very much. It was a name with character. "You have many working for you?"

"I'm a one-man show." He smiled, revealing a black space in place of a right incisor. I admired his confidence. "I prefer it." He knocked on the side of his head. "People can be headaches." He glanced up at the clear sky. "Truth is, I love my job. You meet so many interesting characters."

"Characters . . . ," I repeated.

He looked at my wrist, Sal's watch. "I have to get to my next stop."

I nodded, but I didn't want him to go. I wanted to learn more about him. I wanted to be him. I followed him to the driver's side, and as he climbed into his seat, I asked, "Would you be willing to come back and help me with that room?"

"Happy to." He grinned, and I was certain he was imagining the room filled with pornographic materials, sports paraphernalia, booze, and unhealthy snacks. I would have to make sure to set it up that way for him.

"How about next Tuesday," I suggested, "when my wife has her yoga-for-pregnant-women class?"

"Good thinking. If she sees your room, she's gonna want to turn it into a nursery."

A nursery . . . right. I would soon be a father. The role of a lifetime. Before I could tell him I'd changed my mind, he said, "That's why I never got married. I like having my whole place be my man cave."

"No children?" I asked.

"Not that I know of." He winked and shut the passenger door. "Maybe someday, but for now I like living life on my terms."

*   *   *

On the walk back to the apartment, I thought about how every Tuesday for the past seven and a half months, while Rebecca took her yoga class, I'd waited in the sitting area with the burning incense. Patchouli, that most offensive of odors. I knew lying to Rebecca wasn't an option. Lies only led to more lies, until there would be no trust left between us. I had no choice but to dust off my tool kit and give a Tony-winning performance. After all, I was still an actor.

One last character study before the baby arrived couldn't hurt. Rebecca had her yoga class. I needed this . . . for me.

*   *   *

On the following Tuesday, I kept to our routine. I grabbed Rebecca's yoga mat from the hallway closet, filled the reusable lunch bag with her water bottle and the peanut chocolate protein bars she craved, and like we had done every Tuesday afternoon for the past three months, we walked the five blocks to the yoga studio. Per usual, at the entrance we took off our shoes and placed them in one of the cubbyholes, and Rebecca kissed me on the cheek and went inside for her class.

"See you when you get out."

The instant the instructor closed the door, I slipped on my loafers and ran back to the brownstone. I had an hour and thirty minutes before the end of class, and I didn't want to waste a moment.

As arranged, Just Anthony was waiting for me out front. It had been a while since anyone was responsive to my schedule, my needs. I loved taking care of Rebecca, anticipating her wants, desires. It brought me great pleasure to devote my time, life, and service to her and our baby. But I had to admit I was looking forward to my session with Just Anthony.

"Out for a run?" he asked.

I assumed he was referring to the sweat dripping down my forehead.

With his metal tank in one hand and a backpack slung over his shoulder, the exterminator followed me upstairs to the saferoom. I pressed the side panel and it popped open, exposing the keypad. Anthony stood close enough for me to feel his warm breath on the back of my neck. I punched in 234581, and the faux panel clicked open.

Inside, the distinct odor of death permeated the air. Just Anthony didn't so much as twitch his nose.

"This place is bigger than my apartment," he said. "A train buff?" He lifted his chin to the wall maps of all the Metro-North and NYC subway lines I'd yet to take down.

I nodded.

"What's back here?" He opened the door to the room with the stage makeup mirror and the hot tub. "Love to take a soak in that."

I could see his nose had been broken, several times. "You a fighter?" I asked.

He rubbed the bridge of his nose. "Good at pissing people off when I was younger. Better fighter and runner back then. Out of shape now." He patted his belly. "Gives me character." He turned to show me the other side of his profile.

"It does," I said. "Very much."

"Too bad I can't smell for shit," he said.

"You can't smell that?" I exaggerated an inhale through my nose.

"Your wife smelled something. I couldn't tell. I don't argue with women in her condition." He sniffed and shook his head. "A blessing and a curse. Probably something did get trapped and died in here." He dropped his pack onto the bare mattress, unzipped it, and took out three mousetraps. "I can put these down, but I don't see any signs of mice." He walked around the bed, looking down at the floor: no droppings, nothing chewed. "Definitely no rats." He stepped over to the chute, pulled the handle, and stuck his head inside and then closed it quickly.

"Even with my bad honker, I can smell that. Something died in there. Could be a mouse or a rat, probably a squirrel." He closed the chute. "Where does it lead to?"

"The basement."

"Lead the way." He bowed and swung his arm toward the faux wall.

I glanced down at my wrist. I had less than an hour before I would have to get back to the yoga studio and meet Rebecca, but watching him work was fascinating and I wanted to learn more.

"It'll only take a minute," he assured me. "Sniffing out vermin, pun intended, is my thing."

I flipped the switch at the top of the basement stairs and acted surprised when the light didn't go on. "Fuse blown," I said.

There was the mound of clay Rebecca would use to sculpt her first piece, which she wanted to be of me holding our baby. We'd been looking for weeks for the right consistency, but Rebecca had been displeased with every clay we found until I'd had the idea to mix the contents of my trophies, ash and bone, into generic clay from the art supply store. Testing it, Rebecca had deemed it perfect.

I knew the mound here in the basement was only the raw material she would be using, but she was sensitive about her art. I was the only person she'd ever let see one of her works in progress. Even her former patron, Mother, had never seen a piece until it was done. Out of respect for my wife and her process, I thought it would be wrong for Just Anthony to see it.

I heard him rustling around in his pack, and the next moment I was blinded by a light shining in my face. I lifted my hand to protect my eyes. He put the flashlight under his chin, and his face glowed like a jack-o'-lantern. He smiled at his own humor and trained his light on the kiln.

"That's a monster. I've serviced hundreds of apartment buildings with incinerators smaller than that."

"It came with the house," I said.

"Was this a funeral parlor?"

His intuitive nature impressed me. I never worried about a character understanding the script, knowing the end of their story before I revealed it. In fact, I enjoyed observing them in a state of desperation while they tried to figure out what play was going on and where their character arc led.

"Something this size could cremate a body," he went on, aiming the flashlight at the corners of the room.

"What are you looking for?" I asked.

"A dead body." He shone the flashlight under his chin again, a second-rate actor in a B horror film.

"That's what the incinerator is for," I said, then forced an expected smile.

"Look here, a conveyor belt leads right to the opening of a garbage chute." He stood in front of me with his flashlight probing the area. "I don't see any signs of vermin, but something probably crawled inside, got trapped, and died."

"Makes sense," I said.

He walked over to where the chute connected to the conveyor belt. "Can you turn this on?"

"There's a switch, but I can't find it in the dark." I didn't need light to find it but thought better of turning it on.

He kicked the side of the chute with his steel-toed boots. "Trying to unstick whatever might be in there." He gave it another kick, and something banged against the inside.

"What's that?" I played dumb.

"Dead rodents, I bet." This time he punched the side, and an object fell out onto the floor. Before I could see what body part it was, Anthony dropped his flashlight, and everything went dark.

*   *   *

In the bright August sun, Anthony was outside, running east. I shouted after him, "Your backpack! You forgot your pack!"

He ran faster. It was too hot for a big guy like him to run. After all the hikes Rebecca and I had taken these past months, I could catch up with him without breaking a sweat. He was pulling at the driver's door handle of his van and then banging against it.

His keys were probably in his pack.

"Your forgot this," I said lifting his pack in the air from the sidewalk.

"Stay the fuck away from me."

"I'm returning your pack to you."

"You're one crazy fuck."

A police car drove near us, and Just Anthony waved his arms and shouted, "Help. He's trying to kill me."

The police doubled-parked in front of the van, and two uniformed officers got out, their hands over their holsters.

The one who asked the first question had a clean crease in his blue synthetic pants. Seeing the uniform, I was struck momentarily by the feeling of loss. *Sal.* I missed playing that part, the part that had helped me win over Rebecca.

"What's the problem?" the creased officer said.

"He has a human head in his basement." Just Anthony sounded like he was about to cry.

"Oh, Anthony," I laughed. I was struck by how authentic I sounded. "Is that why you ran away?"

"Fuck yes!"

"Officers, I'm an actor . . ."

"I knew you looked familiar," the sloppy officer said, more to his partner than me.

Of course, he was confusing me with someone else or doing what people do—convincing themselves of whatever idea you put in their heads. He hears I'm an actor, so of course he connects me to something he's seen. It was a New York thing: wanting to believe you were standing in the presence of someone famous, someone you could tell the wife and kids about.

"He has a head in his basement!" Anthony shouted again.

"Sir, please calm down."

"Are you listening to me?"

"I can explain, but it would be better if I showed you," I said. "First, may I see your ID? You never know these days. Too many impostors."

The officers pulled out their badges. Shiny shields. "Officer Brandon," I said, noting the sloppy one. "Officer Franklin." The creased one.

The officers followed me back to the brownstone with Just Anthony trailing cautiously behind.

At the entrance of the basement, I warned of the horrendous odor. "That's why I had the exterminator here. We thought a rodent died."

"A head . . . ," Anthony said, standing behind us.

I flipped the switch. "Needs a new bulb."

The officers pulled flashlights from their holsters. I pointed them to the corner of the room farthest away from the crematorium and Rebecca's art.

There, in all its glory, sat my collection. Sixteen heads to date.

The officers jumped back. Just Anthony let out a sound that sounded more mouse than human.

"See, see!" Just Anthony pointed. "Heads. I only saw one, and got the hell out. The sick fuck has more—"

"Props," I said.

Anthony stepped from out behind the officers and sighed. His breath moistened my cheek. "They're fake?"

"Most of them," I laughed. Of course they weren't real. I wasn't a psychopath who collected human heads.

"Excuse me?" Officer Franklin said.

"He's kidding." Officer Brandon, in spite of his slightly disheveled appearance, was growing on me.

"Go ahead. Squeeze the nose," I said.

Just Anthony did. "Like flesh."

"It's made of fire-resistant foam. Prop masters work with some amazing artists. Let me show you something else."

Officer Franklin handed me his flashlight, and I led them to an area I hadn't visited in years. It was where I kept props from various horror movies.

"This is from *Dead Eat Dead*."

"I loved that one," Officer Brandon said.

"Classic slasher flick," Anthony added. "Is this Dracula?"

"The original."

"Bela Lugosi," said Anthony.

"That was his stage name. His real name was Béla Ferenc Dezső Blaskó," Officer Brandon told us.

"Impressive. Not many people know that."

"My grandmother was from Hungary. A huge fan," Officer Brandon said.

"Was this the head you saw?" I handed him a fake decaying head that was more skeleton than flesh. One that would look closer to Doorboy's, if that was what had fallen from the chute.

"Maybe . . . one glimpse and I was out of here."

"I get them mostly from private dealers, sometimes a Sotheby auction."

"We should let you go about your day," Officer Brandon said.

Metal clanged. Just Anthony jumped. Officer Franklin shined his flashlight. The light moved from the chute to the furnace and down to the conveyor belt. "Look at what we have here," Officer Franklin said.

Officer Brandon's hand moved to his gun. "What is it, Bob?"

* * *

It was a dead squirrel. Two dead squirrels. It turned out a couple of rodents were the cause of the smell.

The officers wished me a good afternoon and all the best with the baby. After they left, Anthony was kind enough to bag the squirrels and take them out.

I walked him out. This time I made sure he didn't forget his pack, and this time I insisted he take the fifty I took out of my wallet.

"You kidding me? I tried to get you arrested."

"Misunderstandings happen," I said. "Those heads look real."

"You're a cool guy," he said, and he took the cash and went on his way.

* * *

I was late to meet Rebecca. This time I ran, but I made it only one block when I saw her walking my way.

"Where were you?" she asked.

"I have some good news," I said.

"What?"

"The exterminator was here, and the smell is gone."

"Dead mice?"

"Squirrels," I said.

"Aw, they're cute," she said.

"And dangerous if they start chewing the electric wires. But that's not the best part of it."

Back at the brownstone, I showed Rebecca the saferoom. "This is huge," she said.

"Our nursery," I announced.

"But this was your father's room. And your special place." I pressed my lips to hers, and when we broke our kiss, I said, "You and our daughter are the only family that matters."

"It could be a boy," she pointed out.

"It could be." I knew it was a girl. Rebecca wanted the sex to be a surprise. I never liked surprises, but to that one I'd agreed. Still, I was certain, even then, that you were a girl.

"What color shall we paint it?" I asked.

"Not blue or pink," she said. "I want you to be able to appreciate it."

I smiled, having forgotten, as I often did, that I was color-blind. "The mint green you showed me in the baby magazine?"

She jumped up and down like a little kid.

"Easy." I put my hand on her belly.

"She likes it." She kissed me on the lips. "You're too good to me." A second later, she added, "The exterminator."

"What about him?"

"His tank. He forgot it."

There, on the floor underneath the chute, lay a metal tank.

"So he did," I said. "So he did."

*   *   *

In the coming days, my plan to get Anthony Donovan back to the brownstone to retrieve his tank when Rebecca wasn't home became solid as a rock. As did my larger plan: I needed one final role, and then I'd be ready to fully embrace my ultimate role of devoted husband and father.

*   *   *

The doorbell rang.

"You're expecting someone?" Rebecca asked.

"It's probably the bassinet we ordered," I said.

I walked down the stairs to the front door, and there he was, Just Anthony Donovan, the exterminator.

"What a nice surprise," I greeted him.

It was definitely a surprise, but it wasn't nice. "You called me about my tank."

"Of course," I said. "Come on up."

Rebecca was folding the baby clothes we'd bought and I had insisted on washing before they came in contact with our baby's developing immune system.

"Mr. Donovan." She looked up from a yellow onesie with a teddy bear design.

"In all the chaos yesterday, I forgot my tank," he said.

"Chaos?" Rebecca twitched her nose at me.

"Again, I'm sorry about the misunderstanding."

"What did I miss?" she asked.

"Found those squirrels, right, Mr. Donovan?" I interjected.

"Yup, crazy squirrels," he said. He didn't miss a beat. He was a smart man. No reason to get the wife involved in our misadventure.

The two of us went into the saferoom.

"She's going to be one happy mommy when she sees you turned your man cave into a nursery," he told me.

"Yes, it will be a great surprise."

"Your wife is a lucky woman."

"I'm a blessed man," I said.

Anthony picked up his tank, and several scenarios flashed through my mind of how I could get him to stay so we could work together, but none of them involved successfully getting Rebecca out of the house. My work couldn't start with her at home.

So I did what I had never done before: I decided to let this one pass.

"I'll show you out," I said.

He took a step toward the door, stopped, and looked up at the ceiling. "You know, I've done a fair share of painting and drywall. If you need a hand, I'm cheap."

"I'll consider it," I said.

*   *   *

At 9:30 every morning, Rebecca—who was convinced the paint and chemicals used to ready the nursery wouldn't be good for the baby—left the apartment.

At 9:40, Anthony would arrive. He scraped and painted and plastered and stenciled ducks on the walls, all exactly equally distant apart. At 12:20, he left, always ten minutes before Rebecca returned for our lunch: steak, rare (her iron was low). Rebecca knew Anthony was helping me with the nursery, the finished state of which was meant to be a surprise. She wasn't to peek until it was done.

She never saw him come or go. My plan was in motion.

A week after we started, Anthony came to me. I was in the kitchen, cleaning the breakfast dishes.

"The trim is done. Project Nursery complete."

"This calls for a celebration."

I went to the kitchen and retrieved two glasses from the cabinet above the sink, grabbed a bottle of champagne, Anthony's favorite (and only) alcoholic beverage, from the refrigerator, and returned to the nursery.

He had done a beautiful job. Even with my color blindness, I could see how the trim enhanced the color of the walls and the stenciled ducks. Rebecca was going to love it.

I popped the cork and poured a glass for each us.

"A toast," I said. "To a man with a broken nose but a great eye."

Anthony lifted his glass and said, "To a smart man with too many heads but one big heart."

We clinked glasses.

I hit him straight between the eyes with the champagne bottle.

He went down for the count.

The pulley-and-lever system had been disassembled after Anthony judged it equipment for some "kinky bondage play" and inappropriate in a nursery. For that reason, it took more maneuvering and physics than usual to get him strapped down to the cushioned rocking chair at the side of the crib.

I made sure to gag him. I knew the room was soundproof, but who'd have thought Rebecca could have smelled anything through the walls? I hadn't ever heard of pregnant women possessing a heightened sense of hearing, but just in case . . .

I left the room and punched in the code. The panel shut, and two arms wrapped around my waist. Rebecca.

I kept my tone steady.

"When do I get the code?"

"Not until the room is done. Come on, let's get you some lunch and a nap."

"You're too good to me."

* * *

On the days Rebecca wanted to skip yoga class and sleep in, I encouraged her not to.

"You always feel so much better afterward. Why only once a week?"

So, every day after Rebecca left, I worked with Just Anthony. He was more cooperative than most. At first, he did the usual begging and pleading for his life and the *Why? Why? Why?* I had to keep him drugged enough so he was able to eat and get to the bathroom but his head remained the right amount of fuzzy so he'd think he was dreaming.

A van with a giant rat on top was, as you know, asking for trouble. There were no long-term spaces available in any of the garages nearby, but eventually I found a garage in the Bronx, blocks from the building where you and I would eventually live.

After a week, he understood that he had become part of my process. After our work was done, I told him, he would be free. That made him more cooperative. He even had the brilliant idea to put in a built-in bookshelf where I had removed Father's bar.

Outside the room, Rebecca nested, and she and I planned for our future.

Inside the room, Anthony and I built the perfect baby crib, identical to the one Rebecca had dog-eared in the new-parent magazine she subscribed to. Except ours was made with better-quality wood.

Most importantly, Anthony taught me the ins and outs of the exterminating business. He showed me how to mix chemicals and how to spray directly into the cracks, and how to distinguish between mouse and rat droppings. He told me that when it came to smart cockroaches—the German cockroach, to be specific—all apartments in a building had to be serviced the same day or they would find their way to the apartments not yet sprayed, their safe havens. He showed me the secrets of salesmanship: how to get new stops and win over potential customers.

"In the multi-occupant buildings, you gotta see the manager. They have the decision-making authority and are usually pretty easy to persuade. Just the hint that their current guy may not be giving them the best service, and you're in."

I gave him anything he wanted to eat or drink. And I rented all the movies he wanted to see.

In time, he relaxed and trusted me.

All was well; the work almost done. I had Anthony's body movements down pat, so much so that Rebecca commented on how my posture had changed and I looked taller. I told her that my love for her and our baby inspired me to carry my head high.

*   *   *

It was time for the dress rehearsal. Would the world believe I was an exterminator? Anthony's overalls were several sizes too large, so I put my costume-design training to work and made the necessary alterations.

When Rebecca was out for her yoga class, I mixed the chemicals as Anthony had shown me and went out to find business, places he had never serviced. (It would have been too risky to visit one of Anthony's existing stops.) Besides, Anthony had told me that the real money was made in the luxury buildings. One he had on the West Side paid well and on time. He never had to deal with the tenants either. The managers let him in or gave him a passkey, he did the work, and he was out of there.

I set out to get my first account. I was feeling confident when I walked into the building where Rebecca had lived with her patron. The doorman was Jack, but when I approached the building, he took one look at my tank and my overalls and blocked the entrance. He didn't recognize me. This was when I first realized exterminators are invisible, only a pair of overalls and a backpack.

"Service entrance. Never come through the front."

"New guy," I explained.

He walked me around the back and showed me the door to use in the future. Then he walked me to the manager's office and went back to his post.

Mr. Credo was on the phone. He waved me in but didn't offer me a seat. I stood and waited.

"Yes, Mrs. Renault, we'll take care of it right away." He slammed the phone down.

"Always something," he said. "What can I do for you?"

"I'm here to offer my services."

"What services would that be?" I assumed he was messing with me, or else he was dense. I was carrying a tank and wearing coveralls with *Donovan Exterminating* on the back.

"I think I can do better than the company you have now," I said, recalling how Rebecca had complained about the exterminator never showing up on time.

He stood. "Please, have a seat."

After we talked for five minutes, I had the account. At the time, I'd thought it was my brilliant sales pitch, but I would find out later that his current exterminator had recently cussed out one of the residents, leaving Credo stuck without a pest killer. I also agreed to sign a long-term contract, which I would later discover was below the average exterminator's rate.

I was so pleased with my performance that I walked all the way from the Upper West Side to the brownstone. On the way I bought a stuffed, plush, yellow duck that matched the stenciled ducks on the mint-green wallpaper in the nursery. I stopped by a local Italian place to get Anthony's favorite dish for our final meal together.

At the brownstone, I went to the basement, changed out of my overalls, hid them and the tank on the other side of the furnace, and went upstairs.

Rebecca wasn't home. Her yoga class had ended over an hour ago, but since I'd stopped waiting for her there, she'd been spending time talking to the woman at the front desk who had three kids, all natural-birthed. I had wanted to take those birthing classes, but Rebecca had insisted we didn't need to. "Whatever we need to know, we know, and whatever we don't, we will find out. You know how I love surprises."

I put the stuffed duck on the coffee table and the linguini with white clam sauce on a ceramic plate and poured a glass of Coke. That had been a hard one to explain to Rebecca. She knew I hated to put anything artificial into my body, but it was the only thing Anthony ever wanted to drink, so I told her it was a daddy craving, connected to a happy childhood memory. She understood and said it was the same reason she was craving Scooter Pies.

I was eager to tell Anthony the great news that I'd gotten my first job. Just Anthony and I were going to celebrate before parting ways.

I punched in the code and entered the room. There, hanging from the ceiling fan we'd installed only the day before, was Just Anthony himself. He'd hanged himself with an extension cord.

To say I was shocked and grief-stricken would have been a lie, my dear daughter. Unlike with Rocco's premature exit, I wasn't devastated. I had more pressing concerns now, like how soon I would become a father and how unprepared I was for that role.

Exhausted from the long walk from the West Side, I let Anthony down from the ceiling fan, sat in the leather chair, and ate the whole plate of pasta, then drank two full glasses of the decaffeinated Coke. It was surprisingly refreshing, but now I was feeling sleepy. I couldn't keep my eyes open. My body wasn't used to all the carbs and sugar. I kicked off my shoes, leaned back, and drifted off.

LINDA

15

B Y THE TIME I arrived at my apartment building, the foul odor of vomit from my shoes was unbearable. I skipped the elevator and hobbled up the three flights of stairs.

Before I could stick my key in the lock, Anne was hovering behind me. *Fuck.*

"Linda, I'm relieved to see you."

I didn't turn to face her, but I could hear her sniffing. "Are you sick?" she asked.

"Can't talk now." I turned the key and opened the door. She followed, one baby step behind. I lacked the energy to ask her to leave, and a part of me didn't want to be alone.

I picked up the *Greatest Dad* mug from the table. It still had coffee in it.

"The police were here," she said. "They made quite the racket. Woke the missus from her nap. And you know that woman sleeps like the dead."

"I'm sorry about that."

Inside, all the lights were on. The police must have forgotten to shut them off.

"They were looking for your father." I could feel her breath on the back of my neck. I wondered what Jess was doing now. Working with her partner to put a case together based on circumstantial evidence that would put my father away for life, and frame me as his accomplice?

I dropped the boutique bag on the kitchen table and kicked off my shoes. "It's been a long day." I kept my back to her. "Don't want to be rude."

Anne walked past me toward the bedrooms. "They think a warrant gives them the right to destroy your home."

"Where are you going?" I followed her down the hallway to Dad's room.

"It looks like they didn't touch anything." She ran her hand along Dad's comforter.

"They made the bed," I said. "Dad never makes his bed. Bedbugs thrive in the moisture created by tucked-in sheets."

"They were cleaning up their mess," she said.

"My mother's sculpture." It had been moved from the center of the room to the far corner.

"What were they looking for?"

"Evidence," I let slip out.

"For what?"

I didn't answer. I couldn't bring myself to say *murder*. I went over to Dad's nightstand. The drawer was ajar. I sat on the edge of the hospital-cornered bedbug-breeding ground, slid the drawer all the way out, and placed it beside me.

"Anything missing?"

I couldn't be sure if Dad's full collection of funeral cards was still there, but right on top was my mother's card. I held it in my hand, rubbing my thumb down the scratchy edges of the Scotch tape holding its two torn parts together. Dad had tried to fix it. Now I felt even worse than I had before. No matter how frustrated I'd been, there was no excuse for ripping my mother's funeral card.

Where are you, Dad?

All of a sudden, Anne screamed and took cover behind Mom's sculpture. I looked up.

It was Sam, tail wagging. He was happy to see me. I was thrilled to see him. I knew his owner would not be far behind. "Sam, what are you doing here?" I scratched under his chin, grateful to have something to keep my hands busy and away from my earlobes.

"He's friendly," Jessica told Anne as she joined us in the bedroom.

I assumed she was here about the case. Still, her pink T-shirt with *Serenity Now* written across the chest and her black sweatpants were far from official police attire.

"It's okay," I reassured Anne. "Sam won't hurt you. He can be trusted."

"I was only trying to help," Jess said.

"You were doing your job," I said.

"You came to the station. I tried to warn you."

Anne came out from behind the statue, and with her shoulders pulled back and looking taller than Jess, though she was several inches shorter than I, she stepped between Jessica and me. "Dogs aren't allowed in this building." Her fierce tone made her sound like a mamma bear protecting her young.

"Detective Jones." Jess extended her hand.

Anne crossed her arms. "Your friends forget something?"

"I'm here to talk to Linda."

I shifted until Anne's body blocked me from Jess's view. "Linda doesn't want to talk to you."

I neither confirmed nor denied it. I didn't know what I wanted. To go back in time before yesterday ever happened? I couldn't deny my feelings for Jess, but how could I ever have let myself fall for a cop who'd put her badge before me? I had no doubt she was here because she wanted me to lead her to Dad. And the truth was, I needed someone to help me find him, help me save the only family I had. We could use each other.

I stuck my head out from behind Anne. "I'll talk to you, Detective."

"You don't have to say anything to her." Anne extended her arm out in front of me, the way Dad would when he had to hit the brakes because some idiot jumped a red light.

Sam barked. Anne fell back onto the bed, and the middle of her spine hit the edge of the drawer stuffed with funeral cards. She winced.

I extended my hand to help her. She didn't take it.

Rubbing the center of her back, she stood even taller than she had before.

Jess ordered Sam to the corner. With his tail lowered and stiff, he pouted over to Mom's sculpture and sat.

Anne shifted her glare from Sam to Jess.

"I'll be okay," I told her.

"You need me, I'm just on the other side." She knocked on the wall that connected to the bathroom for dramatic effect. "Shout and I'll be here with animal control."

On her way out, Anne bumped Jess hard. Jess took it without saying a word. Her shoulders hunching up to her earlobes told me she was screaming inside.

"You two have history?" Jess asked, after Anne had left.

"She's my neighbor's caretaker."

"Seems like she's taking care of you too."

I wasn't sure if I was happy or aggravated over Jess's line of questioning. Did I like that she was jealous? Yes. Did she have the right? No.

"I already told you and your partner everything I know," I said.

"I'm not here as a cop." Sam let out a low whine. "Come here, boy." Jess waved Sam over to her. She knelt at his side and rubbed him under his chin and then behind the ears, which he seemed to enjoy more.

"Then why are you here?" I asked.

She stood. "The initial autopsy report shows Mrs. Lyons died of congestive heart failure. A condition she had for a while but wasn't taking her prescribed meds for, though she had no problem taking a whole lot of other drugs. Her liver was shot too."

I felt the weight of the world lift from my shoulders. "What a relief. Thank you."

"Don't thank me yet. Your father did run away, and there is the question of how Mrs. Lyons's body—"

"What I am going to do?" It took everything I had left in me to hold back the tears.

"The running-away part—well, I'm sure Rita would be willing to overlook that."

"She would do anything for you," I said.

"This would be for you," said Jess. "You have more in common than you think."

"We both love you." It slipped out. "I shouldn't have said that."

Jess leaned in and kissed me. "I love you too."

"I am so glad Dad called you," I said.

"There is still the matter of Mrs. Lyons's body."

"I can't believe Dad had anything to do with what happened."

"Even if he had, a good attorney could try and make the case of temporary insanity. Your father was an abused child . . . He has no priors under either name. He has to turn himself in, Linda."

"He's not answering his cell. I don't know where to find him."

"This is no longer a homicide case."

I turned away. I didn't want her to see me cry again. "I understand."

She stepped in front of me and put both hands on my shoulders. "I'm in this with you. I'm going to help you find your father."

"I never meant to hurt you."

I took a step closer to her.

Sam growled at me.

"No, Sam. Bad." Jess pointed to the corner where the sculpture stood. Sam sulked in the direction he was told. He was a good dog.

"He's defending you," I said.

"That's what you do for people you love."

I was feeling so much rage toward my father for risking everything he, we, had worked for, risking the business. I raised my fist. Sam lurched forward.

Jess gave him the sign to stay, signaling that she'd let me punch her.

Instead, I dropped my arm to my side and plopped face-down on Dad's bed. My body wanted, needed, to cry, but I couldn't let go. The pain was the only thing giving me the will to fight for my father.

"We'll find him, Linda." I felt the vibration from Jess dropping onto the bed beside me.

"I don't know if I want to," I mumbled.

"Can't hear you with your face in the pillow."

I rolled onto my back. "I don't know if I want to," I repeated. I could hear the childlike desperation in my voice.

"You're hurt. Angry. He's your father, and he did a pretty good job raising you on his own. Even if he was the biggest screw-up in the world, you love him."

I nodded. She was right. "I need you as much as you need me if we're going to find my father."

Jess's shoulders relaxed. "Thank you."

"Don't thank me. Help me."

Jess picked up a handful of death cards from the drawer resting between us.

"Funeral, prayer, holy memorial cards. I call them death cards—though not so much in front of Dad."

"Your father collects them like baseball or Pokémon cards?"

"Reminders to pray for those who have passed." Hearing myself say it aloud, I could see how someone who didn't know my father might find it peculiar, whacked, his saving every card from every funeral and storing them in the drawer of his bedside table.

"There must be hundreds." Jess was rummaging through the drawer.

"We go to a lot of funerals. We're Catholic," I said, knowing attending funerals of strangers was more a Dad thing than a Catholic thing.

"A lot of dead Catholics."

"They're not all Catholics." I picked up one and showed her an example. "This one was a memorial service for a woman—well, don't know what her faith was or if she had one, but it's her picture, a younger her, and a few words about her life."

"Where's the card from today?"

"I didn't take one." I had almost forgotten about Mr. Epstein's funeral. Apparently, the cards really did help you remember.

I picked up my mother's card from where it had fallen onto the bedspread.

"A lot of those are from before I was born."

"Matches would be easier." Jess nodded at my hands. I was rubbing Mom's card between my palms like I was trying to start a fire.

I stopped and revealed the card. "This is my mother's."

"I'm sorry," she said.

I dropped Mom's warm card onto the pile of the others. "You can't miss what you never knew."

"Yes, you can." Jess lifted the drawer stuffed with memories of life and death and placed it on the floor by the bed. She scooted in my direction until our thighs touched, and she kissed me. I didn't kiss her back. I wanted to. But I was tired. So very tired. I let myself fall back onto Dad's pillow and gave myself over to Jess and the love I didn't want to lose, not again.

CHAPTER

16

I DIDN'T REMEMBER FALLING asleep, but when I awoke, Sam was in bed next to me and Jess was on the floor, her black sweatpanted legs crossed in an asana pose (to balance my martial arts training, Dad had made me do yoga) with funeral cards fanned around her.

"Are you meditating on death or the meaning of life?"

"I sorted the cards by type, like you said—religious, non-religious, saint, photo—and then there are these." She bent to the right and tapped her elbow against one of the fanned groupings. Her flexibility was impressive.

"They look like standard Catholic prayer cards."

"There are sixty cards with St. Genesius of Rome."

I had never paid close attention to the saints on the cards. Except for St. Raphael, the patron saint of soul mates and happy times on my mother's card, they all felt so generic to me. "A popular saint?"

"Not necessarily. When I Googled him, I learned he's known for having been a performer that mocked Christianity until he found his calling and converted." She showed me her phone.

"Says he was the patron saint of lawyers, clowns, musicians, and actors, and also victims of torture?"

Jess shrugged. "Well, I was a theater kid in high school, and performing comes with plenty of rejection and self-ridicule. Pretty torturous."

"It also lists stenographers."

"I don't get that one. Read it."

I picked a card up and read the prayer silently to myself.

"Now look at the original." She put her phone in front of me.

"The screen saver's on." I held the phone to her face to unlock it.

"Read it."

I read. "They're the same."

"No. This line"—she clicked her short, clear-polished nail against the face of her phone—"isn't the same as the one on these cards."

She read aloud from one of the cards in Dad's collection: *"Intercede for your fellow characters before God that the actors who become them may faithfully and honestly perform their roles and so help others to understand their role in life, thus enabling them to attain their end in heaven. Amen."*

She called up the Googled version on her phone. "The original's a little different: *Intercede for your fellow actors before God . . .* See, *characters* aren't mentioned. I Googled the prayer with *characters* replacing *actors*, and nothing comes up. Yet in all sixty cards he collected, the original prayer's been changed."

"Maybe a printer error. Same batch of cards?"

"For over fifty years?"

I picked up one of the cards resting near her foot. "Nineteen forty-two. That's why no lamination." I looked up at Jess. "My father wasn't born until 1964. He must have kept cards his parents had."

"This last card for a Salvatore . . ."

I grabbed it from her. "The year of death is 1993. The year before I was born." I only pointed this out because Jess sounded so desperate for me to say something, make some connection.

"Why do they all have that one specific change in the prayer?"

I quickly scanned all the cards, the sixty, and the hundreds of others, and I spotted my mother's right away, the only one with tape down its middle.

"They all have the same funeral home listed," she noted.

I was too distracted to read. I believed her, but I didn't see how any of this would help us find my father.

"Bad," Jess shouted, and jumped over to Sam, who had his leg lifted in the air and was peeing on Mother's yellow blob sculpture. "Bad, bad, boy." She stabbed her index finger at him. "He never does this. I'll clean it up."

"Don't worry about it," I said. "It could only be an improvement." I went to the kitchen with the intention of getting paper towels, but instead I pulled two Guinnesses from the fridge and filled a bowl with water. When I returned, I handed Jess a beer and put the water in front of Sam. "He's going to need to replenish." I laughed.

I tried to twist open the beer until I remembered it wasn't a twist off. "I'll get a bottle opener."

"No need." Jess pulled from the side pocket of her sweats a knock-off Swiss Army knife and uncapped both our beers. We clinked, and I raised my bottle to my mother's sculpture. "To Sam, knowing ugly art when he pees on it." I chugged most of the beer. When I went to throw the bottle in the trash, my stomach hurt, and it wasn't the beer. I deeply regretted having torn my mother's card in half. I hadn't meant to hurt Dad, but I couldn't stand another anniversary of focusing on my dead mother while he refused to share much about her life—and never shared much about his life either. He'd lied to me about his own mother being dead, and he'd never told me he changed his name, my name. I was sure he was trying to protect me from the truth about what had to have been an abusive childhood. But until now my father had been the man who never lied. We were supposed to be open and honest with each other because family needed to trust family. He said that a lot. All the time, in fact.

Regret was again becoming rage.

"You okay?" Jess asked. "I don't think it's ruined."

"You kidding me? It's better." I threw the bottle at the sculpture. A piece of clay broke off, but the bottle remained intact. Sam whined and hid behind Jess.

"What's going on?" Jess came over to me and tried to hold me, but I moved away from her and stepped over to the sculpture.

"I never did understand how or why my dad displayed this monstrosity when my mother had so much incredible work."

"Art is subjective," Jess said.

"Homicide detective is an art critic too?"

"I majored in art history as an undergrad." She sounded more embarrassed than defensive.

"Of course you did." I sounded like an asshole. "I'm sorry," I said. "I know beauty is in the eye of the beholder."

"Or in the eye of the art dealer gouging buyers." Jess smiled.

I forced one in response. I knew she was trying to be understanding.

"I want to show you something." I went to Dad's closet and pulled from the back of the top shelf a large wooden lacquer box with a four-digit code lock. I'd figured out the code around the same time I broke the PIN for the parental control on our cable. It had taken me two tries. The second try was 0726. My birthday.

I opened the box and took out the portfolio with pages and pages of sketches and drawings. Mostly charcoals. Some watercolor. All of my father, except for one of a young boy smiling up at a man who looked like an older version of Dad. I assumed it was who my mother had imagined I would be. Dad said my mom was certain she was having a boy, though Dad knew from the moment of conception that I'd be a girl. That was one of the few times Dad had shared a memory about my mother unrelated to her death that wasn't your generic *Your mother was a saint* crap. Those few memories meant everything to me.

"She was good," Jess said. "Really good."

"Amazing, right? So why is the only art of hers Dad displayed that ugly yellow blob sculpture? It would be an embarrassment to any preschool child."

"Different medium," Jess said. "Your mother could have been new to working with clay."

"Look at these drawings." I rapped the portfolio with my knuckles. "This charcoal of my dad sitting on a brown leather couch, reading *What to Expect When You're Expecting*. The sentimentality is a bit much, but the details? Not one missing."

"She even has the bar code on the back of the book."

"I bet you it's exact."

"Her work is precise, like a photograph. I can see why you'd find her abstract sculpture so strange."

"It's as if someone took a big lump of clay and painted it yellow and said that's art." The anger in my voice rang clear and on-key. I couldn't remember a time when I hadn't resented my mother. Yes, she hadn't been well, and she must have suffered so much pain in order to take her own life. But she'd left me, and I'd always hated her for it. A cliché, I knew, but it was my reality.

Right then, though, all I felt for her was a grave sadness. She'd lost out on getting to know her child. My rage was more about my father. He didn't have the excuse of suffering from mental illness. And yet he'd abandoned me.

"Maybe it was a work she was only starting." Jess moved closer to the yellow blob, careful to not step in a pool of urine, and knocked on it. "Hmm. It's not solid clay," she said. "It's hollow."

"Maybe there's another life-altering document hidden inside. Birth certificates of Dad's other children from his second family." I meant this sarcastically, but when Jess sighed, the resentment vaporized, and I suddenly saw this as a real possibility.

I raced to the kitchen and from the junk drawer pulled out a hammer.

Jess blocked me with her body. "You sure you want to do that? Even if she didn't finish it, your father connects to her through it somehow."

"I thought you were a fucking cop. Stop being a therapist." Jess stepped out of the way, and I brought my hammer down onto the head, a baby's soft spot, and one blow was all it took to crack it in half. I couldn't stop smashing that yellow blob into pieces. I kept hitting and hitting. Somewhere in the background I could hear Jess begging me to stop, telling me it would all be okay. I could have stopped, but I didn't want to. I needed this. I heard the doorbell ring, but the building could have been on fire and I would have kept right on banging, smashing, crushing until the ugly yellow blob I'd been forced to worship my whole life, the center of Dad's room, his heart, was nothing but dust. Then I'd sweep it into the trash and throw it down the chute to burn in the incinerator. Years of suppressed anger poured out of me like lava. When I ran out of rage for my mother, it was Dad's turn. Not only had he refused to let me express any of my feelings for my dead mother, but now he'd abandoned me too. Fuck them both.

Sam didn't go to Jess's side to make her feel better. He didn't bark at me to stop. He lay on my bed and watched. He understood. There was no stopping a wounded animal until its body was ready to heal or die.

"What is happening here?" It was Anne's voice. "She's going to wake the whole building."

I ignored her, just another gnat in the room.

"I can't get her to stop." I could hear the strain in Jess's voice, the tears trapped inside her throat. "She thought there might be something hidden inside. Something her father was keeping from her."

Anne came up behind me and, before I could resist, took the hammer out of my hand and me in her arms. "Sweetie, it's empty. Let it go."

I cried until I felt my ribs might crack, and then I sobbed softly to myself.

"You're going to be okay." Anne patted the back of my head, and then Jess stepped in. She did her best to comfort me, including mimicking what Anne had done, but Jess's patting was clumsy and her tone awkward. She wasn't good at this kind of thing, but she cared enough to try.

"Anne's right. It's empty," she said. "Your father wasn't hiding anything. No secrets here."

"I don't know about that." Anne held out a piece of the sculpture.

I took it from her and examined it. "Oh, wow. Remember those kits for kids? They came with a small hammer and chisel. They were from the Smithsonian, or maybe National Geographic. You'd chisel away until you exposed a real fossil, some shellfish or something. Dad and I played paleontologist for hours."

The memory made me smile, but Anne and Jess had never looked more serious.

Jess took the fossil-like object from me. "This is bone."

"Human bone," Anne said.

"How do you know?" I asked.

"If you listened more, you'd know I did two years of nursing school."

My mind swirled, a tornado of possibilities. It all felt impossible until I inhaled some of the clay and bone dust.

"My mother," I said.

The expressions on Anne's and Jess's faces froze like the people of Pompeii when Mount Vesuvius erupted, casting their fear and worry in stone.

"Why Dad loved this crap makes sense now. It isn't a piece of her art. It's a piece of her."

"Your mother's buried in New Jersey, right?" asked Jess.

"Maybe he mixed some of her remains into clay," Anne said.

"That would make sense—why Dad kept it in his room under a spotlight. When I was little, Dad didn't care about any of his stuff. I could touch anything, and if something broke, he shrugged it off. But I was never allowed to get too close to the sculpture. Ever."

"Why wouldn't he tell you about it? It's not as if he wasn't open with you about death," said Jess.

"Maybe he wanted something of her just for himself." Anne seemed to understand more about Dad than I did. "Love isn't supposed to make sense."

"I wish something, any of this, made sense."

Jess cautiously moved closer to me. "I'm going to take the bone fragment to the lab and see what forensics can determine."

"Forensics." Anne rolled her eyes. "They're magic workers on TV, but in real life, some coroners are elected officials
who don't know their hipbone's connected to the backbone."

"The backbone's connected to the neck bone," Jess sang
for my benefit, an attempt to lighten a mood heavier than the
Rock of Gibraltar.

"Doing the skeleton dance," they sang together, and we
all laughed until I had to use Dad's bedspread to wipe away
the snot and tears.

"Our forensic team's good. I don't know if they'll find
anything or if they will be able to tell if this is your mother
or not, but it's worth a try. Maybe the cards can tell us something too."

Anne looked down at all the funeral cards on the floor. "I
know," I said. "My father went to a lot of funerals."

Anne smirked. "My grandmother would put him to
shame. She has half her attic filled with boxes of holy cards
bundled with rubber bands. You can't throw them out. It's a
sin. You pass them on until there's a fire or flood, and that's
that."

It was a relief to hear Dad wasn't a unique freak but part
of a bigger tradition of freaks . . . or just ordinary people.

"Look at these." Jess picked up some of the cards with
St. Genesius.

"I don't know this saint," Anne said. "But I'm the least
religious in my family."

Jess pointed out the discrepancy between the prayers on
two of the cards forty years apart.

"You're the detective," Anne said. "Not for me to tell you
your job, but will this help you find Linda's father right now?
That seems to be the first order of business."

Jess's shoulders were touching the bottoms of her earlobes again. Anne reached out and touched Jess's upper arm,
and Jess's shoulders dropped. "I can see you care about our
Linda. She clearly cares for you. If you remember that, whatever happens will be okay. What God intends."

"I need to pee." A disembodied voice came from nowhere.

"Please tell me that didn't come from Sam," Jess said.

Anne pulled a baby monitor from the pocket of her long red silk robe. She pressed a side button and put the monitor close to her mouth. "Coming now." Without caring whether I wanted it or not, Anne hugged me tight. "You remember," she whispered in my ear, "your father raised you and loves you, and that will always be true. You let the detective do her job. You remember, no matter what, his love is true."

"Chanel No. 5," I said.

Anne looked caught. "Your father gave it to Mrs. Camberi the other day. He knows that's her brand of perfume. He had a client that passed and her family was giving some of her things to the workers. She apparently had a full bottle of perfume, never opened. I know I shouldn't have, but it always smells so nice on Mrs. Camberi, I dabbed a bit behind my ears."

"It suits you," I said.

"Always the flirt," she smiled. Before she left Dad's bedroom, Anne glanced over her shoulder at Jess. "Take care of yourself, and don't get lost in details. The answer is usually the big thing right in front of your face."

Jess and I were silent until we heard the front door close.

"Or your nose," I said. "Did Dad take that from Mrs. Lyons . . . his mother's apartment? He may have known about her death and didn't tell anyone? I don't know if this is making more or less sense."

I knelt and began picking up my mother's pieces, literally or figuratively; forensics would tell me one way or another. "Do you need all of them?"

Jess knelt next to me. She put what I had gathered and the bone fragment Anne had found into a doggy poop bag she had in the pocket of her sweats. "This should be enough. I can have a forensic team come in and look over the rest." She took out another bag. "If it's okay with you, I'm going to take these funeral cards." Before I responded, she had the sixty or so of the cards wrapped in several bags and was on her feet.

"You want this one too?" I held out my mother's card.

"You should keep that one."

"Take it," I insisted. I knew it was time to let it go, and this time not in anger, but in peace.

Jess slipped it in with the others. "I don't know what's going on here. But finding your father is the only way we'll hear his side of the story."

Sam licked my ankle. He had been lying on the floor by my feet. I reached down and rubbed him behind the ears. "Thank you, Sam. I needed that."

"I have to get this guy home," Jess said. "His pills and food."

"Of course," I said.

"You're coming with me." Jess stepped over the cards on the floor.

"Am I under arrest?" I smiled.

"A citizen's arrest." She smiled back. "You'd be doing me a favor. I have a feeling I'll be working a lot of hours, and I'd feel better if Sam wasn't alone."

Jess had plenty of options for Sam, including doggy day care, but she knew the last place I wanted to be was alone in this apartment.

"What if my dad comes back?"

"Anne will hear him. She can call us. I can also have a patrol officer out in front."

"You already do, don't you?"

Jess didn't respond, so I did for her. "Just doing your job."

CHAPTER

17

At one forty-five am, I changed out of my funeral cocktail wear, put on a light-blue T and my most unflattering but comfortable jeans, and left the apartment with Jess and Sam.

We hadn't made it two feet away from the building when Sam peed on the tree in front of our vandalized van.

"*Donovan and Daughter*," Jess read the side logo, the only part of the van not tagged. "You call this in?"

I didn't tell her that Dad hadn't wanted to call the police. I shook my head and shrugged. "The giant rubber rat on top and the Grateful Dead mosaic both scream *Vandalize me*."

"You're blaming the victim." The muscles in her face went up but then quickly down. She clearly realized that what she'd thought was a joke was insensitive and not funny.

We walked over to her car, a 2015 Subaru with a sticker on the back—silhouettes of two parents, three children, a dog, and a cat. "Good for stakeouts," she explained.

"Maybe in suburbia. In the city, it's actually kinda conspicuous."

Jess opened the back door. Sam jumped in. Lots of dog hair on the seats. She opened the passenger door for me. "My lady." She smiled.

I was ready to return the smile when I caught sight of the patrol car parked across the street.

"One minute." Jess reached into the Subaru, opened the glove compartment, and shoved in the poop bags of evidence and funeral cards, then walked over to the uniformed cop, who got out of his car when she approached.

I couldn't hear what either of them was saying, but it was clear from the way the officer stood at attention who was the boss. I watched while he and Jess took turns nodding.

The officer looked over at me, and when our eyes met, he looked sleepy, and I realized that Jess had to be exhausted. I at least had had a nap, but she'd been going since early morning. The officer turned away and got back into his vehicle, and Jess returned and climbed into the driver's seat.

"That cop's not going to shoot first and ask questions later, is he?"

"You have my word," Jess said.

I believed she meant it, but if I had learned anything from the events of the past two days, it was that we couldn't control what others did, no matter how hard we tried.

"Seat belt," she said.

I pulled my seat belt across me but was too flustered to clip and lock it in place. Jess did it for me. It turned out I didn't need a mother, but it sure was nice to have a friend.

*   *   *

This was my favorite time of the day, when Dad and I would do our early-morning restaurant stops, when it was still dark and there were few other cars on the road. It felt like the city did sleep.

Jess and I drove over the Henry Hudson Bridge. Sam was snoring in the back seat when her cell phone rang.

"Want me to answer it?" I knew she was too by-the-book to pick up her phone while driving, and she didn't have it paired to the car's speakers.

"Can you see who's calling?"

I took her phone from where it rested in the cupholder between the driver and passenger seats.

"Unknown number," I said.

"Unknown can just wait."

By the time we got off the parkway at the Seventy-Second Street exit, Unknown was calling for the fifth time. Jess double-parked and picked up. "Detective Jones, and this better not be spam."

There was a long pause while Jess nodded several times, occasionally looking at her rearview mirror to check on Sam or to see if a cop was going to get her for illegal parking.

"Ten minutes." She hung up.

"Everything okay?" I asked.

"You hungry?"

Before I had the chance to tell her my stomach was too flippy-floppy to risk putting anything into it, she said, "I'm starved. Feeling like the special," and we were heading in the direction of Carmen's Diner, which never closed.

There was a space right in front of the diner. "Would you mind waiting?" Jess asked. "I don't want to leave Sam alone."

"No problem." I was more than happy to stay in the car. The last thing I wanted to do was go inside the last place I'd seen Dad and smell the fresh stench of today's special.

I must have nodded off, because when I woke, Betty was knocking on my window. The windows were automatic and I didn't have the keys. I opened the door to talk to her.

"You ever go home?" I asked.

"Had some paperwork to catch up on. Here." She gave me Jess's key fob and her apartment keys. "The detective had to take off. A cop thing. She said to tell you she has a spot in the garage across from her building. She'll call as soon as she can."

Betty had the perfect poker face. She had no tells. Even her voice oscillated the same as it always had, indiscriminately from high to low. Still, I knew she was hiding something.

"What's the special?" I asked.

"The special?" Betty twitched her nose.

"The special," I repeated. "Not liver and onions; that was yesterday."

"The day cook makes the call when he comes in around six and checks the freezer."

"Jess . . . er, Detective Jones. She eats here a lot?"

"More than she does at home, I'm sure." Betty smiled.

"She always gets the special? Like Dad?"

"Unless she comes in after a late shift or in the middle of the night."

"Like now."

"We always run out of specials after the dinner shift. Call anything special and people want it." Betty laughed louder than usual. She was definitely hiding something.

I stepped out of the car, looked down at Betty, and said, "I know it was you who called her. Why? It was about my dad, right?"

Betty shook her head, but before she could think of some plausible explanation, I begged her. "Please, I can't take any more lies, especially not from you."

Betty put her hands on her hips. I knew she was bracing herself to tell me the whole truth and nothing but the truth, as she knew it. "Rob, our delivery boy, was on his way out when Cook got a call. Rob said he'd do it. He delivered a grilled cheese to some guy who said he was family, and he gave Rob two envelopes to bring to me right away. Lives were at stake was all he said, and he tipped him fifty dollars."

"It was Dad, right?"

Betty continued. "Rob said the guy was so calm about the whole thing, it freaked him out. It was one AM. I had just gotten into bed when Rob called. He thought it was either a prank or a real emergency. I got dressed, no makeup—surprised you haven't mentioned that—and rushed over here. Rob handed me both envelopes. He wasn't to give them to anyone else. One envelope had my name on it. The other, the detective's."

"What did it say?"

Betty pulled a folded paper towel out from her apron pocket and handed it to me. It was a note in Dad's handwriting, only his letters were shakier than usual.

My Dear Friend Betty,

I apologize for putting you in this situation of involvement. There is no one else I can trust to help me and Linda. I don't know how much you've been told, but my behavior at the diner earlier should have made it clear that I am in trouble and I need to make things right, not for me, but for Linda. My beautiful baby. She has been the greatest gift of my life and it's time she knows the truth, her family legacy, and takes her rightful place as the head of the family business.

Dad still was holding on to the hope that I would give up my chance to go to college and take over Donovan and Daughter Exterminating? He really was delusional. I continued to read:

There isn't the time to go into this more now. *I hope to someday sit again at my booth and talk about the big things that matter and the small things that matter because they provide us the opportunity to spend time together.*

Right now, I need to ask a favor of you. Rob, a very professional young man, gave you an envelope with Detective Jones's name on it. I need you to please get it to her as soon as possible. Please do not open it. The contents are for her eyes only. You know my feelings about the police: unless they're on one of my shows, I don't trust them. This Detective Jones is someone my daughter trusts, and from the evidence, I believe she loves Linda. For these reasons, I know if anyone can help me make this right, it is her. I trust you will get the envelope and its contents to the detective as soon as possible.

If you see my Linda before I do, please give her a kiss and tell her it will all make sense soon, and I love her.

I ignored the tears blurring my vision until Betty used a dinner napkin to blot them away. "Don't make a habit of using napkins on your face," she warned. "You'll destroy your beautiful skin." She touched my cheek the same way I'd seen mothers caress the faces of their children on television shows and commercials.

I brought her hand to my heart. "What did Dad write to Jess? Please, tell me what was in her envelope."

She sighed. "I don't know."

Of course she hadn't looked inside. Dad trusted her not to.

"All I know is, she opened the note and read it fast and told me to give you all her keys. She never said anything about your dad. She didn't know he'd also written to me."

"Not me."

"You know he and Jessica are trying to protect you by keeping you out of all of this."

"A little late for that."

"At least he's getting help from someone who you know will try." The veins in Betty's forehead pulsed. There was something else she wasn't telling me.

"What is it?" I took hold of her shoulders.

"It's only a feeling. Probably nothing," she said.

It was never nothing when Betty had a feeling about someone.

I tightened my grip. "Tell me."

"When Jessica read your father's note and handed me her keys, she asked me for a glass of water."

"So?"

"She held the glass for a minute, maybe longer, and then put it down on the counter, thanked me, and left."

"Betty, please, what are you saying?"

"She never drank the water. Not even a sip. It was like she needed time to think, consider her next move."

"About whether to help Dad?"

"Or the consequences. If she doesn't call in the information she got, doesn't even call her partner, she's risking her job, her future on the force. If she does call it in, she risks losing you."

"She thinks she has to choose between her career and me."

"Is she wrong?"

I shook my head. She wasn't wrong.

"It looks like she went with love," Betty said.

"I can't let her give up everything. There has to be another way."

"I wish I had advice on that."

"One thing's for sure: I'm the one who needs to protect them. But I have no fucking idea how to find them."

I pulled out my cell and dialed Jess. It went straight to voice mail. I was sure she'd turned her phone off. If she was going to compromise herself, her career, she wouldn't want to be reachable. I dialed Dad. Same thing. Straight to voice mail.

"They could be anywhere. What am I going to do?" I stared at the face of my phone, willing it to respond.

"The phone!" Betty squealed like she'd won the lottery or seen a rat. "I wasn't thinking! I'll be back in one minute." This time it took everything in me not to go inside the diner. But I couldn't leave Sam alone.

I clicked the fob and unlocked the doors. I sat in the back, and Sam snuggled up to me and rested his head on my lap. Petting him calmed me, stopped me from ripping off my earlobes. Maybe there was something to that pet-therapy stuff, beyond enabling people to bring their animals into restaurants and on airplanes free of charge.

Betty came back waving one of those old-fashioned order pads with the carbon copies.

"Cook took that order for the grilled cheese. There was an address. Obviously." Betty ripped off the carbon copy and handed it to me.

There was no street address. "It's only an intersection."

"Sorry," she said with a shrug.

I petted Sam's head. If I'd ever needed a therapy dog for comfort, it was now.

"Hope is found in tiny places," she assured me.

"Betty, you're a genius." I climbed from the back to the front, unlatched the glove compartment, and pulled out one of the poop bags.

"She keeps her poop in the car?"

"It's the cards. Dad's funeral prayer cards. The ones with the wrong line." I pulled a handful out, and the addresses on them were the same, just like Jess said. The location was also in the vicinity, probably one or two blocks east of the intersection where Dad had met Betty's delivery guy.

Why Dad was hiding out at a funeral home was a question I let myself consider for a minute. Were the owners old friends or family I didn't know about?

"What's happening?" Betty's voice stopped me from going down a hole I hadn't the time or the energy to dig myself out of.

I shoved one of the cards in my pocket.

"It's what you said. Hope is found in tiny places . . . or in small print."

"Too early in the morning for riddles."

"I think I know where to find them," I told Betty.

Sam barked, and his energy helped me believe I could do this, though not alone. Before I returned the remaining cards to the stash, I found my mother's card and pocketed it. I'd never admitted to needing her before, but I knew I couldn't do whatever I was about to do without her.

CHAPTER

18

"BETTY," I SAID, glancing at the dog, "Would you mind . . . ?"

"Come on, buddy." She waved Sam to her. "I have some nice steak for you. Food."

Sam jumped out of the back seat and hurried to Betty's side.

I closed the car door and handed Betty the fob. I was in no state of mind to drive; besides, this parking space was too good to give up. I raised my hand to hail a cab. I had no money on me, and my credit card connected to Uber was still over the limit from the overpriced cocktail funeral dress and shoes. Reading my mind, Betty pushed a rolled ten and two twenties into my fist. Then she used her thumb and index finger to whistle for a cab. She was the coolest.

She opened the cab's rear door for me. "Thank you, Betty," I said.

"You don't thank family." She kissed me on my forehead twice, I assumed once for Dad and the other for her. "Now go find your father and help your girlfriend clear his name and keep her job."

Girlfriend.

That sounded, well . . . I wanted more from Jess, from us. "The meter's running," the driver said. "This isn't Uber."

"This is yours." I gave Betty back the paper towel message. It wasn't all kisses and roses and heart-dotted *i*'s, but for Dad, it was a love letter. Probably the only one he'd written to anyone other than Mom. Betty dropped it into her apron pocket.

I got in the cab and told the driver the address from the funeral cards, and Betty waved to me the way moms did when sending their kids off to the first day of school.

Whatever happened tonight, I knew it would be life changing. Nothing would ever be the same, but I'd always have Betty to come home to.

By the time the driver announced, "Here we are," I had called and texted Jess and Dad each a half dozen times, with no response, and had a headache from pulling compulsively at my earlobes.

I looked out the window. We were in front of an orange-brick brownstone townhouse. There was no signage for a funeral parlor or anything similar. The front windows were boarded up, so I assumed the place was abandoned.

"Are you sure this is the right address?" I asked.

"Are you sure you gave me the right address?"

I took the funeral card from my pocket. It matched the address on the building.

The meter was close to exceeding the money Betty'd stuffed in my hand. I paid the guy, tipped him despite his attitude, and got out of the cab. The driver drove off, and I stood at the bottom of the stairs leading to the front door. I gave Dad one more chance. *Where are you? Need you. Urgent. Please. Begging you. Respond.*

Still no response.

19

I PACED THE SIDEWALK twenty-five times, once for every year since I was born in one direction and another twenty-five times for every year my mother had been dead in the other.

Still no responses on my phone. Not a word. Not a dot. I'd been worrying about Dad, and also about Jess putting her job at risk for him, but now I was afraid. Of what, and for whom? Dad? Jess? I wasn't sure. The threat of something bad happening if I didn't find them felt suffocating. I had to go and see if they were inside, abandoned building or not.

I climbed up two steps, and my phone beeped. I picked up without looking, and there was only silence.

"Hello? Anyone there? Dad? Jess?"

"This is to inform you that your insurance coverage—"

I clicked off. Scam calls. I could have screamed, but instead I took a moment to think. If there were any lesson to be learned from every cop show Dad had watched, it was that one should never go into an unknown situation without backup.

I called the diner, but the person, probably the cook, put me on hold. It was five in the morning now, the time when most eateries received their food deliveries for the day. Between that and the early breakfast crowd, I'd have a longer wait than I could stomach. I hung up, ascended two more steps, stopped, and dialed the precinct.

They picked up on the second ring. The voice sounded like the desk officer from yesterday. Was it really only yesterday?

"Detective Frascon. Please."

"One minute." I could hear his chair swivel. No doubt he was checking that damned magnetic in/out board. "She's not in until ten."

"It's about her partner," I said.

"Is it an emergency?"

Not really. Maybe. I didn't know. Dad was in serious trouble. Leaving a message probably would only make things worse for him and Jess. If Frascon learned her partner was helping Dad—not a murder suspect but still a fugitive who had a warrant out for his arrest—without telling her or calling for backup, suspension was written all over the outcome. It also wouldn't be good for Dad. I only saw one ending for Dad: the book being thrown at him. And that was the better of the two possible outcomes.

Maybe I'd been worrying about their lack of communication for nothing. If they were inside this derelict brownstone, they probably had no Wi-Fi or cell signal. Of course they weren't getting my messages.

"Hello? Your name?" The officer was still on the line.

I panicked. "Linda Bennett."

What was wrong with me? Of all the fake names to use, I'd used my real first name and my original surname. If this got back to Frascon, she'd know something was up.

"Is this the number where she can reach you?" He could see my number, of course. Caller ID. What had I been thinking calling the precinct?

"Never mind. It's a personal matter. I'm her cousin, and I was thinking about visiting . . ."

Christ. What was I saying? I couldn't shut up. Instead, I kept rambling, and the only thing that stopped me from telling the desk officer about my three fictitious kids and my farm in Idaho was an incoming text from Dad.

I knew you would find your way to me.

I stared at my phone. He knew I was here? Could he see me?

"I have to check with work about vacation days," I mumbled to the officer and hung up.

Dad, where are you?

I wondered if he was peering through a hole in one of the wooden boards.

Top floor. Back end of the brownstone.

Is Jess with you?

I saw three dots, then nothing. I waited, and there were three more dots and then nothing. And I waited. Finally, I gave up and climbed to the stoop, where the side windows were also boarded. I imagined they had once been paneled with ornate stained glass. I turned the brass knob, and the door opened.

Dad was expecting me.

The inside stairs leading to the second floor were so well lit I could see the layers of dust hanging on the stucco walls and every scuff mark on the wooden stairs. The ceiling was high, and except for the creaky sound the stairs made, the space felt extravagant, giving meaning to the term *a grand entrance*. I assumed this had once been a funeral home for the elite—what we now called the one percent.

If I thought the staircase was impressive, the second-floor living room, with its ballroom-sized chandelier and stone fireplace, was magnificent. This would have been the room where the mourning family received visitors paying their respects.

"Dad?" I called out. No response.

This place was huge. I'd need a megaphone for him to hear me if he was on the far side of the building. I'd started making my way through the living room when I caught sight of a painting at least twice my height of a man who looked like an older version of my dad and a young boy who looked like a younger version of him.

It was my father and his father—my grandfather. They had matching grimaces. So serious, and a little sad. Was this not a funeral home but my dad's childhood home? Maybe that was it; my father's family were morticians. He'd said very little about his youth and never spoken about where he'd grown up or what his father had done for work. Knowing that his mother was a wealthy woman, it made sense. Dad often said there was money in death. I'd thought he was referring to exterminating, but maybe not. Him growing up here was hard for me to picture, unless his mom had been the housekeeper or cook and his father the chauffeur.

It was curious that Dad's mother wasn't in the portrait. Maybe she was the one who had painted it? The artwork covering the walls of Mrs. Lyons's Park Avenue apartment, I thought, had all been created by famous artists, but maybe my grandmother had painted some of the oils. I wished I had paid more attention.

I continued walking and calling out for Dad and Jess. Still no response. I took a wrong turn and found myself in a kitchen larger than our whole Bronx apartment. On an oak table with a bench built into the wall were a teapot and two cups, one full, the other half-empty. It made me smile to think of Dad and Jess having tea together. I knew the full cup was Dad's. He hated tea. He was a coffee drinker all the way. It was sweet of him to have made tea for Jess.

I could imagine him trying to get everything just right for her. Apologizing for not having any biscuits to go with the tea.

I left the kitchen. This place was gigantic, but even brownstone mansions had to end somewhere. I passed four bedrooms and two bathrooms and then hit a wall, literally. There was nowhere to go. For some reason, Dad seemed to be screwing with my head. Was Jess conspiring with him? I was ready to go back—maybe I had missed a turn—when my eye caught a keypad in the upper right corner on the dead-end wall. The cover was flipped up. I didn't need to text Dad for the code. I punched in my birthday and the wall opened to reveal a secret room.

Dad and I had served clients with hidden rooms off their bedrooms or kitchens; some called them saferooms, others panic rooms. I tended to agree with Dad, who said that paranoia for some is reality for others. You'd occasionally hear about home invasions in the news, though these days they seemed to happen in suburban counties like Westchester.

I stepped inside, and the stench of trapped paint fumes and dead squirrels slapped me across the face. It was an improvement over the scent of a rotting corpse or vomit on my shoes, though I would have been less shocked to find a decapitated head or an S&M dungeon with caged rats than this: a rubber-duck-stenciled wall, matching baby furniture, tall and short dressers, a changing table, and a crib, all in gender-neutral sunny yellows and mint greens. And the pièce de résistance for any nursery: a waist-high bookshelf filled with every kid's book I had ever known: "Goodnight Moon," "The Snowy Day," "The Little Prince" (in which Dad had used a black marker to change all the princes to princesses), and many, many others. The books in this collection, though, were not my originals; they were all shrink-wrapped, in mint condition, and unopened, never read. The shelves even held a dozen or so baby-bath books and the complete works of Shakespeare, which I had never owned.

It was clear that the only thing that had ever touched these books, or this room, was time.

Why had Dad asked me to come here? Why had he never told me he'd changed his name, our names? Why hadn't he told me Mrs. Lyons was my grandmother?

And then there was the most confounding question of all: Where were he and Jess now?

I was drowning in a duck pond of *why*s.

Had this crib room been intended for me? I wondered. Was bringing me to this room Dad's evidence that my mother had loved and wanted me?

I looked up and saw a miniature replica of the celestial painting on the ceiling at Grand Central. The stars were even painted backward. Every time we walked through Grand Central, Dad made me stand on the exact spot he and my mother had met, then proceeded to tell me how infuriated she was by an artist going through so much effort to get it wrong.

The ceiling ruled out my mother having been the one who created this nurturing space.

Then who had? And why was it never used?

That's when I thought of Mrs. Lyons. Maybe this was a room she'd created for a baby she'd lost, a miscarriage, a stillbirth, or a horrific crib death. Could that explain why she'd been so distant and cruel, withholding her love from my father? Had Dad brought me here to help me understand why he had severed ties with the woman who was incapable of mothering him? Her pain cut so deep that it slashed into her living child? It wasn't an original story, but it was a story Dad exalted.

"Tragedy, my daughter, connects humanity because of suffering's common denominator: loss."

20

THE ROOM WAS beginning to feel oppressively hot. The ventilation was poor, and there were no windows to open. Panic rooms were only safe when there was a single point of entry and exit, controlled from the inside. I didn't know if my father was ever going to show up, but I felt my only choice was to wait, so I sat on the cushioned rocking chair at the side of the crib.

The chair had side pockets. The one on the right had a bottle of cold water. *Thanks, Dad.* I toasted the empty room and chugged it down, wishing for something stronger.

Looking around the room once more, I saw through the slats of the crib a plush toy duck with a page of lined paper taped to its head. A note:

Under my feet, which are below my beak, are five note-books. Shakespeare wrote his plays in five acts. There are five notebooks, one for each Act.

Shakespeare? Dad hated the theater. If it wasn't on television or in a paperback and a true crime, thriller, or murder mystery, he had no interest.

Looking under the stuffed duck and around the crib, I saw nothing.

Hmm. I dropped to the floor and looked under the crib instead. Bingo. Five journal-style notebooks lay neatly piled in a stack.

I picked up the first notebook and sat back in the rocking chair. The notebook looked like the same brand Dad used to write his customer notes in. Was he asking me to read all our clients' stories? He hadn't made me do that in years.

I read the second paragraph of his note to me.

Please read them in order, every word, no skimming. I will see you when you're done. Now please turn to page one.

I turned to the first page of book one.

My dear daughter,

I know my disappearance has left you feeling abandoned. On my word, I've been close by, watching you.

By the time you've read Act I, your world, as you've known it, will have been turned upside down. You are confused and hurt. I regret the pain I have caused you. If I am anything, I am human. In my desperation to preserve the past, to keep my relationship with you as it always has been, I've acted selfishly. Today, circumstances have forced me to do what I should have done long ago. In these notebooks, you will soon discover the story that belongs to you.

In the beginning . . .

*   *   *

For seven hours I read, getting up from the rocking chair only to retrieve each subsequent notebook. I suppressed my need to pee, risking a bladder infection because I couldn't stop reading.

What started off as a love story morphed into a perverse tale about a deranged man—a serial killer, really—who took on the identities of the people he murdered. I was shaken at first that Dad named the protagonist after himself and the woman he loved after my mother, Rebecca, and it was chilling to read about his darling daughter, Linda. I might have believed this was my father's confession to me if it had sounded anything like the dad I knew, though I was certain the protagonist's childhood abuse was inspired by the father's own tragic upbringing.

It broke my heart to think my father had never felt he could share his pain with me, and that he did so now only by writing a thriller about a character he would have judged too sympathetic and preposterous if we were watching him on-screen.

We'd had a lot of popcorn thrown at us at the movies because of Dad's shouted critiques. He was forever complaining about how writers never did their research, which led to inauthentic characters. Whenever I suggested he write his own story, he laughed. "Working people don't have time to write books. They need to put food on the table."

Well, it seemed he'd finally found the time to put pen to paper.

Maybe the story had holes and the protagonist wasn't entirely believable, but it was all clearly a metaphor for the childhood horrors my dad had suffered. The protagonist's evil father, and his mother, who let the abuse happen, were obviously inspired by my father's parents, especially his mother, whom he'd kept me from my whole life.

My hurt for Dad cut so deep I could now imagine that he'd killed his mother.

I didn't want to read the final book, but again, Dad wasn't leaving me any choice. I had to know how his story ended.

I stood to get the final notebook, but my leg had fallen asleep and I fell facedown on the wooden floor. It hurt, but my nose didn't feel broken and there wasn't any blood. That's when I saw what I'd been missing.

Everywhere in the room, the wallpaper had been stenciled with small yellow ducks in an organized and methodical pattern, the same number of ducks in a row, all equidistant from each other. An inch to the right of the childproofed electrical socket, there should have been a stenciled duck, but there wasn't. I saw only eggshell-colored paint, and it wasn't an exact match. It was the kind of mistake Dad often made because he was color-blind.

I crawled over to the wall and scratched the mismatched paint; underneath, I found a reddish-brown spot. Dried blood?

I took out my phone and used the flashlight app I had reinstalled after the storage area incident and saw there were more dark spots under the paint that led to the tall dresser.

I pushed it to the side, and there, exactly as Dad had described it, was a door the height of a minifridge but wide enough for a human body to fit through.

I pulled the handle, relieved not to find any detached body parts or a dead baby. I could easily climb inside and slide down the ramp, but the stench of dead squirrel had grown stronger than before. Now I was questioning whether it was dead squirrel or a rotting, torn appendage . . .

Wait, I told myself. *What am I thinking?* Was it even possible that Dad's story was actually a letter, a confessional, written to me? The tone was stilted and snobbish, nothing like my father. Was it even possible for a man to be one thing for decades, then turn into someone else? Or was the man I called Dad a monster and the greatest actor of all time?

I felt like I had died. My whole life had shattered. I should be calling the police. Instead, I did something crazy. I picked up the fifth notebook, sat in the rocking chair, and read the final act.

ACT V

I WOKE UP TO the smell of Rebecca's generic soap, which I had always found irresistible. I had to have been dreaming about her, though, because the only other body in the room was Anthony Donovan's.

I glanced down at my watch. I had been sleeping for hours. Turning, I saw that the faux wall was open. I must have forgotten to close it behind me. I rushed around the house, calling, "Rebecca?"

She wasn't in the kitchen, the living room, or the bathroom. I even went to the basement to see if she was there . . . but no. She wasn't anywhere. It was after eight. She should have long been home. There was no message on the answering machine.

I called the yoga studio. They said she had left class early. She wasn't feeling well and needed to rest.

Oh no, I thought. Had she gone into labor? There were still seven weeks left before her due date.

I'd learned at a young age never to panic. Staying calm was always the better option. Before I could let myself worry about Rebecca, I had to finish the work. Anthony's body was in the rocking chair where I had left it.

It had been Anthony who suggested breaking objects up before sending them down the chute. Smaller pieces were easier to slide through than big ones. He had been so helpful,

and he was a wonderful painter. The molding was impecca-
ble. I took a moment to take in the beauty of the room, then I
covered myself in a raincoat and hat, which reminded me . . .
I had almost forgotten. I hurried and got the plush yellow
duck from the living room and put it in the crib, then took
out the chain saw and cut off Anthony's head and limbs. This
step was likely unnecessary. With the exception of Rocco, I
had never had an issue fitting a shell in one piece down the
chute when properly lubricated, but with Rebecca in her sev-
enth month, she'd need my full attention, so as Anthony had
said, "Play it safe rather than sorry later."

After I covered each piece in petroleum jelly and vegetable
oil, my own creation, an alternative to motor oil, I slid head,
limbs, and torso down the chute. I took the sheets and bedding
and my raincoat and hat and put all of them into a plastic bag
and pushed them down the chute as well. I gathered all the
drop cloths, ten in all, and shoved them into another contrac-
tor's bag and pushed that (oiled, of course) down the chute.

I thought I was done until I saw in the corner of the
room a stenciled duck had been splashed with blood, leaving
a line of droplets from its beak to the chute's door. I didn't
have enough paint, so I had to run to the hardware store
to get more. I forgot the empty can and couldn't remember the brand we had used, but I did remember the color
was eggshell. The salesperson explained that not all eggshells
are alike, but it looked close enough to me—besides, I was
running out of time. I finished the painting and covered the
blood, but stenciling another duck would have to wait.

I went to the basement to make sure the body parts had
all come down on the conveyor belt into what I now called
our kiln. All parts were accounted for and were soon cremated
successfully, leaving nothing but ashes and a few shards of
bone. I mixed them into the clay I'd give Rebecca for her to
begin her first sculpture, her masterpiece, father and child.

Now I had to find Rebecca. And my baby.

Three painful days passed with no word from her. I called
her obstetrician's office, but they hadn't received a call from
her. I called every hospital in all five boroughs, including

Staten Island: no person had been admitted with her name
or description.

Desperate, I went to see Mother. I used the service
entrance and went directly to her apartment. I knocked on
her door. She called out, "Who is it?"

"Exterminator." I used my Bronx accent.

She looked through the peephole, and between my overalls and the tank in my hand, she didn't recognize me. She
unlocked and opened the door and with her back to me said,
"I hope this won't take long."

From behind, I covered Mother's mouth. I felt her body
go stiff.

"It's me," I whispered in her ear and pushed her away.

She squinted at me. She'd always been too vain to wear
her glasses.

"It's been a long time," she said. "I see we're playing
exterminator these days."

"Where is she?"

"Who, dear?"

"My wife."

"Congratulations," she said. "I must send a gift. Is there
a registry?"

I wanted nothing more than to slap the sarcasm off her
face. Her tone told me she had seen Rebecca. I also knew if I
dared raise my voice, Mother would go to her room and lock
the door behind her.

"I'm worried something happened to her."

"I'll make us some tea." She walked to the kitchen, clearly
playing the Mother game, her rules, her terms.

If I had any hope of her telling me what she knew about
Rebecca's whereabouts, I had no choice but to go along with
her little charade—that all was well in the world and I was
her loving son, home for a visit.

She steeped the tea in her heirloom porcelain pot and
poured it into matching cups she had never let me use before.
Clumsy hands don't get to touch nice things.

She served us her favorite biscuits, the kind that only
came from Denmark.

We sipped our tea in silence. One of the rules was not to speak unless spoken to. She took a last bite of her biscuit, poured herself and me another cup of tea, and said, "How is my son getting on these days?"

My son from her lips made my skin itch. I sat on my hands to stop myself from scratching. "Please tell me where she is."

She leaned in and stared at the embroidered name on my left pocket. "Antony."

"Anthony," I said.

"You must be in a modern interpretation of Shakespeare's *Caesar*. Mark Antony, Caesar's loyal exterminator."

She was mocking me the same way she had Father. But I wasn't going to let her win. Composure was the only way to handle Mother.

"I would appreciate it greatly if you'd be so kind as to tell me where Rebecca is."

She lifted her porcelain cup to her lips, but instead of taking a sip, she said, "This pretending you do is not healthy."

"I'm an actor," I said with a shrug.

"Please." She put her cup down and grabbed hold of my arm. "None of this is your fault."

"Tell me where she is."

"I know he did unspeakable things to you."

"Where is she?"

"And I'm so sorry for not stopping him."

"You're sorry." I tugged my wrist back and, in doing so, swiped the porcelain teapot and matching cups and saucers to the floor.

"No!" she screamed, and hurriedly knelt on the floor. For several deep breaths, I watched her pick up shattered pieces, sobbing.

With great calm and composure, I asked again, "Where is she?"

"Everything and everyone you touch, you destroy," she said through tears.

I leaned over from behind her, wrapped her hair around my fist, and whispered, "Tell me."

"I don't know!" she screamed.

I released her and stood straight. The fear in her eyes should have evoked my pity, but it only brought me pleasure. I felt myself harden under my uniform.

"This morning, Jack the doorman let her up."

I could barely make out the words through Mother's sobbing.

"Speak up!" I shouted.

"She wanted my help. Money."

I nodded for her to continue.

"I told her it was too late for my help or money."

"Why?"

"She was rambling about a dead man in a chair."

My worst fear was confirmed: Rebecca had discovered Anthony while I slept. I stifled a curse and glared at Mother. "What else?"

"She had a hospital gown sticking out from under her coat. I assumed she escaped from an institution. Bellevue, probably. It was clear she wasn't in her right mind. I asked her to come inside, have some tea." Mother's sniffling began anew.

"Where is she now?"

"She showed me this creature. Shriveled. Tiny. Like a baby gerbil. She had it in a shoebox. She said it was my grandchild. I knew that was impossible. My son couldn't—"

"She had the baby? It's too soon."

"Clearly, it was premature. Like you said, seven months . . ."

"Where is she now?" The desperation in my voice nauseated me.

"She had the nerve to call my son a monster. Good riddance, I told her."

"How could you let her leave? She needed your help."

Mother picked up two broken pieces of china and fitted them together. "I could glue this."

I told her right then that if anything happened to Rebecca, or to you, Linda, it was on her. She would pay. Then I left before I did something I'd regret.

I was so desperate that I went to the police station to file a missing persons report, but they had the gall to insinuate that Rebecca had left me by her own choice. Maybe it was hormones. Postpartum can make a woman irrational, they claimed. I should go home and wait. They were sure she'd come back on her own.

She didn't come back, but the next morning the phone rang. It was Rebecca.

She refused to answer any of my questions. She had to see me in person, in an hour, but it had to be in the place we'd first met, under what she called the "backwards stars."

I packed the black diaper bag with a few things I thought the baby and Rebecca would need—a onesie, a diaper, wipes, a protein bar, a thermos of New York City tap water—and went to the street and hailed a cab.

* * *

There she was, my Rebecca, standing in the exact same place that I first saw her. Only she wasn't looking up, she was looking straight at me, and in her arms was a shoebox. Our baby? Something changed inside me. The passion I had for Rebecca vaporized; the anger at Mother vanished like a magic trick: now you feel it, now you don't. What mattered was the box in her arms. I had never been more certain that fate had brought us together—not for Rebecca to be my mentor, my teacher, but for her to be the mother of my child. This I was sure of. I rushed to her, but two feet from touching the baby, she warned me back: "Don't come any closer."

"What happened?" I asked her. "Where have you been? Why didn't you call and tell me where you were?" I fired many questions at her, but she answered not one.

All she said was, "Do you want to see her?"

"It's a she," I breathed.

Rebecca nodded and removed the blue-striped blanket covering my baby's face and tilted the shoebox in my direction. There you were. The most beautiful creature in the galaxy. You had the tiniest nose I'd ever seen in my life.

"She's not well," Rebecca said.

My heart leapt into my throat.

"She was born premature. Under two pounds. She's not able to keep her body temperature up, and her lungs aren't developed."

"We need to get her to the hospital!"

Rebecca shook her head. "She's going to die."

"Don't say that!" I wanted to slap her, but not as much as I wanted to hold her and love her again. I reached out and cupped Rebecca's face. She didn't pull away as I thought she would. Instead, she rested her chin in my open fist, and her burden, the weight of the world, momentarily lifted.

"It'll be okay," I told her. "We'll get help. She'll live."

Rebecca jerked her head back. "She's better off dead than to have a sadistic, evil psychopath like you in her life."

She dropped something onto the floor. I bent down and picked up a piece of wallpaper with a printed yellow duck with a drop of blood on its beak. She had been in the nursery. "How did you get the code?"

"Your mother."

"Mother didn't have the code."

"She always had the code."

"I don't understand."

"I called her to tell her we were going to have a baby. I thought whatever she did to you could be maybe fixed, forgiven somehow, because not having a mother . . . it's awful. I know. I wanted our baby to have a grandmother. At first, she was quiet, a long silence; I thought she had hung up for a second. I told her how excited you were about being a father and about the nursery. She said she was happy for us and she wanted to give me a gift before the baby arrived. She had something special, a family heirloom, but needed to know if it would fit in the room. I told her I would have you measure it. She insisted I not tell you. She wanted to surprise you. She gave me the code and—"

She stopped, seemingly unable to speak. Her eyes filled with tears as she took a deep, bracing breath.

"How many others have you kept hostage? Murdered?"

"It's not murder. It's my process as an actor. I thought you understood."

"Good-bye," she said.

I reached out and grabbed her. "You're going nowhere but home. Our home."

She was trembling now. She understood.

Then the baby made a sound, a squeak that cracked the surface of my skin.

"She's crying?"

"She's hungry."

"Feed her!"

"You're hurting me."

I released her, and she took the baby out of the shoebox and held her under her left arm. The baby books called it the football hold. Then she lifted my tiny child to her breast.

"She's eating," I said. "She'll be okay."

"She's not able to suck." Rebecca glanced down at my baby and then up, meeting my eyes. Quietly she said, "I hate you." And then she ran.

I kicked the shoebox she had left behind as I picked up the black diaper bag and raced after her. She was a fair distance ahead, but I could see she was headed for the subway.

I finally caught up to her at the platform for the No. 7, the shuttle train that went from Grand Central to Times Square and back.

"Rebecca!" I shouted.

She waved me over, and I moved toward her. At two feet apart, she raised the palm of her hand and stopped me. She was talking nonsense at this point. Calling me pure evil and lots of other names.

I reminded her about the books and how we'd read that some women get sad and depressed after birth. I heard what I sounded like—like the worthless police had when I'd gone to them for help. I shut up and listened.

"I wish I could blame you, but you're a product of your genetics, environment, and two fucked-up parents."

The baby squeaked again.

"She needs help," I cried.

"I never wanted children. And then I met you," she said, edging back from me, her feet passing the yellow line next to the edge of the platform.

"You're too close to the edge."

She repositioned my baby back into the football position, and I could see that tiny face clearly again. My daughter was fragile and beautiful.

The train was approaching. I tried to warn her, but she interrupted me as the roar of the train neared us.

Calling me by my given name, she said, "Foster, I loved you. I did."

And she jumped.

Train brakes squealed, masking the sound of the impact, followed by screams and cries of horror. Mass shock.

The police, the fire department, and subway and Metro-North men and women in uniforms rushed to the scene.

"Step back," a man in the NYPD uniform said.

"My baby," I said.

"You know the woman?"

I lifted the black diaper bag and repeated, "My baby."

When the train backed up, Rebecca lay on the railroad ties, smashed, mangled. Faces looked away. I couldn't bring myself not to look. Rebecca was gone and my baby dead.

I had taken several steps into the crowd when someone shouted, "The baby!"

Heads turned back to the tracks, and now I saw smiles.

I grabbed the arm of one of the firemen. "What's happening?"

"The baby's alive," he told me with a grin.

I pushed through the crowd and jumped down onto the tracks. A firefighter was holding the little bundle in her arms.

"My baby." Again, I lifted the diaper bag.

She handed me my daughter, and as I held you in the palms of my hands, I knew there was no one I had ever loved as much as you, or would ever love more than you.

I glanced up at the name tag on the firefighter's uniform.

Linda.

It was fate.

I would call you Linda.

And "father of Linda Donovan" would be the only role I'd ever play again.

LINDA

CHAPTER

21

I WAS SWEATING, SHAKING with chills, but I didn't have a fever, I had the truth. After reading the final notebook, there was no doubt left in my mind. This was no master storyteller spinning a grisly yarn . . .

My God. My God. Dad.

The man who'd played the role of my father for twenty-five years was a killer, and my mother his victim. He might as well have pushed her in front of that train. I took her card from my pocket.

I didn't know where my father was except that he had to be nearby. What I did know was that he needed to be taken away, far away, and maybe he could be helped . . .

No, that was a fiction I wanted to believe. Men like my father didn't heal; they went on and on, concealing their pain from themselves by torturing their victims, by playing on their will to live, their hope that if they did everything as they were told, perfectly, they would be spared.

Tragically, my father's story was not a new one. It was the ageless tale of a sociopath, a psychopath, a disturbed, delusional mind.

The numbness taking hold of me wasn't because of what I now knew about my father, but because I couldn't help but still love the father I'd believed he was.

It was time to call the police.

I heard something. The door to the shaft was still open. Was the noise coming from it? Voices? Dad?

Jess.

He had her. I was now certain of that. I had to stop him before it was too late.

The basement.

Clutching the five notebooks to my chest, I ran through the brownstone, down the hallway stairs, and found the door leading to the basement level. Of course, the thought ran through my head, this would be the point in every horror movie when the audience shouts, *Don't go down there!*

I had no choice. I descended the creaky wooden stairs and on the last step was accosted. The light from the basement's fluorescent bulbs made me nauseous, dizzy. I gagged.

"Linda, is that you?" Dad was wearing a new fitted suit, designer, his hair cut short. He'd lost the ponytail, which frightened me most of all.

Before I could move, he hurried up to me and hugged me tight, his notebooks punching into my sternum. "My baby girl . . . I had faith you would find me," he whispered into my ear. He took a step back and snatched the notebooks from my hands. "It was long overdue," he said, glancing down at his journals. "I waited far too long." A shrug. "Well, finally, here we are."

"Where is she?"

"She's fine."

"Don't lie to me."

"I've never lied to you."

"My whole life is a lie."

"I'm an actor." He smiled, all front teeth exposed, and the space between story and reality clamped shut. This man was not the dad I'd known. I was looking into the eyes of a malevolent stranger.

He stepped over to the conveyor belt and placed his journals facedown, side by side. "Linda, to your right."

I hesitated, so he moved over and flipped a red switch. The doors of the metal dragon opened and I stared into the throat of hell.

The notebooks rolled forward.

"They can't burn!" I rushed over to save them—not as evidence for the police but as proof that my mother hadn't abandoned me. That she hadn't left me behind, but instead had tried to take me away with her, away from him.

He pulled me back from the furnace and wrapped his arms around me, a human straitjacket. "Careful. It's over a thousand degrees in there."

I felt the heat now, followed by a deep, searing pain as his notebooks ignited and disappeared forever.

My tears were no match for the flames, but if I'd thought jumping into the fire would bring my mother back, I would have gladly sacrificed myself.

"She and I had a lovely tea," he said.

"Oh my God." I tried to pull away and looked around wildly for Jess.

He squeezed me just short of cracking my rib cage. "She's fine," he whispered.

"I want to see her now." I kicked his shin, hard.

He didn't flinch, but he let go. "She's a fighter like you," he said. "A good choice."

I turned to face him, consciously not making eye contact, lest it paralyze me with fear and render me powerless. "Please bring me to her."

"I'm forever in her debt," he said. "Without her, the work might not be possible."

"The work." I tried to control the panic in my voice. He was planning on making Jess his next victim.

"The urgency, and frankly, writer's cramp, forced me to omit some crucial details of the craft. I can show you now. You were a gifted apprentice when I taught you the exterminating business. I see you excelling here as well."

"You want me to watch you?"

"Ideally, if there were time," he said. "We'll have to skip ahead to hands-on training." He looked at me meaningfully. "I may have to go away soon, darling."

"You want me to kill—"

"Did you not read those notebooks?"

The tension in his voice signaled that he was ready to snap. I had to make this better.

"Every word, like you said."

"Then you know we don't kill. We create."

"Characters," I said, hoping to appease him.

"Exactly." He bent down and kissed my forehead.

It was all I could do not to vomit on his fancy new suit. "Your mother."

He put his hand over my mouth. "Don't you ever, ever call her that again, understand?"

I recoiled, and he dropped his hand.

"She was gone when I found her. Dead. Heart. Cancer, Overdose. Aneurysm. I don't know and I don't care. I can't lie; I don't feel remorse. She took away everyone I loved. My father, my Rebecca . . . and she was trying to take you."

"Me? I didn't even know her."

"She knew you. She knew every college you applied to."

Before I could ask how, he told me she had her ways, her spies. Her money bought all the information she needed. She knew that a full scholarship to the one West Coast school I'd applied to would be an offer I couldn't refuse.

"Either way, I lose," he explained. "If I tried to convince you not to go, she would have used it against me. Turned me into a bit player. Cast me as the selfish, uncaring father. I couldn't let her do that." Tears fell from his eyelashes.

When I looked into his eyes, it wasn't fear I felt, but pity, and when I reached out and touched his cheek and felt the wetness on my fingertips, Dad was back.

"I didn't know," I said.

He took hold of my hand. "I went to her to do something I swore on my father's grave I would never do. I was going to get on my hands and knees if I had to, and plead with her to pull the scholarship. I had no intention of killing her."

"You said she took everything from you. You hated her."

"She did. I do. But I am not a murderer. I told you that. Actually, I was quite upset to have found her dead, in that trashy dress. She deprived me of any chance I had to tell her how I really felt. Sometimes we need that to heal. I even considered calling the police. I went to the kitchen to get a glass of water and thought about you and how it was important for me to face my demons if I expected you to face yours. Believe me, that woman was a demon."

"She was dead before the rat . . ."

"How could you even think that about me? I may have despised her, but I never would have tortured her." He shook his head.

"I don't understand. If she was already dead, why would you . . . unless you wanted Credo to fire us."

"My sweet Linda, if only I had your brains." He gently pushed my hair away from my face. I wanted to ask him to sing "What a Wonderful World," the way he had when I was a child to comfort me after I had a nightmare.

"That was an added benefit." He dropped his hand, and the nightmare returned. "I had to get you to stay somehow, and well, we both know if the business was collapsing, you would never leave me." He put his hand on my chest, and I would swear my heart stopped.

"The rat. Was that you?"

"I guess it was the only way I could get some justice."

"A rat. Her face . . ." I was at a loss for words and thoughts.

"The rat," he affirmed. "Mother was a vain woman. She spoke often of how she wanted to be laid out in her Halston dress and her hair and makeup done by the best. Yes, she had it all planned out. But there would be no open casket if there was no . . . well, nothing to work with." This time when he smiled, he showed no teeth.

"I think I'm going to be sick." I gripped my stomach.

He grabbed on to my shoulders. "You are going to be fine. More than fine. Your day, our day, has finally arrived. Now out real work can resume. Your apprenticeship starts today."

"I believed you were innocent," I told him.

"We are all innocent and guilty. Life is a paradox." He put his hand on my shoulder and squeezed. "Your blind faith is what will make you the greatest of us all."

"There were at least sixty funeral cards with this address. You and your father"—I caught myself before the word *murdered* slipped out of my mouth—"worked with all those characters?"

"And my father's father before him. Your great-great-grandfather. You'll be the first woman to carry on the family legacy." He beamed with pride, the same way he had when I'd trapped my first rat. "Long overdue, but here we are, and our training begins tonight."

I remained silent, unwilling to admit I knew what he meant.

"First, I have something for you." Dad took from the inside pocket of his suit jacket a folded piece of paper and handed it to me.

I unfolded the document. "This is a deed in my name."

"This place was the one thing my father left me. I thought we'd return here and begin our training years ago, but there were too many memories connected to your mother, and I wasn't ready to face them."

I glanced over at the furnace's fire, still burning strong.

"When the work is done, their shells are put into—"

"The crematorium," I said.

"You are a quick study." That toothy smile was back.

"I thought you believed in the spirit, the soul."

"Of course I do. Every character I've ever worked with is a part of me. Every character you work with will be a part of you."

"I can't," I said.

"You have no choice."

"This is not my destiny."

The smile vanished. "I have never been as disappointed in you as I am now."

Despite everything, his words hurt me, bad. I had never questioned my own judgment, or myself, more. How could I let the words of this lunatic get to me?

He was still my father. But he wasn't. But he was.

"I know this is hard for you to take in all at once, but you'll come to understand."

"I will never understand."

"I didn't either. I thought I had, but it wasn't until I held you in my arms that it all made sense. It's through our work that I, like my father and his father before him, came to understand: the path to greatness, to our ultimate truth, is the work. My only regret is that I wasn't ready to step up as your mentor until now." He reached out and hugged me tighter than before. "My protégé," he whispered in my ear.

I couldn't breathe and was struggling to pull free when we heard a loud crash.

"That came from upstairs," I said.

"It's time."

"Not until I see her, please."

He slapped me across my cheek. The surprise stung more than the blow. My father had never put a hand on me before now.

"Never beg. Artists who beg get nothing and learn only that they are worthless. Enough talk. Time to get to work."

22

H E LED AND I followed, from the basement to the second floor, through the living room, past the kitchen, the four bedrooms and two baths, all the way back to the nursery. He exhibited no concern that I might run. If I wanted to, I could have easily gotten away without even a fight, but he was as confident as I was sure that I had to follow this to its end.

I told myself it was for Jess. She was here, and I had to find her, save her. But it was also Dad I was hoping to find, the man who'd loved and raised me for the past twenty-five years. I still believed my father lay somewhere in the shell of the well-dressed stranger with the salon-styled hair.

"This was supposed to be your room," he said. I nodded.

"Of course . . . you read your story."

"Where is she?"

He lifted his chin toward a closed door I hadn't paid attention to earlier.

My sweaty palm slipped twice before the knob turned.

There was Jess, hog-tied at the bottom of an empty hot tub. Her mouth ball-gagged, her head flopped to one side, eyes shut.

It must have been Jess who'd made the crashing sound upstairs. Which meant any hope that help was on its way had vanished before my eyes.

"Is she alive?"

He nodded curtly. "We haven't started our work. I always wanted to study a character who was a detective, but I never had the opportunity . . . or maybe the courage, like you, my dear daughter."

I knelt at the side of the dry tub and removed the ball gag from her mouth. "Jess." I patted her cheeks. "Wake up, please." There was no response. She was out cold.

"You found the perfect character in that one. What a challenge for your first study!"

I felt his sinister pride spit out on the back of my neck. "What did you do to her?"

"Gave her something to rest until you were ready."

"I'm so sorry, Jess." I reached in to untie her.

My father took hold of my hair and dragged me to my feet. "Never rush. Do you understand?" He tugged hard.

"Let her go."

"It's important to give the character time to adjust to her setting. Otherwise, there's too much unnecessary drama. Do you understand?"

I considered hitting him, using my judo training to disable him. But if I didn't prevail, I would be guaranteeing Jess's death. I chose another tack.

"Please, Dad, for me?"

He wrapped my hair around his fist and drew me to him. "I asked if you understand."

"Yes!" I pulled away, ripping a chunk of hair from my scalp. I winced, and he slapped me across the face again. Strands of my hair fell from his open hand onto Jess's bruised, exposed stomach.

He'd hurt her. I'd never felt rage like I did then. "I'll kill you if she doesn't make it."

With that, I pushed him hard enough that he stumbled back into the other room, banging his head against the side of the crib.

It took him a moment to get back on his feet. When he did, I was in a fight stance, ready to destroy.

"Brava!" He clapped.

I hadn't thought it possible to feel any more confused. "Nice 'tough cop,'" he said. "See, she's already teaching you." He caressed the welt on my cheek. "This right here is a big reason why I put our work off for so long."

"You're not supposed to make marks where the camera can see."

He shook his head. "I couldn't bring myself to scar you anywhere. I never had my father's inner strength. Or his father's. They understood that without pain, one never reached their potential." He lifted his shirt and showed me the scars I had seen before. "Shards of glass," he said.

"You told me it was from a windshield, a car accident."

"Father and I were in a car crash, but before the paramedics, the police, anyone arrived, Father did this with the broken windshield glass."

"But why?" There was no disguising my horror.

"I was driving. There was an oncoming car. Father told me to drive into it, but at the last moment I swerved, and we crashed into a tree."

"The glass was punishment?"

"Never. Father didn't believe in punitive measures. He wanted me to experience suffering deep in my body. Once the feeling is a part of you, you can access it anytime. These are all tools."

Jess moaned. I moved in her direction.

"She'll be fine," he said loudly. "Metabolisms vary. Some characters take longer to come out it."

I took my mother's card from my pocket. "Dad, see Mom's card?"

He took it from me and caressed its edges.

"She showed you it could be different. You could be different. You wrote all about it."

"Don't you understand what we're doing here? How the work means everything? Your mother understood."

"My mother jumped to her death with me in her arms to get us away from you forever."

"She was depressed. You were so small and sick. She found the exterminator, and she finally witnessed the work I was doing. She understood its importance. So much so she was afraid that you'd both get in my way. Stop me from what she thought was my greater purpose. She needed guidance. She went to Mother. And Mother convinced her it was true: she'd be a burden to me. She's responsible for your mother's death."

"Oh, Dad, it wasn't your mother. It was you. Your actions. You killed my mother."

He took hold of my hand and led me to the small door set low on the wall. With his free hand, he opened it as wide as it would go. He was going to push me down the chute. I tried to free myself, but the more I struggled, the tighter his hold on me got.

"Love made your mother weak." He put her card between his teeth and tore it through the taped middle, then tossed both halves into the chute.

Turning to me, he paused, as if remembering something. "You haven't seen my master stage set." When I didn't react, he continued, "This nursery can be transformed into whatever you want. Police headquarters, interrogation room, a murder scene. Yes, a murder scene. That would be an excellent way for you to learn from this character."

I released a long, drawn-out breath, and with my hand still in his, I looked up into his eyes, hoping they would be unrecognizable, praying he wouldn't be the same man who'd stenciled ducks onto a nursery wall before chain-sawing a man into pieces. But his eyes shone with the same love they had my whole life. How was this possible?

"Linda," Jess called out. Her voice sounded thin and weak, but she'd get through this. I would make sure of that, no matter what it took.

"Dad, I want to be your protégé. I get the importance of the work and our family legacy."

He put my hand to his mouth and kissed my knuckles. "But listen: Jess isn't the one I want. I know of a much better choice." I wasn't sure how I was managing to stay calm, but to save Jess, I needed to play the role of a lifetime: his meek, devoted daughter. "I think her partner would be a much more interesting study."

"The older one, right?"

"She's been on the force for twenty years." I tilted my head at Jess, whose moaning had grown louder. "She's practically a rookie."

He bent over and kissed the top of my head. "Genius."

I smiled, and it was a genuine smile. He would have seen through anything forced. I thought of Sam and Jess and the three of us walking in a park. It was so corny that I couldn't help but smile for real.

It worked. Dad released my hand.

"All this"—he opened his arms wide—"this was you testing me."

"Testing you?"

"I knew after you read my—our—story, you'd understand everything. You'd want to join me. You seek greatness, which is what you deserve. I get your initial resistance. You needed to see what kind of a mentor I would be. You had to be certain I wouldn't be too soft. You had to push my buttons hard to see if I could handle myself. The student teaching the master."

"What's next?" I asked. "Do we call her partner and get her here? Maybe have Jess call? Then knock her back out?"

"I have a better idea."

I glanced over at Jess. Her eyes were wide open, but she wasn't struggling or screaming. She was a trained professional. She was smart. She knew if she created a stir, it would only lead to her being knocked out again. She remained silent, the audience watching, or at least hearing, the actors perform.

"Okay," I said. "But how else can we get her partner here?"

"We need a homicide." He pulled from the back of his pants a gun I hadn't seen. I didn't have to ask where he'd gotten it. I could hear the answer in Jess's rapid breathing. It was hers.

Dad walked over to the hot tub and pointed the gun down at Jess. "We have a body. We call her partner, but we get her here under false pretenses. I say I'll turn myself in, but only to her, and she has to come alone."

It was a ridiculous plan, of course, but no less dangerous for that. I needed to get him back on track.

"If Jess calls and tells her partner to come alone, don't you think that'll be more effective? Then we can shoot her after she makes the call."

"Too risky. You said she's a veteran. She'll know from her partner's voice that something's wrong. She won't come alone."

Like Rita would have come alone if he called in a homicide and offered himself up only to her. Our situation was looking grim. There'd be no rescue. My only hope was to buy time and look for an opening to end this all myself.

Dad clicked the safety off. "Ready?"

"Don't shoot. Please!" I shouted.

"I wouldn't do that to you."

I glanced at Jess, who suddenly looked more confused than scared.

"You have to be the one to shoot," he explained. "It will help when you're studying the detective character to have the full experience." He put the gun in my hands. "Remember, grip it with both hands. Pistols have a kick." He spread his feet on the floor. "Wide stance." He brushed his thigh against mine. "Knees bent."

I followed his exact instructions. "Now, shoot."

I pointed the gun down at Jess, closed my eyes, and said, "I can't do it." I knew that for him to believe my performance, I had to resist.

"Linda, the first time you had to clear a rat trap, you said you couldn't. But you did, and now you don't give it a second thought. We learn from doing."

"Okay," I said, after a long moment. "Step back in case I screw this up."

Dad did as I said.

Again, I aimed the gun at Jess. "Close your eyes," I told her.

"No," he said. "Let her see death coming. Don't deny her the beauty."

I put my finger on the trigger and looked over my shoulder, saw Dad's eyes fixed on Jess in the tub. He seemed to be in a trance.

I whispered, "I love you."

He turned his gaze on me. "I know you do, sweetie."

I pulled the trigger.

What happened next was a blur, like someone had hit fast-forward on the remote and couldn't get it to stop.

I fired. I missed. I couldn't say if it was on purpose or if the kick from the gun threw my aim off. Or if Dad knew it was coming and dodged in time. Before I could fire again, he regained his footing and dived into the chute. I heard his body bouncing all the way down.

A voice came from the entrance to the saferoom. "Drop the gun."

Detective Frascon stepped into view, aimed, called out another warning. But her voice was drowned out by my father's. I heard the man who had sacrificed all he knew for love, for me, scream.

The crematorium. Dad was burning alive.

"No!" I cried, unaware my gun was aimed at Frascon's heart. She fired—a direct hit. And I died.

FINALE

THE DOCTORS SAID I was clinically dead for three minutes and fifty-two seconds. Seconds away from permanent brain damage. I lost a lot of blood, and my heart stopped. The miracle of science and a team of kick-ass paramedics saved me. My father hadn't burned alive in his family's crematorium. The scream I heard was real, though. Maybe he was feigning death to buy time. Maybe it was the only way he knew to say good-bye.

He escaped through a basement door. Cops were everywhere around our block, but he got away unseen.

It's been three years and a worldwide pandemic since that day. The day everything changed, but then not enough changed.

I didn't go to college, obviously.

I sold the brownstone. I gave half the money away. A quarter of it went to research, focused on studying the psychological traits of serial killers. Maybe psychologists or doctors will one day find a definitive answer to how these murderers come to be. After all, science did manage to create a vaccine for a virus that stopped the world in its tracks.

I gave the other quarter of the proceeds to organizations that aid families of serial-killer victims. Detective Frascon—she's now retired—tried to help me find any living family members of the sixty, victims of my father and his father, but we couldn't find anyone except the Metro-North conductor's mother, who since has become my adoptive grandmother.

There was one other woman, a daughter, who we managed to track down, but she'd died of a drug overdose and had no living relatives.

Frascon said targeting victims with little or no family enabled my father and his father and grandfather to go undiscovered for so long. Their being rich helped too. Apparently, when someone's dressed in designer clothing and tips their doormen well, their crimes often go unnoticed.

I'm getting off topic. I do that a lot. My therapist tells me it's a coping mechanism, like the way some people laugh when they're talking about difficult subjects. I get tangential.

I've been approached by every network, cable, and streaming service, dozens of podcasts, including one with three million listeners, and movie producers about my story. One actor offered six million dollars for the movie rights, and a publishing company wanted to give me a two-million-dollar advance to write a book—a memoir—without even knowing whether I could write. I turned them all down. It wasn't because I wanted to protect my privacy or stay out of the public's eye. I already can't walk down the street without someone taking my picture and posting it on Instagram, Twitter, or one of the other social media platforms I haven't a clue about.

The main reason I've declined is that I still don't know the answer to the one question that matters.

I know the story my father believed was his story, and I know all the stories the police, special investigators, and forensic scientists have tried to piece together. I know the story I lived, and the one I've spent endless hours of therapy trying to interrupt, and reinterpret, in order to understand. Those are the parts that try to answer the question of how a person becomes a serial killer. Is it nature or nurture or both? Some theorize that socialization is the key factor to the making of a serial killer. Were they abused as children, traumatized? Such kids often suffer early brain injuries from severe blows to their heads. Others theorize that socialization may be a factor. And yet others assign a greater value to genetics: it's something innate that transforms certain individuals into serial killers.

The part of the story I don't know, the answer I may never know, is how a serial killer stops a lifetime of killing to become a father. And not any father, but a loving one: the perfect parent.

I know in my heart that I will never find him until he wants to be found.

Jess was, still is, obsessed. It's part of the reason we failed to make things work between us. There were a lot of other reasons. I'd like to blame it all on my father, but we had plenty of "doesn't put the cap on the toothpaste" crap as well. We loved each other, we still do, but we aren't compatible. If we hadn't reunited at a murder scene, we would probably never have gotten back together.

I'm doing it again. Tangents . . .

Jess now works for some special task force that involves the FBI and NYPD and Homeland Security, something like that. It's all about tracking down serial killers and other Really Bad People. She's told me a half a dozen times, but I've always been bad with names. We don't talk often, but we text occasionally. She seems happy enough.

I haven't left New York, though some would say I have. I bought a house on Staten Island. It's close enough to the city for when I have a craving for one of Betty's specials, but it feels like a million miles away from my old life. And I don't fear my father will find me here.

Frascon's Realtor niece found me the place. Rita says she's sorry for almost killing me, but I did have a gun pointed at her, so I can't blame her. Besides, if she wasn't as smart as the best TV cops, she might not have thought to track my phone when Betty called her, worried, and the desk sergeant said that her cousin Linda Bennett had called.

It's a running joke between us. (Yes, she and I became good friends.) She introduced me to her third cousin's next-door neighbor Maria, and we ultimately got married. In

Frascon's family, that makes me family. I don't question. I just go along with it.

Maria's an elementary school teacher. She loves kids, and I'm learning to do the same. I'd better hurry, because Maria's five months pregnant. Twins.

She's one of five children. Our kids will have plenty of cousins. Her parents are a little inattentive to their existing grandchildren, but hey, they did raise five kids of their own. I can't blame them for not wanting to ever change another diaper.

I received a note from my father in the mail yesterday, written on torn, lined paper, most likely from another one of his notebooks. It was the first and only communication since the day he vanished. I thought about turning it over to the police, or the task force Jess works for, but there was no return address and the postmark was Los Angeles. I have a hunch he's already left LA. Maybe he was never even there but asked someone he met on his travels to mail it for him when they got to the City of Angels. If I turn it in, I figure it will only lead to more questions without answers.

Besides, his note was more of an afterthought, with meaning only to me:

> *Your mother came into my life to teach the unteachable, or so I thought. I used to think your mother came into my life to mentor to me to perfection. She was going to be my guide to the next level, the same place Father would have brought me if his life hadn't ended too soon.*
>
> *I was wrong. Your mother didn't come into my life to teach me or mentor me. She came into my life so I could see that perfection is not the goal. That in fact striving for perfection only brings out the worst in us, the narcissist that every artist has inside them. She came into my life to help me to see that it's through our mistakes—the chips in the porcelain, the dot of blood on the white rug, or the stenciled duck on the nursery wall—that we find our humanity, find peace, and then vanish among the ordinary, so that our children become fully realized.*

Tomorrow is August 2, the anniversary of my mother's death. Maria and I will take the ferry and the subway to Grand Central, and we will stand in the exact spot where my parents met. We'll look up at the celestial ceiling, with its backward stars, and I will tell her that perfect parents don't always give their children a happy ending.

ACKNOWLEDGMENTS

THANK YOU TO my agent, Cynthia Manson, who never stops believing in me, and thank you to veteran editor Ed Stackler, who helped edit my book and taught me how to make a good story thrilling. I am deeply grateful to Crooked Lane Books: publisher Matt Martz; Terri Bischoff, my editor, who shared my vision for *Her Father's Daughter* and took what was a good story to the next level; Rebecca Nelson, Madeline Rathle, Dulce Botello, and Molly McLaughlin; and the rest of the incredible team.

I am very thankful for the support of my writers groups and friends: Nancee Adams, Kate Brandt, Marcia Bradley, Michael Biello, Susan Bolognino, Kathy Curto, Jeff Faville, Alex Giannini, Crystal Greene, Jimin Han, Gloria Hatrick, Barbara Josselsohn, Deb Laufer, Carmela Leo, Elise Hart Kipness, Maria Maldonado, Jennifer Manocherian, Dan Martin, Tessa Smith McGovern, Alexandra Soiseth, Angela Taylor, Bill Papaleo, and Monica Woo. Extra thanks to Mike Tepper, my website designer and social media manager.

I am grateful to my whole family, but especially to my late father, John J. Dunn, for teaching me about rodents, exterminating, and love, and to my mother, Adrienne Petilli, the fiercest, most courageous, most caring person I know. Last but not ever least, thank you, Allan Tepper, my life partner, for your tireless efforts in reading revision after revision, your mad grammatical and spelling skills, and your faith in this book.